LAUR

Book 1 of
The Thrillosophical Trilogy

By ANTHONY

Choice Publishing

ISBN: 978-1-907107-38-2

A catalogue record for this book is available from the National
Library, Ireland and the British Library, UK

Cover Photography – Terry Collins, Drogheda, Ireland
Cover Design – Terry Collins and Anthony
Cover Model – Nathalia Bianchi, Sao Paulo, Brazil

First Edition
Published 2010 in co-operation with Choice Publishing,
Drogheda, Co Louth, Ireland (www.choicepublishing.ie)
www.anthonywhelan.ie
www.thrillosophy.org

Dedication

To Beauty, Truth and Justice
To Love

To All Those Who Love Me – You know who you
are
To All Those I Love – You might be surprised at
who you are

To You, Dear Reader
To All Those Who Love You
To All Those Whom You Love

To The Search
To The Struggle

To Validation

Table Of Contents

Hunted
September 11th

Bushes crashed against her, scratching and scraping her exposed arms. The Samui sun beat down relentlessly, drying the breath in her throat as she dashed crazily from side to side. The terror was a palpable force in her arteries, pushing the blood to her muscles.

'Fight or Flight' – this was Flight, pure and simple!

Still she could hear her pursuer smashing his (or, please God, no; their) way through the jungle vegetation. Amazingly, even as she fought to escape the ensnaring tropical growth, part of her mind acted as observer, like an interested but aloof critic watching a movie. This critic marvelled at the absurdity of such terror in such an idyllic spot, Koh Samui – one of the many island paradises off the Thailand coast, with hazy lazy summer sun in the June tropics.

Yet here she was, scrambling for her life when she should be relaxing, sipping her Singha beer and sunbathing under the June sun. The critic wondered, How did you get here?, reviewing the past months when she went from being a carefree backpacker, through bereavement, to end up as an international fugitive from unseen but clearly powerful and deadly enemies. She wondered if she was having a nightmare, but she could not deny the reality of the biting and gouging undergrowth, or the stifling humidity that made it so hard to run.

The creepers tried to ensnare her, the shrubs tried to

entangle her, but still she scrambled – up, through, over. The conscious part of her mind sought to penetrate the brush in front of her – all the time trying to decipher the dappled greenery and understand the path of least resistance. All of her senses reached out in front, trying to interpret the moving colours and forms. The dense foliage was both friend and enemy, making it impossible to see an escape, whilst at the same time hiding her. The horror and panic were overwhelming, threatening to overpower her mind. She wrestled, battled and gouged her way forward; all the time hearing the sounds of pursuit, never within reach but always on the point of closing on her.

Again, the critic kicked in, but this time with a suggestion instead of an observation. The jungle was so thick, she could only sense her pursuer by the sound he was making. He sounded like a big man, which meant that he would find the foliage an even more impenetrable barrier than she did. Maybe the trick was to stop running, and stay still – and very, very quiet. Laura weighed and assessed the thought – in one way it was very appealing, as it gave her an excuse to stop, and her legs had become so heavy and leaden. On the other hand, it was terrifying, to stop running, and just hope that her hunter could not find her amongst the foliage as he played hide and seek instead of catch.

Laura realised the decision was being made for her – she simply could not go on, her limbs were starting to shut down from exhaustion. Her legs quaked and she could barely stop them from buckling under her. The sweat flowed from every pore of her body, soaking her clothes and blinding her eyes. Her heart felt as though it would burst if she tried to force the blood through it any quicker. There was a mist roiling in front of her eyes, even though she knew no mist could persist in the midday Asian sun. The pain in her stomach from the combination of exertion and stress was threatening to double her over in agony.

Decision made! As she raced through non-existent openings in the tangled shrubbery, she launched herself off the ground with one final effort. She landed in a bed of soft mulch, formed by rotting leaves. Laura buried her hands into the natural compost, making a hole that she could bury her face in. She wriggled her hands and face as deep as she could, using her hands to keep a breathing space in front of her face.

She tried to force her breathing to be quiet, but it sounded like a turbine in her ears. She lay still, hoping that her manic stalker would neither see nor hear her. As she lay there, she could feel the compost start to come to life. It was as though her intrusion had awoken the spirit of the forest – the entire mixture that she was lying in seemed to crawl and squirm. She could feel movement all over her body, and sensed the incredible life that held her within its grasp. She started to relax into the feeling, with an almost hallucinogenic acceptance of some otherworldly presence. Her sense of peace came crashing down as she felt wriggling around her ears and nostrils. She closed her mouth, through which she had been gulping air, but it was too late. She could feel the invaders within her mouth, her nostrils, her ears. Her hair was moving as if of its own accord, made mobile by the multitude of insects swarming through it.

Laura knew her life depended on staying absolutely still, on co-operating with the forest, blending into it to become part of nature and lying unnoticed until her hunter gave up. Even as she thought this, she realised that she was not going to be able to do it. She had never been a 'girly-girl', afraid of spiders and creepy-crawlers, but she was going to have a phobia after this. She thought about how to escape, wondering if she could quietly crawl to a less infested patch without drawing attention to herself. She decided to creep forward, away from the direction she had come from, to continue to put distance between herself and her pursuer.

She lifted her head out of the damp compost and risked looking around – she could detect no movement, no sound. The entire forest seemed to have paused, to be holding its collective breath. The only sound was that of the surf on the beach that lay a kilometre or so to the east. She blew out as hard as she could out of her nose, trying not to make noise. She spat, and shook her head from side to side to get the insects out of her ears. Finally, she felt that her body was her own again – the invaders had been repelled. She thought of all the books she had read on survival in hostile terrains, remembering the sections on hungry wildlife.

She knew she had to move very slowly, taking care not to disturb the undergrowth around her. It was so still – any movement would be instantly noticed. She had to stay as low as possible, hugging the ground. She must make sure not to snap any of the underlying twigs or frighten any of the forest residents. So much to think of, she nearly froze on the spot. Yet she was caught between two impossible alternatives – stay where she was and be eaten alive; or stand and run, with the prospect of being caught by her heretofore unseen aggressor. She started to move.

Inch by frightening inch, foot by terrifying foot, yard by petrifying yard. Slowly moving her left hand and arm forwards, then joining it with her right. Painfully drawing her right leg up under her, then joining it with her left. Then, oh so slowly, moving her torso forward, spreading the strain across her arms and her legs, so that she would not gasp with the pain and effort. Second after second, minute after minute – it felt like hour after hour. She lost all concept of time, her entire world reduced to the ball of pain that was her body, and trying to move it without moving at all. Aching, hurting, stinging, throbbing, agonising, burning, anguishing, torturing, suffering, racking pain – this was the entire universe of her existence.

As she moved into a deeper patch of shade, the temperature dropped a few degrees. She wondered how far she had come. Was it safe to stand and ease the cramps screaming throughout her body? Still afraid of capture, she resolved to stretch out where she lay, without rising, and let her abused body recover a little. Remarkably, her overwrought mind sought refuge in near-catatonia, and she drifted in and out of semi-consciousness whilst images of the chase raced through her mind. She came to with a start, not sure how long she had dozed. The sun was setting ahead of her in the west, so it was at least a couple of hours since the chase had started.

The forest had settled into its dusk routine – insects chirping, birds coming home to roost, and a gentle breeze blowing in off the sea. For the first time that afternoon, Laura felt she could relax. At last, the jungle felt safe and secure, instead of scary and vulnerable. She didn't know where to turn next. She decided to forsake her belongings back at the room she had hired. Unquestionably the first thing she had to do was get off Koh Samui, back onto the Thai mainland. From there she could use her backpacking experience to get out of Thailand, and hopefully back to safety.

Laura started to stand, slowly and gently. As she rose a couple of inches off the ground, her mind screamed in panic as a heavy body crashed onto her, pressing her back down into the dirt. Her head rapped off the ground, and she was sure she would have been seriously injured if the earth were not so soft. She tried to scream, but a large and calloused hand was smothering her entire face. She couldn't breathe, let alone scream or look around.

Laura realised that this was it – this was the end. She searched for understanding, but could not find it. She had responded to an apparently simple (though strange) request from her dying father; only to be met with exploding airplanes, attacked cabs, and now being hunted through a tropical forest. She felt her consciousness ebbing away, her mind slowly shutting down from suffocation. She tried to kick, to scream, to escape; but her exhausted body was no match for the strength and weight and power that had her pinned to the ground. As the consciousness finally departed, her final thought was that whatever the point of life was, it had certainly passed her by.

A Month Previously

Bedouin
August 11th

Only the previous month, Laura had no thoughts about 'The Meaning of Life.' She considered herself to be young, free and enjoying life. One month to the day before she was chased and caught in the Samui jungle, she was relaxing outside a bedouin tent in the Western Sahara. As she lay back against the animal-hide rugs that served as comfortable recliners Laura thought about how fortunate her life was. Here she lay – young, healthy and living life to the full; out of the rat race that most of her college friends were trapped in, as she travelled the world and soaked up new experiences and cultures.

A young and beautiful twenty-four, Laura was an experienced traveller and had backpacked all over the world. A classic Southern belle from South Carolina, she was tall, slim and gorgeous. Her long, naturally blonde hair was thick and full, falling in waves to the small of her back. It framed a face that Renaissance artists would have loved to paint, with eyes that were slightly almond and of the most startling ice-blue colour – when Laura looked directly at people, her eyes alone took their breath away, whether they were male or female, young or old. Her mouth was curved in a natural smile, with full red lips that begged to kiss and be kissed, whether in friendship or passion.

If her face was striking, her figure was stunning. A perfect hourglass shape, hers was a body that women were envious of and men hungered for. Toned by years of walking and healthy living, she was slim but not thin, muscular but not burly. Her legs, to use the cliché, seemed to go on forever; with perfectly rounded calves and thighs that were poetry made flesh. Her legs grew into shapely hips before narrowing to a slender waist that bore testimony to her active lifestyle. The hourglass then swelled to beautifully proportioned breasts that were spectacularly defined by the T-shirts she habitually wore.

She was in a T-shirt now, but covered by a jilbab out of respect for her Muslim hosts. Jilbab has its origin in the verb jalab, which means covering something with something else, so that it cannot be seen; whilst in the Islamic community, jilbab is meant as apparel, which covers the body of a person. Not only the skin of the body is covered, but also the curves and form of the body are not visible. Laura knew only too well the hiatus that would be caused were she to parade her curves in this community. Her hosts would be scandalised and insulted, and could not possibly treat her as an honoured guest as they did now.

Laura had met the bedouins while bargaining in the marketplace in the city of Laayoune on the coast of Western Sahara. She was mulling over a wooden figure of a man fighting his way through a sandstorm, which she was considering sending home to her dad. Laura picked up the figurine, turning it over appreciatively in her hands and then lifted it towards the trader with raised eyebrows, the international sign for 'How much?' The trader spoke surprisingly good English, 'The usual price my lady, is one thousand dirham.'

In time-honoured fashion of haggling all around the world, Laura blurted, 'Oh my God, that's absolutely crazy!' She quickly did some mental math. Very roughly, the exchange rate was 1 US dollar to 10 Moroccan dirham, so the trader was asking for a hundred dollars. If Laura had seen the piece at home, she wouldn't have hesitated, as the form was truly exquisite – who could have thought that you could sculpt a sandstorm in wood?

'But for you – one as beautiful as a desert dawn – I ask only seven hundred,' came the reply.

Laura examined the piece some more, at the same time covertly studying the bedouin trader. He was tall and regal, with an indefinable presence that proclaimed quietly but firmly 'I Am'. His skin was dark, and his face was weathered from a lifetime in the Saharan wind and sun. A tangible sense of quiet confidence and assurance radiated from him, and made Laura feel thankful to be in his presence. Nevertheless, she wasn't going to let his mystique get in the way of a good deal. She put the piece down with a sigh, and made as if to walk away.

'Wait,' called the trader. 'I think the spirit of this carving is destined for you. I can let you have it for only five hundred.'

'I'll give you fifty,' Laura responded nonchalantly, as though she didn't really want the piece. Yet it was so beautiful, she knew that she would have paid the initial asking price of one thousand if she had to.

'Fifty!' repeated the trader in apparent horror. 'Lady, I have a family to feed, and the desert has been unkind to us this year. Would you see my children starve, because I cannot get a fair price for the work of my people? I could not take anything less than four hundred.'

'Well, maybe one hundred then. Although I am not sure if I really want it or not. It is a big piece, and would be awkward to carry.'

'Lady, give me three hundred, and I will ship it home for you. You are American, yes?'

'I am,' replied Laura. 'If you are going to ship it for me, I'll give you two hundred, but not one dirham more.'

'The fates have decreed that we were to meet. Not only

to meet, but to become brother and sister. Let us agree on three hundred. You and I both know that you were willing to pay more, much more, than this. We will both be happy, and my children will be fed this evening,' said the trader, with a twinkle in his eye.

'Deal.'

They shook hands, and as they arranged the postal address and packed the piece, Laura and the trader chatted. His name was Tahir, and he was the leader or chief of his bedouin clan. They were striking camp that afternoon and moving into the desert to continue the never-ending journey of the ancient bedouin people across the desert sands. Tahir said he was about to pack up his stall, and he invited Laura back to his camp for tea.

Laura knew enough of bedouin culture to know that this was an honour – these nomadic people did not often invite Westerners into their domain – and she accepted gladly, always eager to experience new cultures and ways of life.

When they arrived at the bedouin's camp just outside town, Laura saw a few large tents, bound together from goat-hair blankets, branches and rope. There were a number of camels tethered nearby, and a fire was being used by the women to prepare a communal meal. Laura was invited to sit, and she immersed herself in the conversation that flowed and surrounded her, with Tahir acting as interpreter.

The bedouin talked about their travels through the Sahara, on both sides of the Berm – the second-longest wall in the world, which divides Morocco in two. Tahir's tribe was one of the few bedouin tribes that still lived an almost entirely nomadic life, journeying across the desert, occasionally stopping at a town to sell their crafts and buy necessities with the proceeds. They recognised no borders, national, geographical or military. Their wandering was a purposeful symbiotic exploitation of nature's cycle, as they moved with the water and the grazing; always ensuring that they moved on before they took too much from any one location.

Laura spoke of her travels through the Americas, Europe, Asia and Africa. Hers sounded by far the more exciting and interesting – she had experienced many different cultures, seen incredible sights and had unforgettable experiences. Yet when the bedouin described their harsh life in the desert, Laura sensed that, somehow, theirs was the richer life. There was a feeling of community, a perception of oneness, about their existence that she felt hers lacked. Her perception of her life was that, yes, it was full of people and very busy, but that she was disconnected from the people around her. This was true not only of the people she met on her travels, but even of her family. She somehow knew that this was not 'right', but was unable to express even to herself what was lacking.

As she lay back on the animal-hide rugs, she marvelled at these people. How often in America do you meet a trader at a market who would welcome you into his home as an honoured guest, almost as a family member? She was truly relaxed, and had that rare feeling of being accepted totally, with no reservations or conditions. She luxuriated in the unusual sense of holistic health – not only her body, but also her mind, heart and soul felt at rest and at peace. Unfortunately for Laura, this was an unusual experience. She had never really stopped to ponder it before, but as the bedouins chatted around her, she evaluated her existence.

Hers was a life of busy-ness, of rushing here and there, constantly encountering new places and experiences. Yet, when she thought about it now, she realised that she never really took time to assimilate these experiences – she rushed on to the next adventure without truly learning or growing as a result of the one just finished. She recognised with a shock that she felt isolated – even in the midst of all the activity and people in her life, she felt alone. She thought about her family life, and became conscious that even though she loved her dad dearly and spoke to him often over the phone, she didn't really communicate with him on a truly personal level.

The understanding hit Laura with a physical jolt. As she sensed the harmony and unity of the people around her, she realised her travelling was not about going to places, but running away from herself. She resolved to ask Tahir if she could spend time with him and his people, so that she could learn how to bring this sense of peace, happiness and contentment that she now felt, into her life on a more constant basis. With this thought, she rested in a glow of unaccustomed bliss.

Death!

Into this idyllic setting crashed a technological interruption – her cell-phone was ringing. Laura almost cried at the jarring discordant sound and sensation it introduced. As she scrambled though her backpack to retrieve the phone, she wondered why it is that the more means of communication we are given, the less we truly communicate. There was a time when the only form of communication was face-to-face interaction. Now we have telephone, post, email, texting, web-conferencing and a host of other means by which to be in touch. And yet, many societies experience more 'aloneness' now than at any other time in history. Maybe it is because we are communicating more often and with more people, but less deeply. It is like a man who swaps his single eight-hour sleep each night for thirty-two fifteen-minute naps at equal intervals throughout the day. He is technically getting as much sleep, but eventually he will literally die from exhaustion. Communication is the same – it is not just the quantity, but also the quality, that counts.

Laura finally found her phone, answered it and put it to her ear – and her world came crashing down around her. Her dad. The one constant in her eventful and sometimes painful life; her rock and her foundation; her one calm-weather port no matter what the storm; the only truly stable and steady person she had. No matter how far she travelled, no matter what she did, no matter how she felt, she always knew her dad was there for her. Now the voice on the phone was telling her that this was going to change. It was Dr Perenso, who had treated her as a child when she had the flu, and all the minor ailments that kids have as they grow. His voice came as if from a million miles away, echoing around in her head, the words crashing and colliding; making no sense as words, but with a terrifying and horrifying message that was all too clear.

Her dad was dying! He had been suffering from an annoying cough she knew, but he had assured her it was nothing. Sometimes when she had spoken to him on the phone in recent months, she had heard him coughing, and it hadn't sounded serious. But it was. Lung cancer. Left too late. Terminal. Only weeks to live. Last weeks would be hard. Morphine. Short time to say goodbye. Hurry home!

Homeward

She put down the phone, dazed and confused. Looking around, she realised that her hosts were looking at her with genuine concern – she could actually feel their love and support reaching out to her and enveloping her, holding and sustaining her as the shock set in. There was a feeling of communion amongst the bedouin, and then Tahir spoke.

'We will leave before dawn, and ride to Bir Lahmar. You can get a lift from there to Semara, and fly from there to Agadir in Morocco. You will be at home the day after tomorrow.'

Laura knew her new friends would get her on her way home as fast as was humanly possible. With that, the shock gave way to grief, and she collapsed into convulsive sobbing.

Laura had her own views on death, and they were not conducive to a calm acceptance of the inevitability of our mortality. She did not believe in an afterlife. Having travelled the world, she saw no evidence that any of the religions that espouse life after death had any basis at all. She had discussed philosophy in Athens, had argued the precepts of Christianity, Judaism, Islam, Buddhism and Hinduism at various times in her travels, and saw no reason to believe in some form of universal Consciousness, or any of the other metaphysical propositions that were put forward. As far as she was concerned, death was absolutely final. Her dad would be gone, and no prayer or meditation or altered state of consciousness or medium or anything else would bring him back. She realised with an awful anguish just how much she depended on him. Even though she travelled so much, and had seldom been home since her graduation, just knowing her dad was there always grounded her.

Laura spent the night alternating between the stages of grief – shock, denial, grief and anger – all the stages except acceptance. She couldn't sleep at all, tossing and turning, sometimes getting up to look at the sleeping desert, but getting no consolation from the cold, hard, uncaring stars.

While it was still pitch dark, the bedouin broke camp, miraculously transforming a small village into packs within minutes. Once the camels were loaded, they had a breakfast of bread, made fresh the night before, with goat's cheese and scrambled eggs. The eating was communal, all of them tearing off a piece of bread, and using it to scoop up the cheese or egg – or both, delicious together!

Then Tahir showed Laura how to mount the camel that had knelt for her. When the camel stood up, the feeling was like riding a roller-coaster – a quick, rolling backward swoop that made Laura's stomach instantly leap to her throat. From the camel's back, she looked down on the top of Tahir's head, easily two feet below her own, as he took the lead rope and prodded the camel into motion. The camel moved in a casual saunter that triggered a comfortable swaying for Laura.

She spent the next six hours grieving the imminent loss of her dad, as she swayed atop her ship of the desert. Tahir pushed the group hard during the trek. Rather than stop for lunch, they passed out strips of camel jerky to chew on; but Laura felt too sick to eat. By noon, they were riding into Bir Lahmar. Tahir disappeared as they all dismounted, Laura feeling disoriented by the return to unmoving ground after the rolling motion of the past six hours. Within minutes, Tahir returned, saying that he had found a truck about to leave, bound for Semara, a hundred kilometres to the northwest. Laura could not believe that she had only met Tahir and his community the day before, devastated as she was to leave them now. She hugged all of them desperately, trying to physically draw some of their strength into her body and heart.

Tahir led her to the central square and introduced her to the driver of an old oil tanker. He had no English but greeted Laura respectfully. Tahir helped her into the cab of the truck, and explained that the driver would drop her at the airport in Semara. Laura looked back as the tanker pulled away, tears streaming at the loss of her new friends, compounding and multiplying the heartache for her dad. True to Tahir's word, the driver pulled up at Semara airport, which turned out to be a grass-strip runway. Laura climbed down from the truck and went into the corrugated iron shack that served as both control tower and terminal.

Inside, two young men were playing cards at a small table. Laura asked if either of them spoke English and the darker-skinned of the two replied in flawless English that he had the pleasure of learning the Queen's English in Oxford.

'I need to get to Agadir urgently. Can you help me?' she pleaded.

'Certainly, madam,' was the polite reply. 'Your timing is fortunate, as my good friend Yagoub here is about to fly back to Agadir.'

The young man introduced himself as Nadeem, and proceeded to act as interpreter between Laura and Yagoub. They agreed on a price of one hundred and fifty US dollars, with a departure time of immediately. Laura paid Yagoub and they walked out to the runway. When Laura saw the plane, she almost changed her mind, as it was so ramshackled with peeling paint and a cracked windscreen.

However, the only alternative was to go overland, which would add at least a day to her travelling time. Suppressing her misgivings, she climbed into the cockpit and strapped herself into the work seat.

Yagoub climbed in the other side, while Nadeem busied himself at the front of the plane. Yagoub pressed the starter, and the engine gave an apologetic cough or two before it subsided into obstinate silence. Nadeem spun the propeller and Yagoub tried again. With a weary spluttering and in fits and starts, the motor eventually caught. Black smoke belched from the exhaust, and the old airplane complainingly coughed and spluttered, shaking the entire frame violently, before settling into a noisy, smoky routine.

Yagoub taxied to the end of the grass strip and turned the plane to face into the wind. He opened the throttle and the plane rolled and bounced across the field, almost shaking Laura loose from her seat. As they neared the end of the runway, the bounces grew further and further apart. Laura trembled as the chain-link fence encircling the field grew closer and closer. As they left the ground, she was certain that they were going to crash, and with disbelief saw the fence scrape their under-carriage as they barely cleared the top of the fence.

For the second time that day, Laura found herself in the company of a man who spoke no English. She sank into her thoughts, partly to avoid the stress of being conscious of the erratic flight of the plane. She woke with a start as they landed. Losing no time, she thanked Yagoub and hurried into the international terminal. There, she booked a ticket on the next flight that could get her home to Columbia City in South Carolina, via Paris and JFK. Two hours later, she was on board a Boeing 747, silently thanking Tahir for getting her out of Africa so quickly.

Having changed planes in Paris, Laura crossed the Atlantic completely exhausted and still in a state of shock. While her body had virtually shutdown, and she was almost unconscious from a physical perspective; her mind was out of control. The combination of grief and extreme fatigue had an almost kaleidoscopic, psychedelic effect. As she lay still in the seat, images and nightmares jostled and competed for primacy in her mind.

Her body was apparently tranquil, but in her mind she was racing from The Grim Reaper, who stalked her very slowly at a breakneck pace. She was falling – experiencing time and again that stomach-churning sensation of realising she had just passed the point of no return, that she was going to die. As these scenes repeated themselves, she descended to a hell that she did not believe in. In this awful place, she was whipped and scourged. Her flesh boiled from her bones in the agonising flames, while parts of her body froze and shattered in the absolute cold of deep-space.

There were also more normal anxiety dreams, connected with a sense of where she was. She dreamed that they had landed and she was waiting at the luggage carousel. All the passengers had collected their bags and exited though customs, while she stood and waited. Eventually, the last bag was collected, and she was left alone at the belt, with still no sign of her bag. Armed soldiers gathered around the walls of the room, dressed in full jungle combat dress, watching her. She started to sweat in fear, as still no bags appeared, and the soldiers started to close in on her menacingly.

Laura awoke with a start – the passenger in the seat beside her was shaking her gently by the shoulder. 'You seemed a little disturbed in your sleep.'

Laura could only peer at him, uncomprehending, lost in

that place between waking and sleeping where nothing makes sense and everything is confusion.

She sat in her seat, no longer sleeping, but instead thinking about her father – the one person in her life in whom she had absolute trust. She could not begin to imagine how she could live in a world where he was absent.

After changing flights in JFK, Laura numbly sat through the last leg of this horrible journey, with the two-hour flight from JFK to her hometown of Columbia in South Carolina passing in a blur.

Dad

As she ran out of Columbia Metropolitan Airport, Laura could scarcely believe that it was less than two days since she had received the terrible news. She jumped into a cab and rang her dad's number to let him know that she would be there in less than two hours.

The telephone was answered by an unfamiliar female voice.

'This is Laura. Is my dad there?' she asked quickly.

'Oh, Laura, yes. This is Nurse Rogers. Dr Perenso has arranged for me to provide home-care for your dad. We have been waiting for your call,' replied the kind voice at the other end of the line.

'How is dad? Can I speak to him? Is he OK?' The questions tumbled out.

'He's sleeping at the moment, dear. I think it might be best to let him sleep until you are home – I gave him a sedative a short while ago. I'll ring Dr Perenso, he asked me to let him know when you would be here, so that he can speak with you. How long will it take you to get home?'

'I'll be there in the next hour-and-a-half or so,' whispered Laura, almost afraid to end the conversation. 'I'll see you then.'

Having overheard one side of the conversation, the cab driver asked Laura what the problem was, and she spilled out what was happening – that she had been abroad and was rushing home because her father had fallen seriously ill. The cab driver clearly empathised with her, and took it as his mission to get her home as quickly as possible. Ignoring speed limits and driving on the edge of safety as he sped through the Columbia streets, he had her home in a little over an hour. As he pulled into the driveway of her dad's house, Dr Perenso's car was pulling in just in front of her.

They say that first impressions last, and this is as true in relationships as in anything else. Despite now being in her twenties, and Dr Perenso only being in his late fifties, Laura still saw him as the kindly colossus who went around saving people. This was not a conscious thought of course – Laura saw herself as a mature sophisticated adult and her conscious self thought of Dr Perenso as a middle-aged, competent but not extraordinary, local doctor. Nevertheless, Laura's deepest perception of the doctor was that of the safe giant who leaned over her bed when she was ill as a child, reassuring and curing and ultimately saving her and her family whenever sickness threatened.

And so it was that she now rushed over to him and buried her head on his shoulder, waiting for him to make everything right – even though she knew in her heart that not even our giants can overcome mortality.

Dr Perenso held Laura gently, knowing from experience that the questions would come when she was ready. He knew of many doctors who confessed that this was the one part of being a GP that they really hated – having to comfort family members during a bereavement of a loved one. But for Dr Perenso, this was the most rewarding part of his job. He felt that the purely medical aspect of his practice was technical knowledge – that if you could program a computer, it could do the job as competently as a human doctor. He believed that what really differentiated a great family doctor from the merely competent, was the doctor's interpersonal skills. He knew from experience that when a loved one was dying, the real contribution of the family doctor was not to the patient, but to their family –

comforting and reassuring even when death is inevitable and imminent.

The doctor felt Laura's clutching grip slowly ease a little, and he knew it was time for her to understand what was happening. He gently drew her arms from his shoulders and held her in front of him, looking at the fear in her eyes. 'Oh, Laura, you have no idea how much you have grown since I delivered you twenty-four years ago. Your father is so proud of you, and I know that your mom would have been very proud of you as well.'

'I don't believe this is happening,' she sobbed. 'Surely there is something that can be done?'

'I'm sorry, Laura, but this comes to us all. We all have our time on this earth, and then we must move on to whatever awaits us after this life. It is your father's time, and he has made his peace with that. I know that his only concern now is for you, because he won't be here for you as he always has been. Although ...' Dr Perenso's voice trailed off.

'What is it?' asked Laura.

'I'm not sure,' confessed the doctor. 'There does seem to be something else on his mind, but when I tried to talk to him about it, he refused to discuss it with me. Anyway, the important thing is that you are here now, and you will be able to have some time with him in these last few weeks. Come on, let's go in and see if he is awake.'

Laura felt as though she was walking into the last great unknown. Her mom had died in a traffic accident when she was a child, and her father had quit his government job, taken up the teaching post at the university, and had been both father and mother to her ever since. Laura had no real memory of her mother, but her dad had always spoken about her a lot, showing Laura photos of family outings, although her dad was in very few of them. He had explained his absence as being due to the pressures of his job – apparently he had been a statistician working on economic indicators during the 1970s. Her dad always spoke so lovingly of his wife, saying that she had been a wonderful wife and mother, and that her passing away was a tragic sacrifice. As Dr Perenso walked her into the house, Laura suffered the awful realisation that she was about to become an orphan.

Dr Perenso brought Laura upstairs to her father's room, explaining as they climbed the staircase about what to expect.

'Your father is not in too much pain, as we are sedating him with morphine to keep him comfortable. With such a late diagnosis, that's really all we can do, to try to give him peace and dignity in his final days.'

They reached the door of her dad's bedroom.

'I'll give you some time alone together,' said Dr Perenso. 'Nurse Rogers is downstairs if you need anything.'

Laura thanked the doctor, drawing in a deep breath as she opened the door.

She walked across to her father's bed and sat in the chair that was drawn up next to the bedside. As she gazed at the sleeping man, Laura felt a curious disconnection from the scene. She recognised that she was demolished by her grief and yet she continued to be able to function – sitting, breathing, thinking about the situation as though she were observing it from outside. She supposed this was the safety mechanism developed through aeons of evolution, designed to protect our frail humanity from the shocking intensity of our emotions.

She reached out and took her dad's hand, holding it protectively in hers. It was a strange and unsettling feeling – a role reversal whereby she now felt that she had to guard and protect her father; whereas previously she was always the child, being minded and cared for by her parent. She was shocked at how much weight her dad had lost – she had only been away for three months, yet he looked as though he had lost twenty kilos or more. While he wasn't skeletal, he certainly was gaunt, with a drawn face and permanent worry lines that hadn't been in evidence when she had last seen him. Laura's dad always had a permanent half-smile on his face, although she remembered that he always had a slight frown when he was asleep, as though something was troubling him and he was grappling with some great problem in his sleep. Now, though, there was evidence of a physical pain in his sleeping face, which was troubling and unsettling for Laura.

As she watched over him, he stirred slightly and gradually opened his eyes. As he lay on his back, he looked straight up at the ceiling, but he slowly turned and his eyes softened as he saw Laura at his side.

'You're back,' he murmured, the old smile lightening his pained face.

'Oh, Dad. Why didn't you call me earlier?' cried Laura.

'It's just my time, that's all. It comes to us all sooner or later.'

Laura felt so helpless. 'What can I do?'

'Just stay with me. They tell me I only have a few weeks and I want to spend them with you. I worry about you, you know?'

'You worry about me!' exclaimed Laura, not saying but clearly thinking, 'You are the one who is dying, not me.'

'Yes,' he confirmed. 'I worry about you. I know what is ahead of me – I have my belief, and that comforts me. But I do not know what is ahead of you, and I am not going to be here to help you.'

He paused before continuing. 'But let's not talk of that yet – there is plenty of time for that later. Tell me about the Sahara – it is so many years since I walked those sands.'

'I never knew you had travelled to Africa,' Laura said. Indeed, when she thought about it later, she realised that her father often seemed familiar with many of the far-flung corners of the earth that she visited. She knew he hadn't travelled since her mom had died, so it must have been when he worked in the Government Statistics Office. But always, as now, he dismissed any discussion of his own travels.

'Never mind me. Tell me – what did you see? What did you do?'

And so the evening passed, with Laura relating her tales of the Sahara and Tahir's tribe, and then recalling other adventures and travels she had experienced during her years of travelling.

By the second day, the household was already settling into a routine, although they all know that it would be short-lived. Laura spent the days with her father, in his bedroom when he felt weak, or wheeling him into the garden when he felt a little stronger. Between herself and Nurse Rogers, they tended to his physical and medical needs, with a visit from Dr Perenso each afternoon. As the days turned into one week and then two, her dad visibly weakened, and, by the end of the second week, Dr Perenso was forewarning Laura that the end was very near.

Dying Wish

It was sixteen days since Laura had arrived home. Her father was now so weak that she could no longer wheel him into the garden, as the required movement created too much pain, despite the morphine. Dr Perenso had explained that the level of medication had to be balanced – too little was ineffective, too much could stop her father's heart. Laura now spent her days in her father's bedroom, talking quietly when he was awake, though he slept more and more as the days passed. At night, when Laura slept, tossing and turning fitfully in her bed, Nurse Rogers tended to her father's needs.

It was now late on a balmy August evening, and Dr Perenso called to the house again, despite having made his usual afternoon visit earlier in the day. He examined Laura's dad, and then spoke to her downstairs. 'Laura, you need to prepare yourself. I don't think your father will make it through the night,' he said, confirming what Laura already knew in her heart. She had spent all day every day with her father since getting home, and she knew the end was very near. 'Your father has been very blunt with me,' the doctor continued 'warning me not to shield him from the truth. So he knows that this is likely to be his last night.'

Oh, Doctor,' whispered Laura, 'I still can't believe that this is it. That there is nothing that anyone can do. That this really is the end.'

'I know, Laura,' the doctor murmured gently. 'But there is something you can do. Stay with him. Be close to him. That comfort in his final hours will be your real gift to him.'

It was with a heavy heart that Laura slowly climbed the

stairs, knowing that the next time she walked back down those stairs, her father would be gone from her. She pushed open the door of his bedroom and sat in the chair that was now such a familiar part of her daily routine. Her father was sleeping, although Laura supposed the correct term was probably unconscious. Dr Perenso had warned her that he may or may not regain consciousness before the end. And so Laura settled in for her lonely vigil, knowing that Nurse Rogers was on hand if needed.

As Laura watched over her dad, she dozed lightly on and off. She suddenly came to with a guilty start as her dad stirred slightly in the bed. Not knowing how long she had dozed, she glanced at the bedside clock and saw it was 3 a.m. Her dad shifted slightly again, then slowly opened his eyes.

'It's OK, Dad, I'm here with you,' Laura said softly.

'Oh, Laura,' her father moaned, clearly in pain. 'I failed so much. But after they took your mom, I couldn't risk losing you as well. I had to leave it be.'

'Sssh,' soothed Laura. Her dad was clearly delirious, talking rambling nonsense.

'There was so much, so much power and ambition. What could I do? I was just one man, and I had to protect you. I hid the information, so they would have to leave us alone. But I was powerless to stop them. So much pain and suffering, and all because I was weak.' He paused, out of breath.

'It's OK, Dad, I'm here with you.' Laura wasn't sure if he was even aware of her presence. He seemed to be reliving some pain, something that he felt guilty about.

'It's OK, Dad,' repeated Laura. 'I'm here beside you.'

'I'm sorry, Tracey,' her dad whispered.

Laura made soothing noises, not knowing what else to

do or say, as her dad spoke to his dead wife. A tear rolled down his cheek as he continued. 'I'm so sorry, my darling. I couldn't save you. But I saved Laura. Kept my head down while she was in school, sent her around the world after that.'

Laura stroked his hand and wiped the tear from his cheek as he rambled. Then, he seemed to become aware of her presence.

'Laura, Laura,' he called. 'Please, Laura, forgive me. Please forgive me.'

'It's OK, Dad. There is nothing to forgive. Please, rest.'

'No, Laura. Tell me. You must tell me. Do you forgive me? Please, Laura, please.'

Not knowing what else to say, and not wanting to see him so distressed, Laura told him what he clearly needed to hear. 'Yes, Dad. Yes, I forgive you. Now please, rest yourself.'

With that, her father visibly relaxed. 'Thank you, my darling,' he murmured. 'You have always been a good daughter – I am so proud of you. Please be careful if you decide to take this on.'

Laura wondered what he was talking about, but suddenly it became irrelevant. Her father had been breathing very shallowly, but now drew deep gasping breaths. Laura somehow knew this was the end – there is an instinctive knowledge within all of us, which tells us when we are in the presence of death. He inhaled deeply, then exhaled with a rattling sigh until there was no more breath left in his body.

Laura sat still, hoping against everything that she knew to be true, hoping that her dad would draw breath again. However, as the seconds passed and became minutes, Laura knew that she had to accept the inevitable. Her dad was gone.

She went to the door and called Nurse Rogers. The nurse checked her dad's pulse and respiration and quietly confirmed that he had died. Seeing how physically and emotionally exhausted Laura was, Nurse Rogers told her that there was nothing more to be done that night and that Laura should try to get some rest for the remainder of the night-time hours.

Laura left the nurse tidying the medical paraphernalia that was no longer needed, but couldn't face the thought of going to bed herself. Instead, she made a coffee, laced it with a generous measure of bourbon, and sat in an armchair. She wondered what would happen next – she knew nothing about the formalities or logistics of arranging a funeral. She had occasionally thought about it during the past two weeks, but it had felt somehow disrespectful to her dad to start making such arrangements when he was still alive. As dawn brightened the world outside, Laura's thoughts moved to memories of the good times of her childhood, of her dad coming to see her perform in school plays, of him reading to her at night, and the myriad other little things that seem so insignificant to us when we are adults, but that are so incredibly important to us when we are children.

She didn't know how long she sat there, reliving the past; but she was brought back into the present by the sound of two cars pulling up outside. When she looked out, she saw Dr Perenso and went to meet him at the front door.

'I'm terribly sorry, Laura. I know how hard this must be for you. All I can say to you is that it was a merciful release for him at the end.'

Laura nodded dully, still not sure what she was supposed to do or say, now that the unimaginable had come to pass.

'I hope you don't mind,' the doctor continued, 'but I

thought you might need some support in making all of the necessary arrangements, so I asked Mr Croft, the local undertaker, to call out with me this morning. If there is someone else you would rather use, just say so and I'll let Mr Croft know that he won't be needed.'

'Oh, no, no,' Laura answered quickly, clearly relieved at the thought of someone who could help her during the coming days. 'I think it will be good to have someone to help me.'

The doctor gestured to the man in the other car, who got out and introduced himself to Laura offering his condolences. 'Have you any specific arrangements made for the funeral?' he asked.

'No,' replied Laura. 'Maybe it has been remiss of me, but I haven't been able to bring myself to think too much about it before today.'

'Not a question of being remiss at all,' Mr Croft stated. 'We each deal with bereavement in our own way. If you tell me what church your father belonged to, I will make all of the arrangements for you if you wish. I will, of course, sit down and go through everything in advance with you for your approval. Is that OK?'

'Oh, that would suit me perfectly, Mr Croft. I wouldn't know where to start.'

'That's quite all right, Laura,' Mr Croft reassured her. 'Lets go in and sit down, and we will go through the main items so that I can get everything underway.'

As she sat in the kitchen with Mr Croft, nursing another coffee, Laura marvelled at the apparent normalcy of the scene. She and the undertaker discussed all of the necessary arrangements, from the church, to the placing of a death notice in the local newspapers, to the choice of coffin. It was decided that her father's body would repose in the undertakers overnight, before being removed to the church the following evening. One of the undertaker's assistants arrived during the discussion, and Laura said a personal goodbye to her dad in his bedroom before he was taken away.

By lunchtime, Laura found herself alone in the house, after a hectic morning of making decisions, or rather, of agreeing to Mr Croft's suggestions. The following three days passed in a blur – the church services with their formality lending a structure to an inherently emotional chaos; strangers as well as people she recognised from the university offering their condolences while Laura smiled acknowledgement, even though smiling was the last thing she felt inclined to do. She was glad to see so many of the university students coming to pay their last respects to her dad – it made her feel that his life had been one of value, with his students acknowledging that he had been an important part of their lives.

Two days after the funeral, Laura was at her father's solicitor's office, for the reading of the will. Given that she was the only child of a widowed parent, her expectation was that it would be relatively simple. After waiting only a few moments, a middle-aged man walked into the reception area and introduced himself as Daniel Holden. He ushered her into his office, explaining that he had looked after all of her father's legal affairs and so would be conducting the reading of the will.

When they were both seated at his imposing mahogany desk, he picked up a sealed envelope. 'As far as I am aware, Laura, this is your late father's last will and testament, which we wrote out and he signed here in this office at the end of last year. Are you aware of any written will he might have made since then?'

'No. As far as I am aware, he left everything with you to be looked after should anything happen to him.'

'Very well,' said Mr Holden. 'We shall then proceed on the basis of this being your late father's valid last will.'

He formally opened the sealed envelope, removing a single A4 sheet of paper, and a smaller envelope, which was also sealed.

'OK,' Mr Holden proceeded. 'I can confirm that the will is properly signed, witnessed and dated, and therefore this document is valid.'

He then proceeded to read the will aloud. All was as Laura expected – her father left all of his possessions such as house, car, bank accounts, personal belongings etc to her as his only child. The only slight mystery concerned the smaller sealed envelope that had been filed with the will itself. Mr Holden read aloud the last paragraph of the will.

'"And, finally, I leave my most valuable and most cursed possession to Laura, to do with as she will. Stored with this will is a DVD which Laura is to view in private." Hmmm, that seems a strange wording, Laura! Do you want me to check that this envelope does indeed contain a DVD – it seems about the right size,' Mr Holden asked.

'No,' Laura said, 'that's OK. Whatever about the wording, and I agree that it does sound a bit strange, Dad seemed quite particular that I should view it in private. I would like to honour his wishes, if that's OK.'

'That's absolutely no problem at all, Laura. Indeed, I think you are quite right. Well, that's all there is to it at this stage. As executor of your late father's will, I will handle all the formalities of getting bank accounts switched into your name and so forth. I will keep you updated on progress.'

With that, Laura thanked the solicitor, and returned home. It seemed so strange to call the house 'Home' now that her father was no longer there. Yet his possessions - everything from clothes to books – did seem to lend a resonance to the bricks and mortar, and spoke of him. Laura supposed that over the coming weeks and months she would have to sort through her father's possessions – clothes to a charity, books to the university, etc. Thinking of this made Laura realise that through her dad's illness, and during the last few days since he passed away, she hadn't once seriously considered her future. What was to become of her, now that she was effectively on her own in the world? She realised with a shock that she didn't have a plan – she had no picture of what her future could, or should, look like. She reasoned that the coming weeks and months would be busy sorting out all of her dad's stuff and finalising the legal and financial end of things.

In the meantime, she decided the first item on her agenda was food. She hadn't thought about food properly in almost three weeks, and hadn't eaten properly since her mad dash home from the Sahara. She fixed herself some sandwiches, and sat in her father's study to have them with a coffee. As she chewed absentmindedly, she thought about the unusual wording of the last part of her dad's will. 'And finally, I leave my most valuable and most cursed possession to Laura, to do with as she will. Stored with this will is a DVD which Laura is to view in private.' Very strange indeed, and not at all what she would have expected of her dad, who was a very practical man, not given to flights of fancy.

As she ate, she decided on impulse to watch the DVD there and then, even though she had originally planned on leaving it for a while. She took it out of the sealed envelope and put it into the DVD player, but got a message: 'Cannot read disc.'

After all that, she thought, it turns out to be a dud disc.

She turned back to her lunch, feeling vaguely disappointed. She wasn't sure what she had expected, but she felt a little frustrated that after the cryptic message, the DVD was faulty. And yet, the more she thought about it, the less plausible it seemed. Her dad was particular to a fault - so much so that she had often teased him about being a perfectionist. Laura found it hard to believe that something important enough to be left with his will wouldn't have been checked and double-checked.

With that thought in mind, Laura suddenly thought about her dad's PC – maybe it would work in that. She powered up the computer, hoping that he didn't have a password on it. Happily, the computer booted up to the main screen. Laura loaded the DVD into the drive and sat back to see if anything would auto-play, but nothing happened. Then she listed the contents of the DVD, but there was only one file called Laura, with a file extension that she didn't recognise.

She double-clicked on the file and the screen went momentarily black. Then a message appeared.

'Please Enter Password.'

Laura groaned – the password could be anything. Why would her dad leave her a DVD that she was to look at in private, but then password-protect it so that she couldn't access it?

She tried a few guesses – names of people close to them, family pets from her childhood, but each time she typed in a guess and pressed Enter, the screen simply wiped out what she had typed and stubbornly redisplayed the original welcoming message.

Laura groaned – why would her dad do his to her? As she thought about it, she realised that it really did not make sense. There must be some way that her dad expected her to be able to think of the password. As her eyes wandered from the screen, she became conscious of the fact that she was in her dad's study – the only room in the house with a PC. She wondered was that a hint. Was the password in the study? Would come across it as she tidied her dad's papers? Well, here was only one thing for it – she would have to sort his paperwork sooner that she had thought!

Changing into her 'chore clothes', Laura gathered some spare boxes from the garage and set to work, glad to have something to do to take her mind off the emptiness and loneliness of the house. She sorted everything in the study into a number of categories, boxing each accordingly. Reference books and academic texts were destined for the university library, novels were going to a charity shop, financial statements were filed for the accountant and legal paperwork for the solicitor. Family memorabilia went into a box for her to look at later. Everything else was gathered and tidied.

At the end of a busy few hours, Laura had the study organised and all of its contents categorised and boxed. Famished from the exertion, she heated a pizza and brought it into the study with a cold beer. Still no password, despite all her checking. Still frustrated, but determined to at least get one chore fully completed, Laura started dusting and polishing. As she moved the keyboard to dust underneath it, Laura caught a glimpse of something out of place. Turning the keyboard over fully, she saw note taped to the underside of the keyboard in her dad's neat handwriting. She read and reread it, trying to decide was it a reference to the missing password, and if so, what was it trying to tell her?

'LAURA – A Beautiful Day, ampersand, concatenated.'

She stared at her dad's handwriting. It had to be a reference to the password – what else could it be? But she didn't even know what the last two words meant. She tried typing in the note as the password, using different combinations without and without her name in front, and with and without the last two words, but none worked. Then, she turned to the reference books, and looked up a definition of 'ampersand' – the correct term for the '&' symbol, sometimes used in place of the word 'and'. Moving on to 'concatenate', Laura read the definition: 'To join together two or more words or character-strings to form one big one.' So Laura tried various combinations of the words on the note, but typed them without the spaces between the words, with and without the '&' symbol. But still no luck.

Laura threw up her arms – she was unaccountably angry with her father for setting what seemed to be an insoluble puzzle. He should have left a clue that would mean something special to her, which she alone would be able to decipher. As she fixed her eyes on the note, she felt a slight shiver down her spine. Maybe he had done exactly that! Laura racked her memory – the phrase meant something, something from her childhood. Yes. When she was in elementary school, there had been a Parents' Day at the end of every school year. There would be sports and drama, recitals and quizzes, with all of the children able to exhibit their talent for the appreciation of their parents. Laura's dad had always been there, no matter how busy his lecture schedule in the university. Unlike most kids, Laura only had her dad – for most kids it was both their parents who came, or maybe only their mom if their dad couldn't get off work. But every year, Laura's dad came and clapped and cheered and told her how proud he was of her. And every year as they drove home, he would sing 'A Beautiful Day', and tell Laura that it had been a beautiful day. Laura was elated, proud and thankful that she had finally broken her dad's code.

So she started trying combinations again, but this time concentrating on the words 'Parents Day' instead of 'A Beautiful Day.' She tried Parents Day with and without spaces, but still the computer obstinately refused to allow her access. As she tried different formats of the words one after the other, without success, Laura felt like screaming. She had broken her dad's code, equating his phrase 'A Beautiful Day' with the relevant day from her childhood, and still she couldn't get in!

As she continued trying, and was getting more and more desperate, Laura couldn't see the relevance of the reference to 'ampersand' in her dad's note. There was no 'and' in 'Parents Day', so maybe she was on the wrong track completely. She felt discouraged, and, in truth, a little letdown by her dad, which in turn made her feel guilty. Laura wasn't consciously aware of it, but she was feeling the maelstrom of conflicting emotions that is typical for the ones left behind after bereavement. How could he set her such an obscure puzzle? She had been so delighted to break the code, equating 'A Beautiful Day' to 'Parent's Day', but now it seemed that she was completely missing her dad's hidden message. What did the ampersand mean? How could it be relevant to 'Parents Day'?

Laura thought back to those annual occasions, and the drive home each year at the end of the day, when her dad would be singing 'A Beautiful Day'. Was there anything else there that could help her? She replayed those drives home in her mind as best she could. Again, she felt a shiver run down her spine as a faint memory brushed her consciousness and subsided again. Yes, there was something, something else that was related to those happy days, and that would account for the 'ampersand' in her dad's note. Laura wanted to rip open her mind and get back the memory that had risen so fleetingly. Again, she replayed the drive home each year in her mind, thinking of her dad singing his song and telling her what a beautiful day it had been. And again, the memory allowed a fleeting glimpse, but too short for her to be able to grab hold of it.

Laura couldn't help it – the strain of trying to remember, the frustration of feeling so close to the answer without being able to get hold of it, the emotion of feeling that her dad was depending on her to crack his code, and all of the feelings of loss and abandonment combined to overwhelm her. She fell forward on the desk, heart-wracking sobs tearing her apart. She felt so alone, an orphan, a person without the protection of a close family unit. Laura cried her loneliness out on her dad's study desk, until the pain subsided slightly, and she was able to sit up and think again. She realised that the memory she was chasing was not going to come on command. Laura had known the feeling of trying to recall a name and of being unable to, only to have it pop unbidden into her mind at a later date. So she decided to leave the search for the answer to her dad's riddle until the next day. Exhausted from clearing of the study, but even more emotionally worn, Laura climbed the stairs, showered, and crawled into her bed. As soon as her head hit the pillow, she fell into a worn-out, dreamless sleep.

It was the middle of the night when she woke with a start, a phrase ringing in her head. She woke so suddenly that she couldn't relate the phrase to anything, but she knew it was important. Grabbing a pen and paper from her bedside locker, she wrote the phrase down – 'Dad and Daughter Day.' As she looked at the words she had written, a smile brightened her beautiful face – something that had been mostly absent from that face for the past few weeks. She had it now – she knew the answer to her dad's riddle. And it was a message just for her – nobody else would ever have been able to work out the code.

Again, Laura replayed in her mind the memory of those drives home from Parents Day each year. Her dad would sing his song, and he would tell her that it had been a beautiful day. Like all good parents, he would focus on what Laura had done well, telling her how good she had been and how proud he was of her, regardless of whether or not she had actually won. He always told her that it was a special day for them, and so they should give it their own name. And so he would call it 'Dad and Daughter Day', because it was always just the two of them. Then, he always went on to talk about Laura's mom, telling Laura what a beautiful person her mom was, and how her mom would be so proud of her as well.

Laura jumped out of bed, threw on a dressing gown and raced downstairs. She had to try it now, she couldn't wait until morning. As she sat down in front of the PC, the same message awaited her – 'Please Enter Password'.

Laura started combinations of 'Dad and Daughter Day', with and without spaces, and sometimes using the ampersand symbol instead of the word 'and.' When she typed 'dad&daughterday', the message on the screen changed for the first time since the previous evening, after the hundreds of different combinations of different words that she had tried since the previous evening.

Laura jumped a little, taken unawares by the sudden change. The screen now read: 'Hi, Laura. Remember your fourth grade teacher's admonition!'

Laura gasped as she read the new message – this was the first confirmation that she was definitely on the right track. She racked her brains about fourth grade – her teacher had been Ms Helmott, a kind young teacher whom all the kids had loved. Laura had been a bright student, academically strong and doing well in all of her lessons. The one thing that Ms Helmott had to repeatedly remind Laura about was her grammar – Laura could clearly remember her teacher gently but firmly telling her that the number of mistakes in her written work really wasn't good enough.

With that memory in mind, and taking account of her dad's reference to ampersand and concatenation, Laura typed in 'Dad&DaughterDay.'

Hardly daring to breathe, she pressed Enter.

Video

Laura gasped as her dad appeared on the computer screen in front of her, sitting in the very chair that she now found herself in as she looked at the screen. It seemed almost ghostly, that she was looking at a dead man sitting in the same chair.

'Hi, Laura,' her dad said, straight into the camera, obviously mounted on top of the computer. 'I'm sorry I had to lead you such a merry chase to open this video – I'm sure you were tearing your hair out trying to figure out the password, but I knew you would get it eventually. I'm sure you are wondering why all the cloak and dagger stuff is necessary. Well, I'm afraid it's because what I am about to tell you will be surprising to say the least, probably shocking – and you must not tell anyone about it. I will explain everything and then I have a request, but I must warn you that your life will be in danger if you decide to take it on.'

The image of her dad on the screen smiled sadly and quietly, as he paused, clearly gathering his thoughts to present them to her. Laura leaned forward in her chair, simultaneously fascinated and a little frightened. She didn't know what to expect – it was clear from her dad's face that the video had been made relatively recently. Had he gone a little bit crazy as his illness had set in, or was there indeed something behind all the strange things he seemed ready to lay out before her? Laura listened intently as her dad continued.

'I don't know if I am right or wrong to do this – and even if I am doing the right thing, I'm not sure that I am going about it in the right way. But, anyway, I couldn't go to my grave without leaving even a hope that things might be put right, and so I am going to pass the torch to you, to carry or extinguish as you feel best. I am going to spare you the background, because it hurts me too much to think of it, and I don't believe it would be useful to you anyway. Suffice to say, that this feeds back into my younger years, and the terrible sacrifice of your mom. If you decide to take this on, then from this moment forward, your life is in danger. You must talk to nobody about what you are doing – you have always been a world traveller, so simply say you are going travelling because staying here reminds you too much of your recent bereavement.

'Just before I tell you what the task is, I have to tell you two other things – one to emphasise the importance of this task, and the other to reassure you that I have not gone crazy. In terms of its importance – this is literally world-changing stuff. I know your natural reaction will be to think that ordinary little people like us couldn't possibly change the world, but, believe me, this will. On a personal level, it is incredibly important to me – this would literally put right the terrible wrong that I have had to allow to be left in place for the past thirty years.

'In terms of reassuring you that I have not gone crazy, there are some funds in place should you need to draw on them. If you go to the Banque Generale de Commerce in Avenue de Chatelaine in Geneva, your fingerprints will give you access to a deposit account. To verify this, you can ring the bank and ask them to tell you the balance on account 030705/76987831 – they will ask you for a password, which is the same password that you used to access this DVD. The current balance in that account is in the region of sixty million US dollars.

Laura gasped, clicking the pause button as she tried to let

her father's words sink in. Sixty million dollars? It was impossible. There was no way that her father could have amassed such an incredible fortune on his professor's salary. Unable to make any sense of it, Laura clicked on the play button to see what would come next.

'OK, Laura, now to the task in hand. Remember that you have the choice to walk away, to destroy this DVD and live out the rest of your life in whatever way you wish. But if you want to take this on, bear in mind the danger involved, and realise that I have given you no definitive reason why you should, other than my assurance that it is important – both to me personally but also to the world at large.

'The task is simply this – I want you to go to Bangkok and collect a package from an old friend of mine and deliver it to another old friend. The package should be collected from my friend Mwai, who runs the Five Seasons brothel in Patpong in Bangkok. Mwai will tell you to whom it needs to be delivered. You will have to make the delivery personally, as it is not something that you can post or courier.

'Laura, I tell you again – this is dangerous, so the decision is your own. Regardless of what you do, know this above anything else – I love you more than life itself, as did your mom. I am happy to be going to the next life – I believe I will be reunited with your mom there, although I know you don't share my beliefs. Anyway, please be happy in your life, and be true to what you know to be right.'

Her dad seemed to blink away a tear, as he quietly said again, 'I love you Laura.' With that, he leaned forward and the picture went blank. Laura sat motionless for a long time, simply staring at the empty screen whilst her mind was in turmoil. Questions chased one another in her head, whirling around so quickly that she didn't even have time to consider one before another would take its place.

Slowly, a few key thoughts crystallised in Laura's mind. Her father wanted her to collect a package from a brothel owner in Bangkok – Laura resisted the temptation to start wondering just how the hell her dad came to be friends with a Thai brothel owner. He said it was dangerous, but important for him personally as well as for the world as a whole. He had to be crazy! And then there was this business of a bank account with sixty million dollars in it – clearly insane stuff. And then Laura thought that at least that one was easy to prove or disprove – all she had to do was to ring the bank, if it existed at all. It was now 5 a.m., which by Laura's reckoning would be noon in Switzerland.

She rang international directory enquiries and asked for the number, half-expecting to be told that there was no such bank, but there was. Laura tentatively dialled the number, which was answered by an automated voice system. Following the voice prompts, she pressed 3 for account balance and then keyed in the account number that her dad had given her. There was a pause, and then a male voice addressed her. 'You wish to check the balance of an account?'

Laura wasn't sure if she really did, but forced herself to confirm the request.

'May I have your name and date of birth please?'

Laura provided both.

'May I have the name and date of birth of the joint account-holder please?'

Laura hesitated – her father hadn't said it was a joint account. She guessed that if it was, then presumably he was the other person. She gave his name and date of birth.

'Thank you, Ms Whiteland. Do I need any further information from you before I process your request?'

Laura presumed he was referring to the password that

her dad had specified.

'Yes,' she said. 'You cannot do anything without the password.'

'OK, that's fine,' the as yet unidentified man at the other end of the line said. 'Can you tell me what the password is please?'

'Absolutely,' said Laura. 'The password is 'Dad and Daughter Day'.'

'That's perfect,' said the man, confirming that the account existed, and that the password was as detailed by her dad. Laura was getting seriously freaked out at this stage.

'Allow me to introduce myself, Ms Whiteland, as I have not had the pleasure of speaking to you before now. My name is Herr Speigle, or Mr Speigle if you prefer. I am responsible for managing your account, so please feel free to ask for me at any time. As I discussed with your father at our last meeting, we have upgraded our security systems to include voice recognition. In future, your voice will be sufficient for you to access your account. Now, you wanted to check the balance of the account. Would you like that in American dollars or Swiss Francs?'

'Dollars please,' said Laura, hardly able to believe that she was having this conversation.

'Certainly. The current balance of your account as of this morning is 61,024,433.60 US dollars.'

Laura let out an involuntary gasp. 61 million dollars! It simply wasn't possible – her dad lived on a university professor's salary. Where could all that money have come from?

Herr Speigle's voice brought Laura back to the present.

'I'm sorry Herr Speigle,' apologised Laura. 'I didn't quite catch that, could you repeat it please?'

'Yes indeed. I was enquiring after your father. He told me he was seriously ill at our last meeting, and that it would be after his passing that you might enquire about the account. I was wondering how your father is?'

'He passed away four days ago,' said Laura, still completely shell-shocked by the information she had just received.

'Ah, how sad. Please accept my personal condolences and the condolences of the bank on your bereavement. Mr Whiteland was always a very pleasant gentleman to deal with in all the years I have known him,' said Herr Speigle.

'Thank you,' said Laura simply. She continued 'This will probably sound like a very strange question Herr Speigle, but could you tell me where all this money came from?'

'Your father said you might ask that, too,' said Herr Speigle. 'He explained to me that you were not aware of the existence of this account. I'm afraid he also explained to me very specifically that I was to provide no information to you on any account other than this one. I can tell you that this account was created a little over a month ago, with an opening deposit of 60,824,433.60 US dollars. Those funds were transferred from an existing, long-standing account that your father held with us in his own name. I'm afraid that is all of the information that I can provide for you. Is there anything else that I can do for you at this time?' asked Herr Speigle.

'No, I don't think so,' Laura murmured.

After she had hung up, Laura sat back, deep in thought. There was obviously much more to her father than she had ever realised. It was clear from the conversation with Herr Speigle that he had known her father for quite a few years. Therefore, this money must have been there since she was young, if not before she was even born. The presence of the money threw into sharp relief everything else that her dad had said to her in the video. The next question was around this brothel owner – did he exist? This time, Laura turned to the internet, and more quickly than she had expected, she established that there was a 'club' in Bangkok called the Five Seasons. There was however, no way of finding out who the owner was, and the website had no contact details other than the address of the club. She tried international directory enquiries again, but there was no telephone listing.

Laura played the DVD again, listening to her dad's words, which sounded even more shocking now that she knew that at least some of what he was saying was true. And now, the danger element that her dad referred to a number of times now took on a frightening significance. Her dad had an account with over 60 million dollars – she couldn't see how that much money could have been obtained legally. And it was more than enough money to present a lot of danger in the avaricious world of today, particularly if it had been obtained illegally and criminal elements were somehow involved. As she played the video again, Laura realised that she was going to honour this last request from her father. It seemed too important to him personally for her to ignore it, and it seemed somehow tied up with the loss of her mom all those years ago. And there was the off-chance that it might even make a difference to the world.

She decided to use the approach her dad had suggested in the video. She would tell the solicitor and the accountant and Dr Perenso that she needed to travel for a while. It was true in any case that she found the constant reminders of her dad in the house unsettling. And so, over the next three days, she tidied all of her dad's affairs that needed urgent attention, and arranged for someone to check the house weekly to make sure that everything was OK. She booked a flight to Bangkok, from Columbia Airport via Chicago and Tokyo.

One week after her dad had passed away, Laura locked the front door of the house, not knowing what to expect from her coming journey. She had gone from being a carefree backpacker to being an orphan engaged in a venture that she did not understand, and which could potentially be dangerous. Added to trying to come to terms with the loss of her last surviving parent, was the knowledge that she knew very little about him and how he could have amassed a 60 million dollar fortune. She didn't really know what she was getting herself into, but she knew she had to do this in honour of her dad's memory.

As she walked around the house to make sure she had closed all the windows and doors, Laura ticked off a mental checklist, as she always did when leaving on one of her travels. Passport, ticket, visa, cash, credit card, camera and a small backpack with a few changes of clothes and some simple toiletries. She walked to the cab that was waiting to take her to Columbia Metropolitan Airport, wondering what would happen before she was back home again.

It was early morning, when the cab pulled out of the driveway, so they should be able to make it through the city before the rush-hour traffic clogged the city's arteries. Laura rested in the back seat of the cab, knowing from experience that it's always a good idea when travelling to take any opportunity to catch forty winks. As she dozed, she wondered again about the 'mission' she was on. Was it simply a matter of collecting a parcel and delivering it? What was the danger her dad had spoken so emphatically about, and from whom or where would that danger come, if it did materialise? Just who exactly was this man that she had called 'dad' all her life?

Laura's thoughts were interrupted by the cab driver. 'Excuse me, Miss. Despatch are saying there's been a major pile-up on Knox Abbott Drive, right on the bridge. I'm gonna try crossing the river on the interstate instead, to see if we can get around it. What time is your flight?'

'The flight leaves at nine forty, but I am supposed to check in by seven o'clock. You know what security is like these days!'

'OK. Well, we still got an hour-and-a-half. We should be OK,' the driver said, before launching into a monologue on the shortcomings of everything from airport security to the city's road infrastructure. Laura was only half-listening when the driver interrupted her thoughts again. 'I'm sorry, Miss, but we might have a bit of a problem.'

'What? What is it? What's wrong?' asked Laura.

'Well, it seems everyone decided to use the Interstate when they heard about the Knox Abbott pile-up. And now, an eighteen-wheeler has just lost a load of lumber at the junction between the Interstate and State Street. Problem is, that's a real bottleneck. If they don't get it cleared pretty quick, then hitting the airport by seven is gonna be next to impossible.'

'Oh no,' groaned Laura. It didn't bode well for her mission if she couldn't even get to the airport on time. 'Well, see what you can do – surely there are some shortcuts and side roads you can use? There will be a good tip in it for you if you can get me there in time for my flight.'

'Oh, I'll definitely do my best, Miss, don't you worry about that. But I can't guarantee nothin' though.'

With that, he slipped down a side-road, and proceeded to trace a maze-like way through the city. Sometimes, he was able to head directly south-west towards the airport, whilst at other times he had to track east or even north to get to another road that would once again allow him to move south. At times he was able to make good speed, whilst at other times he would be held up in traffic before ducking down another side-road. Laura watched the clock, as it became increasingly clear that she was not going to make her flight.

As the clocked ticked past seven, they were still a long way from the airport. Laura knew she would have a certain grace period within which to check-in, but the airlines were becoming increasingly strict about late check-ins as the global 'War on Terror' escalated. As the clock ticked past eight thirty with still about five miles to go, Laura knew she was in trouble. They pulled into the airport at nine o'clock. Laura paid the driver as quickly as she could, grabbed her backpack and scrambled out of the cab, running into the terminal as quickly as she could and making her way to Departures.

She scanned the screens to see where she needed to check in, only to see with dismay that her flight was marked as closed. Hoping to be able to talk her way onto the plane, Laura rushed over to the check-in desks, composing her face in a suitably tearful little-lost-girl look. As she walked up to the desks, she chose the only one that had a male attendant.

She tearfully explained about the traffic chaos and how important it was that she make the flight, but the attendant was adamant that the flight had closed.

'I'm sorry, Miss, I really am. I would like to be able to help you out, but we are simply not allowed to exceed the check-in times. I'm afraid the best I can do is put you on stand-by. The good news is that the next few flights to Chicago are not too fully booked, so you shouldn't be delayed by more than an hour or two.'

Laura knew that she couldn't do anything else, so she agreed to go on stand-by. It actually turned out to be three hours before there was a seat available on another flight. As she fastened her seatbelt for take-off, she was thankful to be finally underway, but upset that she would now miss her connecting flight and would be on stand-by flights all the way from Chicago to Bangkok.

When she landed at Chicago, she once again made her way to the stand-by desk. As she crossed the main arrivals hall to make her way to the International Terminal, she became aware of agitation and alarm sweeping across the crowd. People started to gather in front of the TV screens dotted about the hall, murmuring and holding each other. Laura moved to the nearest TV, to see a CNN report about an airline bombing. Laura watched aghast as the newsreader repeated the terrible news – two hours earlier, flight UA7268 out of Columbia City to Chicago had apparently blown up in midair. Laura almost sank to the floor with shock, as she realised that this was the plane she had tried so desperately to get on. If it hadn't been for the pile-up, Laura would have been on that plane!

She watched numbly, feeling the contradictory combination of relief and guilt that is common to survivors of tragedies as she took in the news. The newsreader was confirming the number of dead, and giving details that had already been released by the US government. Apparently, they had already confirmed that this had been a bombing, a terrorist attack launched against a random target within the US. The authorities were saying that the attack was the work of an extremist Islam militia grouping calling itself The Iron Fist of Islam, a little-known and previously not very active terror cell operating out of Syria. The FBI were saying that the members of the group had been tracked immediately after the explosion, using CCTV footage from the airport; and had been surrounded in a house near Edmund, only a few miles southwest of the airport. When the FBI had approached the house in the remote heavily forested area, a firefight had ensued in which no FBI officers were lost but all four members of the terrorist group had been killed.

The newsreader gave details again of the flight and the numbers lost, saying that they expected to have a reporter at the scene of some of the wreckage shortly. In the meantime, they ran interviews with various airline representatives and security consultants. How the attackers had managed to get a bomb on board given the scale of security measures was as yet unknown, but everyone was reassuring the travelling public that the various intelligence agencies were all saying that this was a once-off isolated attack, not the start of an orchestrated series of attacks. CNN gave details of the messages of sympathy coming in from various world leaders, as well as messages of muted congratulations from various political figures on the rapid success of the security forces in tracking down and bringing the perpetrators to such rapid justice. There was an interview with Syria's ambassador to the US, who maintained that Syria had never heard of The Iron Fist of Islam, and had no knowledge of such a group. The ambassador said Syria joined with all civilised nations in condemning such indiscriminate attacks on innocent civilians. Almost immediately, another US government spokesman was on, saying that the US accepted Syria's assurances of their non-involvement, and that the incident would not affect relations between the two countries as they worked together on a process of dialogue to help bring peace to some of the most troubled parts of the world.

Lacking any other hard information, CNN started

recycling the news that had already been presented. Laura moved off to one side, to try and assimilate what she had just heard. The plane she was supposed to be on had been blown out of the sky – was it possible that this was the danger her dad had warned her about was already threatening her? But as she thought more about the news, she realised she was being ridiculous. The US government had themselves attributed the attack to a known terrorist group, and had said it was a random attack. So it couldn't possibly concern her – not unless the FBI and the government were in some sort of conspiracy against her, which was clearly a preposterous idea.

Calming herself with the thought that she was the lucky survivor of a random incident, Laura continued on to the stand-by desk, where she again explained her predicament. She was paged four hours later, to be told that a passenger on a flight from Chicago to Tokyo had failed to show and so Laura could have his seat. She would then have to go on stand-by again in Tokyo, where she would be able to get a direct flight to Bangkok. Laura paid using her credit card and, thirty minutes later, was once again airborne – this time headed across the Pacific for Tokyo.

In Tokyo, she had to wait eight hours for a spare seat. She again paid with her card, and was back in the air. She slept most of the seven-hour flight, waking when they were less than an hour out of Bangkok.

Masters of the Universe

It was almost midnight when Laura's plane landed at Suvarnabhumi – better known as Bangkok International Airport. She disembarked and queued at Immigration and Customs, joining the line for non-Thai nationals. As she often did when she was travelling, Laura had purposely dressed down a little, so as not to appear too attractive. She was all too familiar with the perils of a beautiful young woman travelling alone, although she had never to date experienced anything other than annoyance from being pestered by unwelcome advances. Nevertheless, she often travelled in nondescript clothes, with little or no make-up and her river of blonde hair tied up in a loose bun.

She was well used to travelling in Asia, and expected no difficulties at Immigration or Customs. She was queuing near the centre of the long bank of Immigration Desks, with a line of one hundred or more weary travellers in front of each desk. As always, the people queuing covered the entire spectrum. There were the young Western males, bound for a relatively innocent holiday or a hard-core rendezvous; you could never tell. There were the mostly male business travellers of all nationalities, dressed in suits, with briefcases in hands, checking their cell-phones as they regained mobile coverage. There were the family groups, some Thai retuning from abroad, others being foreigners destined for two weeks of sand and sun to make a holiday that would live in their memories for years to come.

As Laura casually looked over the crowds of people, she felt a sight frisson of anxiety. It seemed that the closer she got to the Immigration Desk, the more Thai soldiers seemed to gather near the very desk that she was queuing for. She was sure it was a coincidence, but her dad's dire warnings of danger in his video, combined with her close escape from the bombed plane, had her jumping at shadows. As she looked around the Immigration Hall, she didn't get any sense that any of the armed and uniformed men were looking at her or were particularly interested in her. Yet there was no denying that there was now a concentration of soldiers around the desk that she was heading for.

Laura waited her turn, trying not to look worried or nervous, even though she was unquestionably unsettled by the apparent show of force at the desk. When she was called forward, she handed her passport to the immigration officer with what she hoped was a casual disinterested glance. As he had done with the previous travellers, he scanned her passport and read his computer screen. However, all the arrivals Laura had watched being processed before her had been asked a question or two, then had their passports stamped before being waved through. Now, however, things were different. After scanning her passport, he passed it back to a middle-aged man behind him. Laura had not noticed him previously, as he was not in uniform and seemed to have no official purpose. Yet as the two men spoke briefly, it was clear from their voices that the immigration officer was taking orders from this man. The passport was handed back to the officer, who then addressed Laura.

'Ms Whiteland?' His tone made it a question.

'Yes, that's right,' Laura answered, not sure what else to say.

'What is the purpose of your visit to Thailand?' he asked.

'Just a holiday, a brief visit,' said Laura. 'I fly back out in one week.'

'Are you travelling alone, or do you have any companions with you?'

'Alone,' said Laura, wondering why this might be relevant to Immigration.

'It is unusual for a young lady such as yourself to be travelling on her own,' he said.

Laura said nothing, as his comment hadn't been phrased as a question, and she wasn't sure if he expected a response or not.

'Are you visiting anyone in Thailand?' he asked after a pause.

'No,' said Laura. 'I'll just be spending the week sightseeing around Bangkok. Some of your wats are very beautiful.' Laura used the Thai word for the Buddhist temples, hoping that her familiarity with the term and her appreciation of a facet of Thai culture that most Thais were very proud of would make the official think a little more kindly of her.

'Where will you be staying?' he asked, apparently untouched by her conversational gambit.

'I was just going to get a taxi to Khao San Road – I was told there are a lot of hostels there that backpackers use.' This was true. Laura hadn't booked anywhere specific in advance of her arrival, preferring to rely on the information provided by fellow backpackers over the years.

'Hmmm,' the official paused. The man behind him said something – again it sounded like an order. 'Have you baggage to collect?' the officer asked her, apparently in response to the instruction from the man behind him.

Laura only had her backpack with her, which she had brought onto the plane as cabin baggage. She hated having to wait at luggage carousels, jostling with the crowds waiting to reclaim their suitcases. More importantly to Laura, she liked to travel lightly, as it gave her the flexibility to be able to make rapid changes to plans, such as when she had met Tahir and his bedouin tribe in Laayoune. Nevertheless, she was unsettled by the number of questions being directed at her, particularly as the people who had gone though before her had only been asked one or two, if any. So it was an instinctive fear of giving away too much information that made answer, 'Yes, I have to get my suitcase from the baggage carousel before I go through Customs.'

At last, he seemed satisfied. Handing her passport back, he waved her through. The six or eight soldiers standing near the desk seemed to ignore her as she walked past them, following the signs for Baggage Reclaim and the Exit. As she move out of the Immigration Hall into the Baggage Reclaim area, Laura couldn't help glancing backwards. What she saw caused her heart to race a little faster than it already was. The group of soldiers were moving in her direction, and the man who had been instructing the immigration officer was now talking animatedly to a be-medalled soldier, whilst pointing in her general direction. Laura moved towards the information screens saying what carousel each flight's baggage was to be collected from, telling herself that she was imagining things and to calm down.

When she looked to see what carousel the baggage from her flight was to be collected from, she saw that no carousel number was up for her flight. This was strange, as flights that had landed after hers already had carousels assigned to them. Laura thought worriedly that if she were paranoid, she would suspect that the luggage was now being searched for her non-existent suitcase. With that reminder that her sense of fear had foolishly prompted her to lie to the immigration official, Laura resolved to get out of the airport as quickly as possible.

She moved quickly from that point on. Walking past the baggage carousels, Laura walked straight through the Nothing to Declare channel, and out into the public access part of the airport.

As always when a Westerner walks through the arrival gates in Bangkok airport, she was immediately accosted, albeit gently and respectfully, by a horde of young men wanting to sell her everything from taxi rides to accommodation. Normally, Laura would walk past them, knowing that the regular taxis queuing outside the front of the airport terminal would be cheaper. This time, however, she simply wanted to get away from the airport, to give herself a chance to calm down and recover from the undoubtedly childish scare she had given herself. She focused on one of the one young men calling to her about taxis.

'Yes,' she said, walking up to him, 'I need a taxi. But I am in a hurry – I want to get going immediately.'

'Oh, that is no problem, Madam,' the young man said. 'My cousin's taxi is just outside, ready to go'

'OK, lead the way,' said Laura, making to follow the young man. She didn't even try to haggle with him to get a better price, as she normally would – she just wanted to get away from the airport. The young man walked out of the main doors and to the left. As always when she arrived in a hot country, Laura revelled in the blast of heat as she left the air-conditioned airport building. It was like walking into the heart of an oven. Laura knew many of her friends and countrymen who complained about the heat when they travelled to particularly hot climates, but she absolutely loved it. Feeling the heat already starting to work its way into her flesh and bones, she was already starting to relax.

They walked only out fifty metres from the door, and the young man stopped at a large Mercedes car. 'This is my cousin's taxi,' he proclaimed proudly. 'A beautiful carriage to transport a beautiful lady,' he recited with a smile. 'And this is my cousin. His name is Rannachai.' With that, the young man quickly headed back for the main door of the airport, leaving Laura wondering how many 'cousins' he was drumming up business for.

'Hello, Miss,' Rannachai said shyly. 'Where is it that you wish to go this evening?'

'Hello Rannachai,' Laura replied, smiling to reassure the shy young man. 'Let's get going first, and then we can talk about where I need to go.' Laura felt a little ridiculous as Rannachai looked somewhat perplexed at her strange request. Nevertheless, even though she was starting to relax, and was now ninety-nine per cent convinced that she had imagined the apparent interest of the security forces in her, she still wanted to get away and give herself time to loosen up. Within a few seconds, they were underway, with Rannachai taking the main road leading out of the airport towards Bangkok.

'Thank you, Rannachai,' said Laura, from the passenger seat. She always liked to sit beside rather than behind the driver when she was the only passenger in a taxi. 'I would like to go to Khao San Road. I am told that there are a lot of hostels there. I am looking for somewhere cheap, clean and safe.'

'Oh, you are going to the very right street, Miss,' said Rannachai enthusiastically. 'There is a very fine hostel there that a lot of the American backpackers use, called The Green Door Hostel. It is cheap, but it is clean and completely safe for a young lady such as yourself. It is a quality hostel,' he declared, putting a strong emphasis on the word quality.

Laura smiled to herself – Rannachai would be telling her that his cousin owned it next! She knew how the local population in many poorer countries had developed a complex network of commission-based selling, and she strongly suspected that Rannachai would be on an extra earner if he brought her to the Green Door.

'OK, Rannachai,' replied Laura, smiling despite herself. 'If The Green Door is as good as you say, then that is where I will stay. But you have to promise that it is a good hostel – would you allow your sister to stay there?'

Given the very strong ties of the family unit in Asian society, Laura knew that this would be close to an 'honour question' for Rannachai – he would find it very difficult to be anything less than one hundred per cent honest in his answer.

'If my sister stayed there, she would be safe,' he answered. 'However, in my family, it would not be a good thing for my sister to stay in such a place unless her brothers were with her.'

'I understand,' Laura reassured him, not wanting to offend his sensibilities on religious or moral grounds. 'I am sure your good sister would never do such a thing as to stay somewhere overnight without someone from your family to stay with her. OK, Rannachai my friend, on to The Green Door.'

Laura relaxed back into the seat, laying her head against the headrest; content to listen peacefully while Rannachai chattered on about the Green Door Hostel, and about all the things she should see and do while she was in Bangkok. Naturally, he had contacts in all of these places that would be able to get her a 'special price'. Laura smiled as they drove towards the city in the night, cocooned in the speeding sphere of the comfortable Mercedes.

As she settled down in the seat, she noticed that Rannachai's patter had fallen silent, and she looked over towards him. He was frowning now, glancing from his rear-view mirror to his side-wing mirror.

'What is it, Rannachai? What's wrong?'

'Oh, nothing I am sure, Miss. I thought we were being followed, like in the movies! It is an army jeep that is behind us, but I have done nothing that would cause the army to be after me. We have a very peaceful society here in Thailand under our Glorious King, may Buddha smile on him; but we still get a bit nervous if we see soldiers approach us. I am sorry if I alarmed you – it is nothing.'

Laura wondered if her life had always had little moments like this, that in the normal course of events she hadn't noticed, because they meant nothing. Now however, the possibility that a Thai army jeep was following her suddenly had the potential to be very bad news indeed. But then Laura rationalised to herself that nothing had been done or said that would indicate that she was being followed. Surely she was just overreacting. She felt she could be excused some minor paranoia, given events of the past week.

'Oh, OK,' Laura tried a nonchalant answer. 'Listen Rannachai, I'm really, really tired, and I want to try to get myself into a bed as soon as I can. Do you think you can try to go a bit faster?'

'Certainly, Miss,' Rannachai exclaimed, and speeded up, changing lanes to overtake the slower vehicles. Then he slipped back into the middle lane, to let faster cars behind him pass by. As he turned left off Soi Phrasawat, Laura glanced back to see the army jeep turning into the street behind them. This street was quiet, there was just one lane in each direction, and theirs was the only car on the road, except for the jeep that was now right on their tail.

As they neared some waste ground on the left-hand side of the road, the jeep pulled into the oncoming lane and came up beside them, as if to overtake on the driver's side. Laura and Rannachai looked across and saw a uniformed soldier driving, and a man in civilian clothes in the passenger seat. With a shock of recognition, Laura realised it as the same man who had been instructing the immigration officer who had questioned her.

As their eyes met, the jeep swerved sharply towards them and slammed into the side of the Mercedes. Unlike taxi drivers in the movies, Rannachai had never experienced anything like this. Totally unprepared for the smashing sideways impact, he lost his grip on the steering wheel and the Mercedes shot off to the left. Laura grabbed the door handle to steady herself as the car bounced wildly across the waste ground. Her terror intensified when she realised that there was what looked like a sheer drop at the end of the plot, towards which their car was now racing. She screamed at Rannachai, who was desperately trying to regain control, but, as he slammed on the brakes, the car skidded and fishtailed, so that it was now sliding sideways towards the drop.

The two wheels on the driver's side dropped into a small trench, but the momentum of the car carried it on. It wheeled side over side once, twice, before dropping over the edge with its wheels in the air.

For a moment, it felt as though the car hung suspended above the chasm – Laura had no way of knowing if the drop was two metres or two hundred. She gasped as the car hurtled downwards. It was not a sheer drop but a very steep slope, and the car careened down, a blur of movement. Laura felt herself being crashed in every direction, with the seatbelt cruelly digging into her shoulders, chest and thighs. Her neck took a similar hammering, as her head whipped backwards and forwards as the car spun.

It felt like a fraction of a second and like all of eternity before they came to rest. Laura froze, afraid that any movement might set them off again. She gingerly twisted her head to get her bearings. The car was on its side, with Laura hanging by her seatbelt above Rannachai below her. Looking out the front of the car where the windscreen used to be, Laura could see that they were on flat ground at the bottom of the slope. Thankfully, the steep hill had only been a few metres high. She could see headlights piercing the sky above them – the jeep must have parked at the edge of the cliff. She couldn't see the jeep itself however, as low bushes growing profusely on the slope screened them from view.

'Rannachai,' she called gently, so that the men above couldn't hear her. 'Rannachai, can you hear me?'

He groaned, slowly twisting his head to look up at her. 'I don't know what you have done, Miss, but we are in extreme danger. We have to move, now, quickly, before they reach us.'

He struggled with his seatbelt, managing to get it undone. He crouched up underneath Laura, supporting her weight as she jabbed at the seatbelt release, trying to get it free. She caught her breath as the mechanism released and she fell down on top of Rannachai. He was ready for her to drop, and gently lowered her to a kneeling position beside him. They both crawled through the windscreen space, pausing outside to get their bearings.

'They cannot see us,' whispered Rannachai. 'But they will quickly make their way down here. We must leave this place. Follow me.'

Laura, thinking of her passport, grabbed her bag before creeping after Rannachai as he crawled along the bottom of the slope, hidden from above by the leafy bushes just over them. They moved slowly for about a hundred metres, until they moved around a retaining wall. Gradually, they stood upright, being careful not to make any noise.

Rannachai put his mouth next to Laura's ear. 'You must not make a sound. Follow me.'

He quietly led Laura away from the crash, along a narrow alley that ended in a deserted side street. They walked along quickly, but without running.

'Where are we going?' Laura asked, realising that for the fifteen minutes since the crash, she had been blindly following Rannachai, without having any idea about their destination.

'I am trying to think,' he replied. 'We need somewhere you will be safe. It has to be somewhere that the army would not expect. And somewhere that they could not just go in and take you. It is not easy to think of such a place, Miss, because of who you are being chased by. That was a soldier in uniform driving an army jeep. That means that it is the army who are after you. If it was the police, then the cause could be a simple affair, maybe a misunderstanding over a little hashish or something. But when the army chase you, that is different. And that man with the soldier, he did not look like he was a soldier. That means CIB – the Special Branch. Yet you do not look like a terrorist, which is the only reason I can think of that they would be after someone. Why are they chasing you, Miss? Maybe I should not be helping you, although I feel this is the right thing to do.'

Laura hesitated. If Rannachai abandoned her, she didn't know what she would do. For want of a better idea, she told him the truth, albeit the summarised version.

'I honestly don't know, Rannachai. My father died last week and asked me to collect a parcel here in Bangkok and deliver it to an old friend of his. He said it would be dangerous, but he said it would be good for the world, whatever that means. I do not know what this parcel is. But I think I will have to face the fact that my dad's dying request is the only logical explanation for what is happening to me.'

Rannachai looked at her long and hard, as though trying to see into her soul. For a fleeting instant, Laura had the strangest sensation that he was indeed doing exactly that, and could see into her innermost self.

'It is good, I think, that I help you,' he said, to Laura's intense relief. 'It is lucky that my car had false licence plates – a little necessity for me at the moment; so at least they cannot identify me. Now, where to take you? Think, Rannachai, think,' he urged himself.

While Rannachai thought, they kept walking, all the time moving in a generally southern direction, towards the centre of the city. As they passed the ornate gateway into a wat, Laura could see the beautiful golden roofs of the temple reflecting the moonlight. She paused, exclaimed to herself in a whisper, 'Oh, that is so beautiful.'

Rannachai stopped to see what she was long at, and a look of wonder crossed his face. 'Of course,' he declared. 'That's it.'

'What?' asked Laura, wondering what he was talking about.

'That is Wat Nák Tong Tieow, the Temple of the Traveller. The Buddhist monks here always helped travellers, and have travelled always themselves. We will ask them for help.'

Laura wasn't sure that this was a very practical solution

to their problem, but felt that she was in no place to tell Rannachai what was and what was not a good idea. She followed Rannachai quietly across the street and waited with him after he rang a little bell set into the wall beside the gate.

Almost immediately, a small door set into the gate opened. A monk stood inside, dressed in the long loose, flowing saffron-coloured robes of the Buddhist monks. Laura expected him to ask what they wanted, and was assuming that Rannachai would have to translate for her. But the monk asked no questions, he simply stood aside and gestured them into the courtyard. Rannachai and Laura stepped through and the monk closed the door behind them before setting off across the courtyard. Rannachai moved off after him, so Laura followed.

She quickly lost all sense of direction, as they moved alternately through ornate gardens and warrens of passages within the buildings. Laura couldn't help but marvel at some of what she saw. The gardens were oases of peace and tranquillity – despite everything that had transpired in the past couple of hours, Laura still felt the call of peace that was exuded by the gardens as she followed the monk and Rannachai through the meticulously kept paths. In the buildings, she often had to duck to get through the passages. Now and again, they would pass through rooms. Many were small and plain, occasionally with various baskets and boxes stacked neatly along the walls. Some of them, however, were very ornate affairs, sometimes small and sometimes large. Statues of Buddha were in each of these ornate rooms, and incense burned wherever they went in the building.

As well as her sense of direction, Laura also lost her sense of time as they weaved through the temple. Eventually, they came to a plain wooden door at the end of a passage. The monk knocked on the door and opened it inwards into the room beyond. He stepped back and gestured Laura into the room. She stepped forward, finding herself in a small room with whitewashed walls – almost a cell. Sitting in a chair at a small desk in the corner was another monk, although this old man was wearing plainer robes. Laura whirled around as the door closed behind her and she found herself alone with this man – Rannachai had not followed her in!

'Do not fear, child,' said the man at the desk. 'You are in no danger while you are within the walls of Wat Nák Tong Tieow. Please, give me one moment to finish this passage of my text, and I will be with you.'

He continued to write for another couple of minutes, before putting down his pencil and stretching his back. 'Ah,' he sighed 'I am getting too old for bending over our beloved manuscripts all day. You should value your physical youth, young lady. Even though wisdom comes with age, it is always sad to see your physical self on the wane. But enough of my chatter. We will have tea.'

As he made this remarkably mundane statement – without yet having asked who Laura was or what she wanted – the door opened and a young man brought in a simple wooden platter with a teapot and two small glass cups. He poured two cups of the green tea without speaking and then left, closing the door gently behind him.

'Now, a toast,' smiled the old monk. 'To peace and happiness.'

'Peace and happiness,' echoed Laura, sipping at the hot tea. She wasn't sure exactly what type of tea it was but, at that moment, it seemed to be the most refreshing thing she had ever tasted.

'Now, my dear, maybe you would like to tell me what

has brought you to our care?' asked the monk.

As with Rannachai, Laura could think of nothing simpler or better than to tell to the truth, so she repeated the story to the monk, but with a little more detail this time.

The monk let her speak without interruption, listening intently. When she had finished, he asked, 'And from whom are you to collect this package?'

This was one of the details that Laura had omitted, but she felt that at this stage she had nothing to lose from being open and honest with the monk. 'A man called Mwai, who according to my dad owns a...' Laura paused, then went on '...an establishment, in Patpong.'

The monk blinked, for the first time seeming surprised. Laura assumed that this was due to the obvious nature of 'an establishment' in Patpong, one of Bangkok's biggest and best-known red light districts.

'I apologise,' said the monk after a pause. 'I should have introduced myself. My name is Chanarong.'

It felt strange to be only introducing themselves at this late stage in the conversation, but nevertheless Laura reciprocated with, 'I am very pleased to meet you, Chanarong, and I really do hope you might be able to help me in some way, though I am not sure how. My name is Laura, Laura Whiteland.'

This time, there was no mistaking Chanarong's surprise, although astonishment might be a more appropriate word. He was clearly taken aback at Laura's name.

'What is it, Chanarong?' she demanded. 'How do you know my name?'

'Ah, Miss Whiteland,' said Chanarong, 'that is for another time. For the moment, we must concentrate on what has happened to you, and how we might be able to offer assistance, as we do to all true travellers. Tell me, given what has happened to you, and given that you believe it can only be because of the mission you are on for your father, do you now intend to see it through? It is clearly very dangerous, as indeed your father predicted it would be.'

Laura wasn't sure why, but the more that happened, the more important this mission was becoming to her. It was her beloved father's dying wish, and he had said that it was important to the world as well as to him personally. Laura was damned if she was going to run away now, just when her dad needed her most. And so, when she spoke, she did so with certainty and with conviction. 'Absolutely. This is what my dad wanted, and I am going to see it through for him.'

'Spoken from the heart,' said Chanarong. 'This is good, for the heart is true. Well then, we need to decide how we can help you. You will stay with us for the next few days while we reflect on this situation.'

The door opened again, and a different young man stood waiting. 'Kasem will bring you to a room that you may use for the next few days. In the morning, Kasem will bring you to the dining room for our morning meal. Goodnight, child.' With that, Chanarong turned and took up his pencil once more.

Laura wanted to ask him more – What was going to happen? What would they do? Why did her name seem to make him react? – but she knew that she had been dismissed, even though politely and gently. And so she followed Kasem through more corridors, until he stopped outside another small door. When he opened it and gestured to Laura to go inside, she saw a small room not unlike the one she had been in with Chanarong. Laura went in and the door closed behind her. She saw another little door to one side and when she looked through it, there was a rudimentary toilet, sink and shower. All the comforts of home, Laura thought to herself ironically, before preparing for bed. As she snuggled down under the light sheet, she thought about everything from happy childhood memories with her dad to the terrifying events of recent days. Trying to make sense of all that had happened, she fell into a light sleep and dreamt of her father.

The next morning, just as Chanarong had said he would, Kasem brought her to the dining room. There were about forty monks, ranging in age from teenagers to old men. None seemed surprised to see her, even though she was the only woman. They all seemed happy to chat with her, and she was grateful for their company, and for their acceptance of her in their midst. She remarked to one of the monks that she was surprised that all of them spoke excellent English with little or no trace of an accent. He replied with a cryptic, 'It is essential if we are to see the new mission of this temple fulfilled', but refused to elaborate any further.

Over the coming days, Laura spoke with many of the monks across a variety of topics, though all conversations seemed to return to a theme of happiness, and how to have peace in your life. Laura would sometimes ask where Chanarong was, as she never saw him, but the reply would always be that he was meditating, or gardening, or writing, and that he would be with her in due time.

And so the next few days passed, with Laura waiting for Chanarong, and listening to the monks discuss their view of the universe. The outlook they held on life fascinated Laura.

The monks explained to Laura that the reason for all of the unhappiness in the world is that people misunderstand the source of happiness. People think that happiness comes from what you have, or from what happens to you, or from your circumstances, or from the love of the people around you. In truth, there is a very fundamental error in this thinking, which many people unconsciously use as the basis for all of the thinking that they have about happiness. In fact, said the monks, happiness is a purely internal phenomenon. 'Happiness comes not from the world around us, but from ourselves. We are each 'Master of the Universe' – all we have to do is believe that, and it will be so. Each of us lives in a separate universe of perception, and each of us is thus God.'

In some of the discussion around the rationale for this view of life, the monks pointed to the fact that people's happiness clearly does not depend upon the person's circumstances, but on the person themselves. For example, they said, we all know people who are poor, or sick, or alone; yet who smile and face the world cheerfully and with goodwill and with a giving heart. Similarly, we all know of people who are rich or successful or healthy, or people who are surrounded by people who love them; yet they are sad, or angry, or frustrated, or they feel alone.

As the monks discussed this, Laura thought back to the feeling she had while sitting with Tahir and his bedouin tribe on the Saharan sands outside Laayoune. In truth, she was much wealthier than they were, healthier with a much higher life expectancy, more successful on any measure that she could think of, and she had the love of her dad. And yet, she had felt immeasurably poorer than they were, missing out on the sense of place and belonging and serenity and community that they seemed to carry with them so effortlessly.

Laura sat in one of the beautiful gardens on her third afternoon in the temple, luxuriating in the heat and basking in the atmosphere of peace and harmony that seemed to envelop her within the temple. Three of the monks were with her and Laura picked up the threads of a conversation from earlier in the day.

'You know, in some ways I can understand what you are saying about happiness coming from within rather than from what you have or what is happening around you. Yet, at the same time, I find myself thinking that it's almost too easy. If you believe that, then aren't you simply denying the reality of what is happening around you when things are not going well in your life?'

'I do not think that one leads to the other', said the eldest of the three monks who were sitting with her. 'But I can see that you have lived your life under the assumption that happiness comes from outside of yourself, and so it is very hard for you to accept a proposition that is so radically different from what you have always believed. The secret of happiness is to realise that you and only you see the universe through your eyes. Therefore no one can judge you, and by the same token you can never judge someone else.'

'But that way of thinking is a recipe for anarchy,' Laura argued. 'We need order and rules if we are to maintain a working society. If I simply say no one can judge me, and I cannot judge other people, then how are we supposed to maintain a functioning society? Everyone could just do as they please, knowing that they would not be judged.'

'We agree with you that the rule of law is necessary in any society, not least to protect the weak and vulnerable,' one of the younger monks replied. 'But our view does not preclude the rule of law. Rather, it means that when judging an accused, we should judge the action, not the person who carried out the action. There are many practical real-life examples of where people had acted in ways that most people would find reprehensible; yet when we look at the background behind the person and behind the action, the action became understandable and forgivable, though still not something that could or should be approved of. In essence, we often find it difficult to judge the rightness or wrongness of our own actions – how arrogant is it, then, to presume that we could ever judge the heart or soul of another person?'

'In order to be happy,' said the third monk, picking up the flow of the conversation effortlessly and seamlessly from his companion, 'all one has to do is to think positively about any event or circumstance. For example, an apparently negative event, such as losing your job, or being sick, or being in debt, can always be looked at with a positive eye.'

'I'm not sure that's correct,' Laura said questioningly. 'Isn't that simply self-delusion – a refusal to face facts? When you're sick, for example, you're sick. No amount of positive thinking can miraculously make you well.'

'Many would actually argue that point,' laughed the older monk. 'But even if you are correct, and the mind does not have power over the body, let us tell you of a poem, or prayer – a proverb, if you will. This is to be found in one form or another in every religion and philosophy. It is one of the most powerful distillations of mankind's wisdom ever to be found in such a short form.'

'Now you have me totally intrigued,' Laura smiled. 'What is it?'

With that, the monks recited together:

'May I have the strength to change what I can,
The serenity to accept what I cannot change,
And the wisdom to know the difference.'

'If we could but be true to this,' continued the older monk, 'then happiness is the natural and effortless by-product. Listen again to the first line. "May I have the strength to change what I can." Many people waste large proportions of their time and energy bemoaning their circumstances, instead of changing them. If you can change something, then just go for it. In doing so, you will be happy that you are at least working on changing it. If we cannot change something, then there is nothing to be gained by being unhappy about it. Rather, we should strive for the serenity of the second line – "The serenity to accept what I cannot change" – that is, the serenity to accept the things we cannot change, whilst at the same time looking for the positive within those things. Meditation is a very powerful tool in achieving this serenity. If you can cultivate this serenity and courage, then all you need is the third line – "And the wisdom to know the difference" – to be able to tell the difference between those things that you can change and those things that you cannot.'

Laura found it difficult to absorb all that she was being told. She sensed that a huge fundamental truth of life was in front of her, within her grasp, but she couldn't articulate it. In one sense, its simplicity was an obstacle in itself. The secret of happiness should be something very complex, but the monks seemed to be saying that there was nothing complicated about it – all you had to do was be happy! The monks explained this by using the metaphor of stopping smoking. What could be simpler, they asked – all one had to do to stop smoking was not smoke. It was extremely simple, yet extremely difficult due to the combination of the addictive properties of cigarettes added to the habit that had to be overcome. They said that Laura was facing a similar challenge in her thinking – she had a lifetime of habit whereby she believed that happiness depended on things external to herself. Naturally, it would take time for her to come to grips with the idea that the truth may be the diametric opposite – happiness and peace come from within. They smiled indulgently as they assured Laura that in time she could come to realise this for herself, and then she could have a much more fulfilled life of happiness and peace.

On the fourth day, Laura was walking in one of the beautiful gardens, pondering the words of the monks. Without Laura being aware of his arrival, Chanarong was suddenly walking alongside her.

'You know,' he said, 'they are right.'

Laura intuitively knew he was referring to the discussions she had had with the monks. 'Yes, I sense that they are,' she answered. 'Yet I cannot seem to simply accept it, and be happy. Which is what I understand should happen.'

'Ah, Laura,' laughed Chanarong. 'As many people do, you are confusing 'simple' with 'easy'. The secret of happiness is very simple, but it is not an easy one to embrace. Particularly for someone like yourself, who has spent a lifetime in a society of such extraordinarily extreme materialism. It will take much reflection for you to be able to overcome the patterns of thought that have been inculcated in you since the day you were born. But be assured that all things are possible, and much stranger things have been known. If you choose to reflect on what you have heard here, then I am sure that in time you will come to a realisation of your own truth.'

They walked in companionable silence for a while, before Chanarong spoke again.

'For the immediate future, however, you may need to give consideration to more practical matters. The powers that be are most anxious to find you. They have said that you are involved in terrorism and drug-running, which, of course, I know not to be true. All security services in Thailand have been alerted to look out for you, and capture you. It may be that they will come to know that you are here. If that happens, you will be in danger here.'

'If that happens,' said Laura thoughtfully, 'all of you would be in danger as well, is that not so?'

'Indeed,' sighed Chanarong. 'That is so.'

'Then I must leave,' Laura stated simply. 'I will not bring trouble into this beautiful place – such ugliness does not belong here. I know I will be able to get help from some of the backpackers – there always seems to be a code that we help each other out. I will leave in the morning and get a train out of Bangkok. Once I am clear of the city, I will see if I can make contact with any friends to get out of the country somehow. If I can do that, then I'll collect that package and make a run for it.'

'I will be sorry to see you go,' said Chanarong. 'But it might be that we will meet again sooner than you think, for the Universe moves in very strange ways. Evening time, when it is at its busiest, will be the best time to get a train from Hualamphong Station. I will walk you to the station tomorrow evening. In the meantime, let us not think of it, but relax and enjoy your last twenty-four hours with us, and the conversation that will come with it.'

That evening, Laura dined with the monks, not speaking much, but content to listen to them and their fascinating conversation. That night, she slept deeply and peacefully, much to her own surprise.

The Hunt Continues

Laura spent the next day sitting in the beautiful gardens of the temple, occasionally chatting with one of the monks as they went about their daily routine. That evening, she made her way to the temple's dining room. As always, the monks ate with an intense appreciation and enjoyment of their food, whilst all the time engaging in lively and spirited conversation and debate. Chanarong beckoned Laura to sit at his side.

'Mealtimes should always be a time for relaxation, a time to appreciate and give thanks for all of the things the Universe has given us,' said Chanarong. 'Eat now with a happy heart, thinking neither of tomorrow nor yesterday; but only of Now.'

Consciously putting the future and the past out of her mind, Laura concentrated on keeping her attention on the present. As she was passed some jasmine rice by the monk on her other side, she savoured the atmosphere amongst the monks in the temple. She had become familiar with the contradictory ambience – at once contemplative and relaxed, while simultaneously being lively and active. Food certainly seemed to be as important to the temple community as it was to Thais in general, with the meal consisting of choices from a wide range of common serving platters. There was everything from tom yam soup, to rice dishes with pork, chicken and curry, to stir-fries and fruit. The monks ate with gusto, using their fingers for most dishes and a spoon for the soups.

When they had finished eating, Laura and Chanarong stood to leave. Much to Laura's astonishment, all of the monks stood and bowed gravely in her direction. Laura was warmed and deeply proud that they should accord her such a gesture of group respect. She bowed back to them with solemnity and dignity, before turning to follow Chanarong from the room.

Following Chanarong back to her room, Laura collected her backpack and they made their way to a side gate of the temple. Chanarong cautioned her to let him check the street outside first, and he slipped out quietly into the twilight evening. It was only about thirty seconds before he opened the gate and beckoned Laura out to join him. But in those thirty seconds, Laura could already feel the peace she had known for the past few days start to desert her. She now knew that she was being chased by the Thai security forces as a supposed drug-runner and terrorist, although at least they had not made any public mention of this. Undoubtedly, it had to involve her dad's request in some way, but Laura felt lost because she didn't even know what she was to collect – What was in this 'parcel'? – nor to whom she was to deliver it. Being so in the dark left her feeling powerless and unsure as to what she should do next. For the moment, all she could think of was to get out of Bangkok to somewhere quiet, try to arrange to get out of the country somehow, and then collect the parcel and go.

Laura followed Chanarong out of the gate and down the street. The streets were bustling as tourists wandered through the sidewalk stalls, and workers made their way homeward. The stallholders were selling everything under the sun. The food stalls looked and smelled delicious and were particularly busy, with many of the locals buying snacks on their way home from work.

The crowds increased as they neared the train station. Soon, Laura saw the imposing main entrance of the railway station, with its curved central superstructure flanked by two squat towers. Chanarong and Laura passed between the pillars of the main entrance and through the main doors. He asked Laura to wait in the middle of a very busy part of the main hall while he bought a ticket. Laura watched the hustle and bustle all around her, and she knew that, for the moment at least, Chanarong's strategy of hiding in the midst of the crowd was a good tactic. After a few minutes, Chanarong returned, ticket in hand.

'I hope I have been guided well,' said Chanarong. 'I felt that Koh Samui would be a good place for you to hide out. It is a long way from Bangkok, and yet there are enough tourists there that you will not stand out. I have bought you a second-class ticket, so that you will not have much contact with staff during the journey. Also, I know that many of the backpackers use these tickets, so again you will not be noticeable on the train.'

'Oh, thank you, Chanarong,' Laura said, feeling that such an oft-use phrase was a poor expression of the gratitude that she felt towards Chanarong and his community. 'I wish I could tell you how much your sanctuary has meant to me.'

'I understand,' Chanarong assured her. 'Believe me when I tell you that there are few expressions more powerful than 'thank you'. The strength of the phrase comes not from the words themselves, but from the way they are uttered. And I can see the sincerity in your eyes when you say it. Now, then,' he went on, business-like, 'it is time for you to go. It is an overnight train, and you will arrive in Surat Thani early tomorrow morning. You must get the ferry to the island immediately, and then you can see what you want to do from there.'

Laura knew that words couldn't express what she wanted to say, so she simply bowed reverently towards the old monk. Chanarong bowed back to her briefly, then turned and disappeared into the crowd. Laura looked after him sadly, wondering if she would ever see him again – as he had certainly seemed to think. With that thought, she turned and made her way towards the platform for the train to Koh Samui. Her sadness at the parting from Chanarong was cut short when she saw the sight of uniformed and armed soldiers at the top of each of the platforms leading to the departing trains. Laura doubted that this was a regular arrangement, and worried if they were looking for her.

Everything that Chanarong had said led her to believe that once on the train, she would be safe for a while at least. She just needed a way of getting past the soldiers and onto the train without being noticed. Laura looked around. She knew that her height and long blonde hair made her stand out in a crowd and decided to do something to be less conspicuous.

Laura looked around the cavernous hall, and her eyes lit on a sign in Thai and English – 'Pharmacy'. She made her way over to the shop as quickly as she could without drawing attention to herself. Moving up and down the shelves, she hunted amongst the Hair Products section, trying to pick out an English language hair dye, so that she could be sure of having a 'normal-looking' result. Having picked a brunette hair colour, she made her way to the station's restrooms. There, she proceeded to dye her hair, making plenty of mess in the process. As she was working the dye into her hair, two young girls also in their early twenties, came in. They were chatting away to each other in English, with what Laura suspected were Irish accents.

Laura straightened up from the sink, ready to start towelling her hair dry.

'Hi, girls, howya doin?' she asked, in a friendly tone of

voice.

'Hi, yourself,' said one of the girls. 'You hiding from a boyfriend?'

'Huh?' asked Laura, not sure what the girl was talking about.

'Dying your hair in a railway station restroom – seems a bit extreme,' clarified the girl.

'Oh that,' answered Laura. 'Nah, nothing so exciting I'm afraid. No, I'm just heading down to Samui for a week, and I felt like a change, know what I mean?'

'Yeah, sure. I sometimes get bored with the colour of my own hair – mousey brown my boyfriend calls it. Say, we're going to Koh Samui as well. Are you going on the train?'

'Sure am,' said Laura, not believing her luck. 'Say, I'm a bit nervous about travelling on my own on an overnight train. Do you mind if I travel with you – if you're in second-class as well that is?'

'Sure, not a problem,' answered the girl. 'We're travelling with three friends of ours – blokes, if that's cool with you. By the way, my name is Pauline and my friend here is Anne.'

'I'm very pleased to meet you Pauline, and you too Anne,' said Laura. 'I'd shake hands, only I need to finish washing this gunk off first. Where are you girls from?' asked Laura as she turned back to the sink. She wanted to try to keep the girls in conversation for another few minutes until she was ready to go. She felt that she would be much better concealed if she were able to board the train as part of a group.

A short while later, Laura left the restrooms in the company of her two new friends. They moved back into the main hall of the station, where the girls' friends were waiting for them.

'C'mon ladies,' called one of the young men as they approached. 'Time's a-wastin'.'

'Hold on to your horses,' called back Pauline. 'We've plenty of time yet. Oh, and we have a new travelling companion as well.'

Pauline did the introductions – the three boys were Richard, Sean and Tom. As Laura had suspected from the girls' accent, the group were Irish. Having done the introductions and explained that Laura was going to Koh Samui as well; Pauline suggested that they board the train straightaway, so that they could be sure of getting seats. It seemed that Tom was the organiser of the group. He had all the train tickets in his wallet, and he took them out as they approached the platform. Laura watched the soldiers – with all that had happened to her, she was now in no doubt that they were on the lookout for her.

As they queued to have their tickets checked and get onto the platform, Laura turned to Tom. 'Sorry, Tom – do you mind holding my ticket for a sec – I just need to get something out of my bag?'

'Sure, no problem,' said Tom, taking her ticket from her and adding it to the five he already held.

Laura started rummaging in her backpack, holding it up and slightly in front of her face to obscure the view that the soldiers had of her. The group of six young English-speaking backpackers moved to the gate and Tom handed over all six tickets. The ticket-clerk barely glanced at the tickets or the travellers, punched the tickets and gave them back to Tom. With that, the group moved past the soldiers and down the platform.

Laura breathed a sigh of relief as she took a pair of sunglasses from her bag and put them on. The group moved down along the train until they found a small empty second-class carriage, and boarded with much passing back and forth of bags. They got themselves settled comfortably, and the boys broke out a six-pack of Singha beer to share around. As they chatted and got to know one another a bit better, the train eventually started and they rolled out of Bangkok on the long southward journey to Surat Thani.

The rest of the evening passed through a combination of chatting, reading, eating and drinking. They played some card games and relayed some stories about previous travels and adventures that they each had undertaken. As evening turned to night, they slowly dozed off one by one in their seats using their bags as pillows and supports. Laura was the last one to fall asleep, looking at her new companions and marvelling that, less than four weeks ago, she had been as innocent and carefree as they were. As the night wore on, Laura fell into a fitful sleep.

The next morning, Laura woke with aches and pains in her neck and shoulders from sleeping awkwardly. She thought about the date, September 11th. It was a date that was etched on the consciousness of every American, recalling the terror and carnage of the attacks on the World Trade Towers and the Pentagon. Laura for the first time could personally identify with that perception of personal threat and danger, having narrowly escaped a downed airplane and being run off the road by an army jeep. She hoped that her flight to Samui signified the end of the fear, despite a shiver at the thought that the date could be a bad omen.

As her friends woke to the new day, they excitedly discussed their plans for Koh Samui – which seemed to involve a lot of lying on the beach, drinking cold beers by the pool, and the three guys talking about hiring a four-wheel-drive to get around the less accessible parts of the island. Breakfast consisted of the last of the cold meat and cheeses belonging to the Irish group, fruit that Laura had with her and water and fruit juice bought from the sellers moving through the carriages.

At six o'clock in the morning, the train pulled into Phun Phin, fourteen kilometres from Surat Thani. Laura and her friends got off, and caught the bus to Surat Thani, making their way to the ferry terminal as a group. Laura had asked Pauline if they had a place booked on the island yet, and Pauline had confirmed that they had two rooms booked in a hostel just behind Chaweng Beach. She had invited Laura to share a room if she wanted to, an offer which Laura had gladly accepted. They rode up on the deck of the ferry from Surat Thani to Koh Samui, chatting and enjoying the sunshine. When they landed on the island, hawkers trying to sell cab rides and accommodation surrounded them. Having been on the island before, Laura was able to negotiate with a driver of a pick-up to take all six of them to Chaweng. Her friends were delighted when they realised that they would have happily paid three times the fare that Laura negotiated for them. The six of them threw their bags into the back of the pick-up, climbed in themselves, and revelled in the feeling of the wind in their hair as the pick-up sped along the sometimes quite narrow roads across the island from the ferry to Chaweng.

When they arrived at the hostel in Chaweng, they unloaded, booked in and made their way to the local Irish bar for celebratory drinks. While her friends settled in for a meal and a few beers, Laura felt the need to spend a little time on her own. Now that she had successfully escaped from Bangkok, she wanted to have a little time to reflect on what had happened, and to try to think practically about how she could get out of the country. She made excuses to her friends, muttering something vague about a headache and a walk along the beach and left them to their merriment.

Laura cut through the narrow streets to Chaweng Beach, and started to stroll north across the sand, aimlessly wandering as she thought about her situation and about what to do. She knew from casual conversations during previous visits that anything could be bought in the 'Golden Triangle' of Thailand, Laos and Burma if you had enough money. Somehow, she had to contact someone who could facilitate some black-market transactions, without putting herself in danger. If she could arrange a false passport, then one plane trip could get her back home, hopefully with her dad's package in hand – although that was assuming that the intended recipient of the package was in the States. Laura had seen enough on her travels across four continents, to know that while it seemed farfetched, these things were an everyday part of life for wide strata of society from illegal immigrants and refugees to drug-runners and other criminals.

As she reached the end of the sand at the northern end of Chaweng Beach, Laura wanted to get out of the sun, so she climbed up from the beach into a wooded area. She started planning how to put her plan into action. Firstly, she would chat to a few locals, to score a hit on some marijuana – she knew from past visits that while some Asian authorities could be extremely harsh on enforcing drug control, a little personal use by tourists tended to be overlooked in Thailand. She could then use that contact to try to make her way a little deeper into the criminal fraternity. She would have to get money wired to her from the Swiss account so that she would have funds ready to pay for a false identity, so that she could travel home in relative safety.

Laura's thoughts were interrupted by the unmistakable

sound of a branch cracking a little behind her. She froze in position, unable to believe that somebody might be following her. She stood without moving a muscle, scarcely daring to breathe, ears straining to hear any indication that there was someone else nearby. Laura knew tourists would be unlikely to walk up this far from the beach, as the area was unattractive by the high standards of Samui, consisting of bushes growing a little more than head height, with plain trees scattered profusely among the growth. It was an area that would attract mosquitoes at dusk and dawn, and there were no tracks or facilities.

Reassured by the absence of any other sounds, Laura slowly started to move forward again. Now, however, she was no longer moving aimlessly, she was consciously trying to angle back towards Chaweng, to the safety of a crowd. She wanted to make as little noise as possible, and so she walked relatively slowly. After she had gone for maybe 300 metres in five or six minutes, she heard the sound that she had been desperately hoping she would not hear – an undeniable rustling of the bushes a short way behind her. Again she froze. The sound behind wasn't repeated – was her pursuer now listening for her, as she was listening for him – or them? Laura almost moaned out loud with fear. How had she come to be on this tiny, heavenly island and the object of a manhunt?

By her best guess, Laura reckoned that she had to be fairly close to the edge of the wood. If she ran, please God, she could get to people before the person or people behind her could catch her, assuming that was their aim. With that thought, Laura started to race forward, no longer worrying about the noise she made.

As she raced through the thick shrubbery, she heard indisputable proof that she was being pursued. Because of the speed at which she was moving, the person behind her now had no choice but to run at least as quickly as her if they were to catch her. She could hear them smashing a path through the undergrowth, trying to gain on her. From the sounds, Laura believed there was only one person after her, not more. It sounded like someone big – presumably a man. She ran and she ran and she ran. Desperately, she realised that she had lost her sense of direction, and she was no longer sure which way she should run if she wanted to get out of the wood into the populated part of Chaweng.

As she ran in the burning Thai sun, with not a breath of wind finding its way into the wood to cool her, she could feel the toll being exacted on her body. Laura was a fit young woman, but even her toned and muscled body couldn't keep up this level of exertion in this heat and humidity for long. Crashing though the greenery sapped huge amounts of energy, especially given the speed she was racing at. Laura could feel her muscles start to ache and tremble with the unceasing demands being placed on them. She knew she could not keep going for much longer, but she did not know how close she was to the beach or a road or the outskirts of Chaweng. Coming close to collapse from exhaustion, she knew she was going to have to try to hide from her pursuer – she could no longer outrun him.

Spotting a slightly less dense barrier of foliage to her left, she launched herself into the air, hoping to clear the bush and thus leave no trace of where she had disappeared to. She landed in a patch of rotting forest detritus and lay as still and as quiet as she possibly could. She could hear the hunter coming close to where she lay and then stop and swear quietly. He had obviously been chasing her by sound rather than by sight – she thanked her lucky stars that he hadn't been close enough to see her. There was silence for a few minutes, as he listened to pick up her trail by her noise again. As she lay like stone, Laura felt the decomposing pile of leaves and wood that she was half-buried in, come to life. It was full of an army of scavenging insects, that had been happily munching on the mouldy decaying leaves until she landed in their midst. Now the bugs started moving over her body. Exhausted as Laura was, it was like being transported into the spirit of the forest, and Laura started to slip into semi-consciousness.

Just as she heard the pursuer start to move slowly forward, in the direction that she had been going in; she jerked awake as the insects moved into her mouth, ears and nose. She froze again, forcing herself not to move, desperately hoping the man hadn't heard her movement. She listened frantically, hearing the sound of the man fading into the distance ahead of her. How long could she stay where she was? Not long, she knew. Even though she wasn't scared of creepy-crawlies, there was no way she could make herself lie still as they violated her body with their disgusting intrusions. She tried to move achingly slowly as she spat the insects out of her mouth and shook her head to get them out of her ears and nose. She couldn't hear any noise of the man chasing her now – he seemed to have moved a good distance ahead.

Slowly, bit by bit, Laura crawled to the left again, hoping to move at a right-angle away from the monster that was after her – what else but a monster could cause such dread and horror? The pain in her body was overwhelming – in some ways it was harder to move slowly than to run. The strain of moving so carefully, almost hysterical with the need to make not a single sound, was both physically and psychologically devastating. After she had crawled a good distance, Laura simply could not go on. She collapsed in a shaded patch of undergrowth, and slipped into semi-consciousness.

When she came to, it was dusk. Laura thought it must be at least two hours since the chase. She believed that her pursuer must have lost track of her completely. She was by this stage seriously reconsidering the vow she had made to Chanarong – maybe she would abandon this mad quest that her dad had launched her on – it was simply too crazy, too scary, too bloody dangerous. She would slip into Chaweng that night, try to make contact with an intermediary into the black market as she had planned, and just get the hell out of Thailand.

Resolved to put an end to the madness, Laura started to lift herself off the ground, slowly and gingerly. Her sluggishness was partly because she wanted to be quiet, just on the unlikely chance that the man chasing her was still in the vicinity; but it was mostly because she couldn't move quickly anyway. Her body was bruised and battered, her muscles were strained and sore, and her psychological state of mind was not much better.

Then her heart almost stopped beating with shock, as a heavy body crashed into her, forcing her back onto the ground. She could not believe it – he must have circled around and been listening so that he could pinpoint her location once she started moving again. Laura was completely trapped by his weight, unable to move.

As she started to black out, losing consciousness for what she believed must be the final time, her mind screamed at the hopelessness of it all. When she had spent time with Tahir and the bedouin, she had felt that there was something missing from her life; and when she had spent time with Chanarong and the monks, she had seen a glimpse of what she was missing – a meaning in life. Now, she was dying, was being murdered, for reasons she did not understand. She had failed her dad. And she would never know what the purpose of her life had been. She would never know how she should have lived. She would never know the peace and happiness that Tahir and Chanarong and their peoples seemed to experience effortlessly. With these thoughts ravaging her soul and making a desolate wasteland of her heart, Laura blacked out, believing she was dying.

She fought waking up. Being unconscious was soporific, it was safe, it was calm. But she could feel herself being pulled back to consciousness. She didn't want to – being conscious would mean having to think, having to feel. And Laura was ready for neither.

She became aware that she was lying on her side. She could not move her arms or legs – they must be tied. There was something in her mouth – she tried to spit it out, but couldn't; and so she opened her eyes to try to make sense of what was happening. The man sat at the other side of a small clearing, about three metres away, watching her with what appeared to be concern, if that could be believed. He spoke, stumbling slightly on the words as though horrified at what he had just been forced to do. 'Laura, I'm terribly sorry. I have tied your ankles – I hope it's not sore. And I have a gag in your mouth. Don't worry, it's not tight enough to risk choking you or anything, but I need to be sure that you can't scream or run, until I've have had a chance to explain.'

He paused, obviously trying to gather his thoughts before continuing. Laura lay still, too scared to move or protest. She hoped he would go on talking, as talking was infinitely less scary than what he might do to her once he was finished talking.

'Laura, my name is Greg Donaldson. I worked with your father Ben in the army in the 1960s and 1970s until he …

retired. I know you're probably thinking I'm talking about some man other than your father, because you think he was a statistician, but that is the first of a few new truths that I have to explain to you. Until you understand all of this, you won't be able to trust me, and you won't be able to do whatever it is that Ben asked you to do - if he asked you anything. But I think he did. Why else would you be back here, where it all started? And why would they be trying to stop you so badly?'

At first his words didn't sink through to Laura, as she was too scared to really hear his words, or to hear the meaning they conveyed. Gradually, however, the message started to get through.

'Laura, your father and I were part of a team that worked the Golden Triangle for Army Intelligence during the Vietnam War. After Saigon, we were transferred to the CIA and we kept working on the same mission. For a long time, we didn't understand the true nature of that mission. For too long, we didn't understand.'

He paused again, seeming to be weighed down by some terrible regret or sadness.

'When we finally realised what was going on, we tried to stop it. But by then, the plan was too far along and we were powerless. When we started to try to get information about what was really going on out into the outside world, they...'

He paused again, seeming to struggle for words.

'I'm sorry, Laura, so help me God, I am. When they couldn't frighten us into shutting up, and then they couldn't find us because we had gone underground, they issued an ultimatum. Either we came to an agreement with them, or they would start to kill our nearest and dearest – one person a week would be murdered until we gave ourselves up. Laura, the first person they killed was Tracey, your dear mother. Ben was devastated. That day we gave ourselves up to them. They would have killed us and disposed of our bodies, except that Ben had hidden documents detailing exactly what they had done and how – and who was involved. He said that if any harm came to him or me, that the documents would be made public. They had no choice – they agreed to let us go, provided we left our old life behind and became 'ordinary' citizens. For the past thirty years, I have been a librarian in Dallas – I always loved books.'

He looked wistful for a moment, perhaps relishing a brief memory of a different life.

'Laura, I know this must be terribly confusing for you. The documents that Ben hid are like a time-bomb from the old days. They tell a story that no one would have believed possible. They detail agreements between the CIA and the Viet Cong, whereby the CIA orchestrated the American rout from Vietnam, in return for permanent access to the Golden Triangle. We couldn't believe it at first – that either the CIA or the Viet Cong would work with the other. They were so bitterly opposed, with absolute ideologues on each side, but I'll explain later how we found out about it, and how it came to be that these total enemies came to work together. The CIA wanted to use the drug trade to fund 'Black Ops'. This was sanctioned at the highest levels of our government – and by that, I mean presidential.

'Laura, many of the people involved in that decision are still around today. They are at the highest levels of our government and they are very senior figures in business. They will stop at nothing to prevent those documents from being found and made public. That is what has been happening to you since you left home. The 'terrorist bombing' of the airplane you were meant to be on – that was no coincidence, and it was no random act of terrorism. I saw the attack in Bangkok, although I couldn't get close enough to help you – they have enlisted the help of some rogue elements in CIB – the Thai Secret Police. They are terrified that you have come here – back to where it all began – because of some deathbed conscience of Ben's. They are afraid that he asked you to get and make public those documents.'

He stopped, seeming to wait for a reaction from her. Laura shook her head – she couldn't say anything with a damned gag in her mouth!

'Of course, I do apologise,' said Greg. 'If I take the gag out, will you at least promise not to scream? I know this is all a terrible shock to you, but we must not be heard, in case they followed you to Koh Samui as I was able to do.'

With that, he approached her slowly, non-aggressively, and gently removed the gag, looking into her eyes as he did so. Apparently satisfied with what he saw, he retreated again to the far side of the clearing.

Laura coughed quietly, at which he immediately passed her over a water bottle. She drank greedily, only realising as she drank how parched her mouth and throat were. Her mind whirled – everything he said made sense, it made sense of her dad's dying request and everything that had happened since. But yet it was so unbelievable! Her dad – her quiet, loving, unassuming dad – a spy! And some conspiracy among powerful men in government and business to stop her from revealing a decades-old secret about the CIA organising the American defeat in Vietnam – though if true, she could see how explosive that would be.

She just didn't know how to decide if anything this man was saying was true. How could she know whether or not to trust him? Not knowing what else to do, she put exactly that question straight to him. 'How do I know I can trust you –

every word you are saying might be a lie?'

'Yes, yes, I know,' he answered, sounding as though he felt a little out of his depth. 'I am not sure how I can make you accept what I am saying as the truth. When I heard that Ben had died, I knew I had to check you were OK, as Ben would have done for my two children if I had died first. All I can tell you, Laura, is what I know – you will have to decide if you can trust me or not. Given that you are here, I am assuming that Ben asked you to recover documents – he may have asked you to publicise them, or to pass them to me or someone else. He would have warned you, I hope, that this was dangerous. He may have mentioned that the world needs this to happen. He almost certainly would have referred to Tracey's death – her loss hit him terribly hard. After she was murdered, he stopped everything immediately – he was like a broken man for a time. But he did enough in hiding those documents to ensure that he and I, and our families, would be safe. He would have told you about the Swiss bank account – he had the access, because we felt it was better to limit it to one person, but there should be tens of millions in that account. Ben loved you more than life itself, Laura – after they killed Tracey, he felt terribly guilty that we could not stop them, but he put your safety above everything else. That is why I knew I had to go to his funeral to see you, and keep an eye on you for a while.'

Laura thought back to the delirious ramblings of her dad as he lay dying. This new information shed those mumblings in an entirely new light. He hadn't been delirious at all. He had referred in one way or another to many of the things Greg was talking about – she recalled the phrases he had said.

'I failed so much ... But after they took your mom, I couldn't risk losing you as well. I had to leave it be ... There

was so much, so much power and ambition ... I had to protect you. I hid the information, so they would have to leave us alone ... I'm sorry Tracey ... I'm so sorry my darling. I couldn't save you. But I saved Laura.'

And then in the video – some of the things he had said there.

'I couldn't go to my grave without leaving even a hope that things might be put right ... this feeds back into my younger years, and the terrible sacrifice of your mom ... If you decide to take this on, then from this moment your life is in danger ... this is literally world-changing stuff ... it is incredibly important to me – this would literally put right the terrible wrong that I have left in place for the past thirty years ... I want you to go to Bangkok, and collect a package from an old friend of mine and deliver it to another old friend.'

It all fit with what Greg was telling her. Laura was awestruck. After all that had happened, it had to be true. What could she do? And was Greg really on her side – maybe he was working for these enemies of her dad's – the people who had murdered her mom all those years ago.

'Tell me about dad,' she ordered. 'And did you know my mom?'

'Oh, I knew Tracey, all right. I was newly married to my wife, Susannah, at the time, but I used to joke with Tracey that she and I would elope. She would laugh and say, "Ah, Greg, I do love you as a friend, but how could I elope and leave a man as wonderful as this?" And then she'd squeeze Ben's arm or hand, and laugh and laugh and laugh. She had a truly beautiful laugh.' Greg stopped or a moment, taking a drink of water and wiping the back of his hand across his face. Laura couldn't be certain, but she suspected that he was hiding an involuntary tear. 'God, they loved each other like no other two people I have ever known.

'It was a funny thing about Ben – he was a real man's man OK, could hold his drink and could party with the best of us. But he had something – nearly like an aura or something. You knew that he could handle anything – I think that came from your mom, and their love. After she was killed, he was a changed man. It was all he could do to hide those documents. Then the only thing he could think about was you – he had to protect you. Of course, I was thinking the exact same about my wife and two girls. He used to say to me, "Greg, I have to protect Laura. Tracey and I had planned our Family Days. Now, they'll just be Dad and Daughter Days."'

Laura gasped as Greg unwittingly spoke the words from her childhood – the password that it had taken her so long to think of. Now she knew that he must have known her dad – must have known him very well, must have been a really close friend. With a low cry, she started to sob, feeling once again the loss not just of her dad, but of her mom as well. Greg moved closer to her, seeming unsure as to what to do or say. Laura grabbed on to him and buried her face in his shirt, feeling protected and with an ally for the first time since her dad's death.

Now, at last, she knew what was going on. At last, she understood her dad's request. And at last, she had someone else who shared her love and respect for her dad, someone who wanted to help her and who wanted to protect her as her dad had done.

The Package

Laura gave herself a shake, and drew back from Greg. The thought reverberated around her brain – 'Now, I know.'

'Greg, it's time for me to take this on properly,' she stated, clearly and calmly. 'Until now, I have been running around like a little girl, not sure what was going on, and not sure what I should do. But now, I do know. Now, it is all clear to me. Now, I am certain.'

Laura paused, and Greg watched her carefully, apparently not sure how to take this change in her. Suddenly, she seemed confident and composed, certain and convinced.

'When you were following me just now, and I thought you were another person trying to kill me, I had just about decided to give up on dad's mad request – this deathbed mission that he sent me on. But now I know differently. There is just one question that I need you to answer for me. Knowing what you know, about the history behind us and the danger in front of us, will you help me?'

Greg seemed relieved, answering quickly, 'Of course I will, Laura. That is what I am here for. That is why I followed you. I will help you, because I feel obliged to honour Ben's memory, and also because the mission that you are on is a good mission. Having lived more than five decades, and having seen my two children safely reared, now it is time for me to make amends for the unfinished business that Ben and I were forced to leave behind all those years ago.'

Reassured, Laura immediately began planning, acting now like a commander-in-chief, detailing the broad strategy whilst leaving it up to Greg to work out the tactical details.

'OK, here is what we are going to do. We will get back to Bangkok – I will leave it up to you to decide on the safest route – and we will collect these papers and see who they have to be delivered to. If that person is here in Thailand, we will simply deliver them, end of story. If we have to go abroad to deliver them, then we will have to work that one out once we know where we have to go. Either way, I need you to get us false passports and anything else we need to leave Thailand. Once we have delivered those papers, then I will go home and forget that any of this ever happened. If you think I need to stay in hiding somewhere, then I will disappear somewhere for as long as is needed. Can you get us everything that we will need?'

'Absolutely,' Greg answered, clearly delighted that Laura was at last being so decisive, responding positively to the challenges and dangers that lay ahead. 'I will need some of the Swiss funds to pay for false documents and travel arrangements. Other than that, I can't see any major problems ahead. The bad guys won't expect you to have company, so that should make it easier to stay a step or two ahead of them.'

'OK,' said Laura, still forging ahead with the planning and organising. 'What do you think is the best way to get back to Bangkok?'

'Without doubt, the way you came,' Greg answered positively. 'It is the least monitored and the safest. What made you decide to come to Koh Samui, and especially what made you decide to do it by second-class train ticket?'

'A friend picked the ticket for me,' said Laura, not wanting to talk about Chanarong and his community of monks in the temple – somehow that seemed to be a private and special memory, which would be in some way lessened if it were shared.

'Well, your friend gave you good advice,' said Greg. 'I lost you after you were attacked in Bangkok, and hung around the train station in the hope that you might surface there. You very nearly gave me the slip, you know.'

'Well, hopefully that should mean that I gave the authorities the slip as well,' said Laura.

'Absolutely,' confirmed Greg. 'There was no trace of you being followed either in the train station or on the journey down here.'

'So our first job is to get the train back to Bangkok. When does the next ferry leave Na Thon, do you know?'

'Yep, the next leaves a little after eight o'clock tomorrow morning,' said Greg. 'If I can advise, I think you should stay with your new buddies tonight, then separate from them in the morning. I will meet you at Na Thon tomorrow morning at eight o'clock, and we can catch the ferry across to Surat Thani in plenty of time for the train.'

'That's perfect,' Laura replied. 'In the meantime, will you walk me back to the hostel?'

The two of them walked back through the trees together, emerging onto the main road north of Chaweng. In the moonlight of the midnight hour, amidst the scent of the sea and the flowers, they strolled in the lessening heat and talked and started the slow process of building a friendship and trust. When they reached the hostel, Greg took Laura's hands in his for a moment, warning her to keep an eye out for danger, while reassuring her that he honestly believed that she was safe on Samui. As he turned to leave, he brushed her cheek gently with the tips of his fingers, and then walked into the night.

Laura went to bed, only waking briefly as her Irish friends came in from a late night on the town. She chatted with them for a short time, as they regaled her with tales of the bars, the transvestites, the stage shows. Laura laughed with them, envying them their innocence and their carefree lives. She told them that a friend had phoned and was in Phuket and that she would be going to the airport the following morning, to catch a flight across Thailand to the western side to meet her friend. She felt guilty about lying to these trusting young people, but didn't want to take a chance that a careless word in a bar might point someone in her direction.

The next morning, Laura woke early, packed her backpack and left a note for the Irish crew, wishing them well in Samui and on the rest of their travels. She got a taxi across the island to Na Thon and walked onto the jetty. Waiting there was her new protector, her knight in shining armour, her Greg. When he saw her, he raised an eyebrow and then turned and sauntered off to the far corner of the jetty, a little apart from the small crowd waiting for the ferry to dock. Laura strolled in the same direction, eventually leaning on the rail and looking out to see the ferry approach.

'We're still in the clear,' he whispered out of the side of his mouth, lips not moving. 'We'll travel as separate tourists while we're on the ferry. When we reach Surat Thani, delay leaving the ferry while I check out the lie of the land. When you get off the ferry, keep an eye out for me and we'll play it by ear then. While we are on the ferry crossing, I will be keeping an eye on you all the time, but at no stage should you do anything that might indicate that we know each other. And don't worry, I'll be close to you all the time, OK?'

With that, Greg moved off towards the ferry gates, rolling a cigarette as he went. Laura stayed where she was, watching the docking process and waiting for most of the incoming travellers to disembark before she walked over and got on board the ferry with the rest of the departing passengers. She took a seat near the front of the ferry in the open air and glanced around casually. With a little sigh of relief she saw that Greg was sitting in the back corner of the front section of the ferry, close enough that he could see her, although she couldn't see him unless she turned around. She surmised that he wanted to be able to watch the other passengers, to check that no one was showing any undue interest in her.

Laura sat back in her seat, facing into the breeze as the ferry moved away from Na Thon into the Gulf of Thailand in the South China Sea. She felt that, mentally, she had moved into a different place since she met Greg. Now she was reviewing their situation, thinking and planning about how to proceed, confident in the knowledge that she had an experienced ally to ensure that she didn't do anything stupid. She thought ahead – ferry, train, Bangkok, collect parcel, deliver parcel (probably abroad), go home, disappear for a while if necessary. Examined like that, it didn't seem impossible. However, Laura remembered a favourite saying of her dad's – 'The Devil is in the detail.' There was still plenty of scope for things to go wrong, so they would have to continue to be extraordinarily vigilant and careful.

When the ferry docked in Surat Thani, Laura fussed about with her bag, taking things out and putting them back in again. She was one of the last passengers to disembark, and she walked down the gangway confident in the knowledge that Greg was waiting for her. As she walked off the ferry, she saw him standing as though he was waiting for someone. When he saw her approach, he smiled and waved, so Laura knew he had decided that they should now travel together. She walked over to him and he took her hand with a smile.

'Hi, darling,' he grinned. 'I have our tickets. Let's hop on the bus straight away, so that we can be sure of getting a seat.'

Laura knew she should simply play along with Greg's lead, and that she could talk to him in more safety when there were fewer people milling about them. They boarded the bus that brought them to the train station and, when they arrived, Greg walked towards the platforms, holding Laura's hand. They boarded the train, and, Laura noticed, this time they boarded a second-class sleeper carriage. Greg walked through the door into the carriage itself, and threw his bag onto the first seat on the left-hand side. Laura put her bag down on top of his and they sat side-by-side in the air-conditioned comfort.

Now that they were on their own, Greg explained his tactics to Laura.

'Anyone looking for you is searching for a blonde girl on her own. I think we should travel as a couple, so that they will be less likely to pick you out of the crowds. The change in hair colour will be a great help as well – congratulations on that. You'd make a perfect Mata Hari!

'Keep your hair tied up all the time, so that the length is different as well. Don't wear sunglasses – they will be expecting you to wear shades to try to make yourself less recognisable. Always try to anticipate what the enemy will expect you to do, and then do something completely different. I would normally have travelled in a non-sleeper carriage as you did on the way down – there are more crowds, and it's easier to hide in a crowd. However, always avoid repeating the same strategies – you travelled non-sleeper on the way down, so I booked this sleeper for the journey back. A side-benefit of course is that we get bunks, so you will be able to sleep properly tonight. You must have had a terrible time trying to sleep on your way down from Bangkok.'

Laura relayed the tale of her trip down from Bangkok – how she had dyed her hair in the toilets in the train station, meeting the Irish girls and their time on the train. As they chatted about the past, the conversation ranged from near to long distant. Laura told Greg about her dad's passing, and about the video and the password. Greg told Laura war stories (literally!) from the time he and her dad had worked in South-East Asia in the 1970s. As the train chugged northwards, they sat in close contact, talking quietly with their heads bowed together so that they could not be overheard. They ate when they felt hungry, drank when they were thirsty, the only constant being their never-ceasing dialogue.

Laura felt truly comfortable for the first time in a long time. She knew they were not safe – far from it – but now she knew what was happening, she knew why it was happening, and she knew that she had an expert ally in the mature handsome man beside her. As they talked, Laura cuddled into Greg, relishing the warmth and safety of his proximity. At some stage during the afternoon, she laid her head on his chest as they talked, and Greg put his arm around her protectively, holding her close to him. As the day waned into evening, their conversation became more personal as they told each other about themselves.

Laura talked about the feelings of isolation and disconnectedness she had felt with Tahir's tribe, in comparison to their sense of community. She spoke about the discussions she had with some monks (though without telling him when she had met them) about the 'Meaning of Life', and the feeling she had that these guys were onto something – some eternal 'Truth' that she could sense, but couldn't quite pin down.

Greg spoke about his life since he had left the army – his quiet life as a librarian in Dallas, his children, and the loss three years earlier of his wife of thirty years to cancer. He told her of the loss and loneliness of his life without her. As he spoke of his deceased wife, a few tears slowly rolled down his craggy face, telling her volumes about how much he had loved his wife.

Laura's heart went out to this gentle, lonely man – at once so vulnerable and so strong. She knew he was old enough to be her father, but that didn't prevent the feelings that were starting to rise in her heart for him. She gazed up at that furrowed face, the face that told of a lifetime of pain and joy, love and loss, victory and defeat. As he looked down at her, she knew that he was experiencing similar feelings for her.

He whispered, 'Laura, I am so much older than you.'

'I don't care. It doesn't matter.'

'Are you sure? I don't want to hurt you.'

'I don't think you ever could, not if you tried.'

Knowing that he was still reluctant to put any pressure on her and needed to be convinced, Laura reached up to him and pulled his face down to hers. Their lips touched for a fleeting instant as she kissed him so gently. There was no rush here, no immature urgency, no unseemly haste. It was as though they had all the time in the world, even though they both knew they were heading back into the danger zone.

'Please, Greg, make up our bunks.'

Greg did as she asked, wordlessly putting both bunks in place. Laura put their bags on the top bunk and slid into the bottom bunk, holding her hand out for Greg to join her.

'Are you sure about this?' he asked, his chivalrous hesitation making Laura think how different he was to the younger men that she had known.

'I have never been more sure of anything,' she said quietly but with assurance.

Greg joined her on the bottom bunk, lying alongside her on the narrow bed. Laura put her arms around his neck, whispering encouragement and reassurance to him as she started to kiss him slowly. Her actions were unhurried, deliberate and incredibly sensuous. She knew that he would be nervous, not having been with a woman since his wife had died. She slowly kissed his mouth, then his eyes, his nose, forehead, cheeks and neck. She pulled off his T-shirt, revealing a body that was in great condition and stroked his back with long leisurely luxurious caresses, trailing the barest tips of her fingernails along his skin.

Slowly, Greg responded, finding this gorgeous girl to be the most stimulating thing that had happened to him in a long time. His initial anxiety seemed to fade, as he became lost in the rush of sensations that enveloped him as Laura worked her magic. She paused to strip off her own T-shirt, and he was electrified by her body. Her breasts offered themselves to Greg, and he worshipped at that alter. As the night wore on, they came together in an almost soundless cacophony of feeling and emotion, as they delved into this incredible pulsating reservoir of human love and lust.

Through the night they made love, dozed in each other's arms, talked quietly and then repeated it all again. They greeted the dawn with joyous solemnity, paying homage to each other and to Life as the sun rose into a wounded sky. They laughed softly in shared happiness, and cried tenderly as they shared sad memories. As they heard people starting to stir beyond the curtain of their heavenly haven, they made ready to start the business of the day. When they were dressed, Greg got their bags from the top bunk, and they shared a simple breakfast of fruit and water. They planned how to approach Mwai, and discussed possible scenarios that might develop once they had collected the papers.

The train pulled into Bangkok with a screaming of brakes. Laura and Greg left the train, no longer simply playing the roles of lovers on vacation. Laura stayed close to Greg, holding his hand and leaning into him as they walked. They walked through the station and into Rama IV Road without attracting a glance from anyone. It was now late morning, so they walked to Khao San Road and had a leisurely late breakfast whilst they watched the tourists marvel at the bustling hive that is Bangkok. They had decided to approach Mwai late at night when the Nana complex would be at its busiest. In the afternoon, they strolled down to Chinatown, and through Little India, looking at the stalls and haggling with the vendors, though they bought nothing except for an occasional snack.

Laura felt that the time crawled but, eventually, it was close to midnight. Greg hailed a tuk-tuk and they sped towards Bangkok's main red-light district – towards Laura's appointment with destiny. Laura's mind was a whirl of emotions – anxious but no longer panicked. Greg's reassuring presence was a bolster to her composure, and she felt that she had a protector. At the same time, she knew that this was it – this was the meeting that had caused these shadowy figures in business and government to try to have her killed before she could make the rendezvous. And while all of this spun through her mind, she actually enjoyed the tuk-tuk ride, revelling in the manic speed and amazing dexterity of the drivers as they threaded the three-wheeled motorbike-car hybrid through near-impossible gaps in the traffic.

With a flourish, the driver pulled up on Silom Road. Laura stared in a combination of wonder and curiosity – she hadn't visited this area before. Covering a couple of blocks between Silom and Suriwong roads, the area was home to a vibrant mix of bars, go-go joints, hotels and shops. At this time of night, the famous night-market was in full swing, with lines of stalls along the street selling everything from clothes to electronics. And in front of most of the bars, the beautiful Asian girls and lady-boys were boisterously calling to passers-by, trying to entice them into sampling the delights of their particular establishment.

Laura and Greg walked along the street, looking for the Five Seasons. They wandered around for a while, before finding it tucked away in a corner – a small entrance with a barely noticeable sign above the door. Unlike most of the bars and brothels, that had girls outside urging potential customers to enter, the Five Seasons had no one on the door. Greg and Laura drew back a little to consider the best approach.

'I'll go in first,' said Greg, talking clear charge of this part of the operation. 'Follow me in, after a minute or two – I don't want you out here too long on your own. When you get in, get a table in front of me, so that you will be directly in my line of vision between me and the stage. Order a beer first, and when it is brought to you, ask for Mwai.'

'OK, Greg,' answered Laura. 'What will I say to Mwai?'

'I think all you can do is tell him who you are, who your dad was, and about Ben's dying wish. Don't tell him anything about me – we'll keep my presence as our ace-in-the-hole. That means you shouldn't let him know that you are aware of any of the background to all of this – you are simply collecting the papers as your dad asked you to.'

Greg kissed her briefly and then started to move off towards the Five Seasons, before thinking of something else and whispering back to her, 'And don't let him take you into a back room or anything – insist that you want to talk in the bar itself.'

Laura slowly counted to a hundred before moving to the Five Seasons herself. She walked and paused to give her eyes a moment to adjust to the dimmer lighting inside. She glanced around as she paused for that moment to get her bearings. There was a raised stage in the centre of the floor, with stainless steel poles stretching from floor to ceiling. The small bar was in the back, attended by a young Asian girl, with an older lady seated on a high stool behind her. The other three sides of the stage were surrounded by seating – five rows, with a low wall separating each. Laura could see Greg in the back row on her right-hand side, with another young Asian girl handing him a beer. She took a seat at a table two rows in front of and slightly to the left of him, so that he could easily see her while he pretended to look at the stage. A beautiful young Asian girl approached Laura immediately, asking if she would like a drink. Laura ordered a beer, and only as the girl left did she really take in what was happening on the stage.

Three of the most beautiful girls Laura had ever seen were on the raised platform. One was in a bikini, one wearing only a g-string, and the other was completely naked. They were dancing to the pulsating music, although as Laura watched them wide-eyed, she thought that what they were doing was as much like gymnastics as like dancing. These girls were incredibly flexible, twisting and contorting their bodies into the most incredible positions, using the poles as props. The effect was mesmerising, with their sinuous movement being incredibly erotic.

Laura's attention was taken from the stage by the arrival of her drink. The girl set the beer down on the table, and then looked shyly at Laura. 'My name is Dani. Would you like to buy me a drink?' she asked, looking up at Laura through the most amazingly long eyelashes. 'I could keep you company while you watch the sexy girls.'

Laura kept a neutral face, not wanting to offend the young girl. She was making a pass at Laura, but Laura knew she was only doing her job. For a fleeting instant, Laura wondered what it would be like to have one or two of these expert girls take her to bed, but she shook the thought away. 'I'm sorry, honey' she said sweetly, 'but not just now. Actually, I came here to see Mwai – is he around?'

Laura held her breath, not sure what to expect – would it be a blank look, would there be pandemonium, she didn't know. The normality of the girl's response was the most surprising thing.

'I'm not sure if he is here, but I can check. Who will I say is asking for him?'

'Tell him it's Laura Whiteland. My dad was Ben Whiteland.'

Dani walked over to the bar and engaged in a lengthy exchange with the older lady behind the bar. Laura assumed she must be some kind of manager, as she did no serving, simply watching all that was happening and seeming to bark the occasional instruction to one of the girls. Dani pointed back at Laura as the older lady asked her questions. Then the older lady walked out from behind the bar, and came over to Laura.

'You look for someone called Mwai?'

'Yes,' answered Laura, 'that's right.'

'What makes you think that there is anyone of that name

here?'

'My dad, Ben Whiteland, asked me to see Mwai, here at the Five Seasons.'

'He is not here.' The older lady's speech was staccato, as though she had a lot of other things to do, but she had to attend to this matter before anything else.

'I don't understand,' said Laura. 'My dad asked me to see Mwai. I think Mwai will be very upset if he hears that I was here and he was not told.' She was gambling now, speaking on instinct, trying to find a weakness in the woman's armour. The implied threat in her last comment seemed to do it.

'He is not here. You will be brought to another house. If there is someone called Mwai, he may or may not agree to meet you there.'

'No way,' exclaimed Laura immediately. 'I will meet him here, where it is busy and there are people. My father's instructions were to meet Mwai here. That is what Mwai will expect.'

The old lady was clearly taken aback, unsure of how to proceed. 'Wait here,' she commanded, and walked off behind the bar and through a door that was cleverly concealed among the shelves of bottles behind the bar.

Laura watched the stage show, only once glancing casually around the room to confirm for her own peace of mind that Greg was still sitting behind her. He had a gorgeous girl sitting beside him, presumably to fit into the scene and not draw attention to himself. In the meantime, the antics on stage moved from being merely suggestive to being acutely explicit, with vibrators and various other props being called into action as the girls engaged in a live sex show for the mostly Western audience. Laura was interested to see that while the audience was predominantly male, there were three of four mixed groups, as well as one group of four white girls – presumably tourists who just wanted to be able to say when they returned to their homely suburbia that they had experienced Bangkok's famous sex shows.

Abruptly, the lady was back at her side.

'I am sorry you have been kept waiting, Miss,' she said. Her manner was now quite deferential – it seemed that she had been told to treat Laura well. 'Mwai is on his way. He may be a little while, as he has to cross the city. Is there anything else that I can get you while you wait?'

'Would it be possible to get a coffee?' asked Laura. She wanted to have something to do with her hands while she waited, but she also wanted to be a sober when Mwai arrived. Hopefully also, seeing the coffee would alert Greg that she had established a contact of sorts, but that she would be waiting a while.

'Certainly, Miss. Is there anything else?'

Laura felt very exposed, sitting there on her own. She thought a little company would make her feel less ill-at-ease, whilst also making her less conspicuous in the bar – at the moment she was the only Western girl sitting by herself.

'Yes,' said Laura, now feeling in charge. 'I want one of your girls who has good English to sit with me while I wait. She can tell me about Bangkok – having someone to talk to will pass the time. I will, of course, pay for her time.'

'I will send Naran to you. Her English is excellent. You will not need to pay her – you are a guest of Mwai.'

With that, she went back to her stool behind the bar to survey her domain. After a few minutes, a very beautiful young girl arrived at Laura's table with an elaborate silver tray with all the accoutrements for a perfect coffee. As she started to pour, she introduced herself.

'Hello, Miss. I am Naran. My mistress says that I am to

sit and talk with you.'

'Hi, Naran. Thanks a million for the coffee. Yes, I am waiting for Mwai, and I just felt a little conspicuous sitting here by myself, know what I mean?'

'Indeed, Miss, we often get beautiful Western ladies such as yourself visiting our humble premises with their partners, or, occasionally, a group of girls will visit, such as those ones there.' Naran pointed at the group of four girls that Laura had already noticed. 'However, it is unusual for a single white girl to visit on her own. Are you just here to meet Mwai, or are you looking for some 'pleasure' as well?'

'Just to meet Mwai, Naran, that's all.'

'OK,' said Naran happily. Laura suspected that it might be an unusual treat for one of the girls to be able to chat to someone in the bar, knowing that it wouldn't end up in them having to offer their body for the visitor's gratification before the end of the night.

'So, Naran, tell me about life here in Bangkok.'

Laura sat back and listened, as Naran started to regale her with stories about a prostitute's life in Bangkok. Laura knew the stories had to be heavily sanitised versions, as they made the girls' lives seem exciting and filled with fun. There were stories about drunken tourists getting upset when they discovered that they had just had sex with a lady-boy – Naran told of one aggrieved customer who howled, 'No wonder she, I mean he – whatever! – was so fucking tight.'

Naran's stories passed the time quickly for Laura. Naran told her tales about some of the girls and lady-boys on stage. She played a game, where Laura had to guess which of the 'girls' performing were actually men in the process of preparing for gender reassignment surgery. Laura found it hard to believe that some of these statuesque and beautiful girls were actually men, but Naran signalled to one of them and she got off the stage and sashayed over to Naran. Naran whispered to her, and she discreetly flashed Laura a quick glimpse of a penis hidden between her legs and expertly camouflaged with flesh-coloured body-tape. Laura was amazed that these very beautiful and totally feminine 'girls' were actually men undergoing a drawn-out surgical process.

A short while later, Naran rose to leave. 'Mwai is here. I will leave you now to have your meeting. It was fun talking to you.'

Laura thought Naran looked a little wistful. Laura took Naran's hand and thanked her genuinely for her time. She slipped Naran a one thousand Baht note – more than she would normally earn for an hour's sex. Naran leaned over and gave Laura a quick kiss on the cheek and Laura hugged her impulsively, knowing now how so many Western men so easily fell 'in love' with their Thai girls. With that, Naran was gone and Laura could see an old Asian man approaching her.

'Miss Whiteland, I am Mwai.'

He sat beside her, and observed her for a time without talking. Laura sat, waiting for him to speak, and taking the opportunity to look at him. He was undoubtedly elderly – he looked to be in his eighties if not older. He was dressed very well, wearing a tropical cream two-piece suit with a white shirt and a red tie. He was totally bald, but had a sweeping handlebar moustache. He looked wise somehow, maybe because of his advanced years, but Laura felt it was more than that – he seemed to emit a sense of completeness. This man knew his place in the order of things – understood and agreed with it.

'You came back from Samui sooner than we expected.'

Laura nearly jumped up with surprise, and couldn't help a quick backward glance to make sure that Greg was still there. 'How do you know where I was?' she asked. 'And what else do you know?'

'The universe is a very strange place, Miss Whiteland. It lives according to its own rules. And it arranges and orders things, events, people; in a way that we often cannot understand. Your father sent you to me to collect something, to deliver it to the right person, because now is the right time. Fate, Buddha, call it what you will. Fate delivered you to 'the package' as you call it, instead of delivering the package to you. You spent four days very close to the package that you have to collect, though you had no way of knowing this.

'We wondered if we should simply deliver the package to you there and then; but on reflection we felt that part of the correct order of things was that you should seek me out as your father instructed. That is why we waited until now. The package that your father left in my safekeeping required special care – as events developed, it required a type of care that I could never provide. Accordingly, I entrusted it to someone who could care for and nurture it properly. Chanarong has looked after this precious merchandise.'

Laura wondered if she would ever be able to look at life in the same way again. How was this possible – that she and Rannachai should pick out the temple at random, meet Chanarong there and now discover that Chanarong had been looking after the parcel all this time?

'How? Why?' she stuttered.

'I can understand your surprise,' smiled Mwai. 'I know that Westerners are often ignorant of the ways of Fate, expecting everything to follow only the rules of the physical world. I have, for my own curiosity, studied physics a little. It amuses me to see how scientists become increasingly puzzled the more they delve into the detail of the laws of the physical universe. The reason for their puzzlement is simply that there is more to this world of ours than physics. Now, we need to go to see Chanarong, so that you can take custody of your 'package'.'

Laura hesitated. She had agreed with Greg that she would not allow Mwai to take her out of Greg's sight. 'Why not simply give the parcel to me here?' she asked.

Mwai laughed gently. 'This is no fitting place for this parcel. Chanarong said that you might be nervous about leaving with me to go to Wat Nák Tong Tieow. He said if I need you to trust me, I should simply remind you of how much you enjoyed the kuaytiaw naam – he said that he will have some hot and ready for you when we arrive at Wat Nák Tong Tieow. If you like, I can arrange for Kasem to meet us outside and drive us to the wat.'

Laura thought for a moment. His reference to the chicken noodles – the kuaytiaw naam – that she had liked so much at the temple, meant that he must indeed know Chanarong, and Chanarong must have told Mwai all about her visit. Laura recalled her conversations with Chanarong. He had been surprised when she had said that she was to collect the package from Mwai, a brothel owner, and he had been astounded when she told him her name. That made perfect sense if Mwai had entrusted care of the package to Chanarong after her father had left Asia and started his new life as a simple university professor in the US. She thought back to her conversations with Chanarong, and the time she had spent in Wat Nák Tong Tieow. She decided that she could trust Mwai.

'I think that would be best, Mwai, if that's OK. Not because I don't trust you, but because I have a friend with me, and I will need to reassure him that what we are doing is safe.'

'Chanarong told me you were resourceful,' Mwai smiled. 'So who is this friend? Where is he?'

'He is here with me,' Laura answered. 'Just give me a minute.'

Laura rose from the table, leaving Mwai for a moment, and walked back to Greg's table. She could see the look of consternation on his face – she guessed Greg was not a guy who liked to see plans being changed midway.

'It's OK, Greg,' she said, as she stopped at the table. She turned to the prostitute holding Greg's hand and said 'Honey, can you give us a minute please?' Laura was amused, putting the lessons she learned from Naran to good use.

'Do you know, darling,' she whispered as the girl left the table, 'that gorgeous lady that was holding your hand – is a lady-boy!'

'No way' Greg whispered fiercely. 'Look, what the hell is going on? We agreed that you would say nothing to Mwai about me.'

'Don't worry,' said Laura. 'I'm not going to say anything about you. Even though I trust these guys, especially the person we are going to see shortly, I think it's no harm to play our cards close to our chest. So I will say nothing about who you are, except that you are my friend, but I do need you to come with me now.'

'But what's happening?' asked Greg. 'How do you know you can trust this guy – I assume that's Mwai?' He nodded in Mwai's direction.

'Yes, it is,' said Laura. 'But the parcel isn't here – it is in a temple that I know, being looked after by a monk whom, coincidentally, I also know. Believe me, Greg, I am not being stupid. We can trust these men. We need to go with Mwai – another monk I met before will drive the car. When we get to Wat Nák Tong Tieow, we will collect the parcel.'

Reluctantly, Greg allowed Laura to take his hand and pull him up from his seat. Together, they walked back down and joined Mwai at his table.

'Mwai, this is a friend of mine. He will be travelling with me.'

'Hello, friend of Laura's,' said Mwai. 'I do not know how much Laura has confided in you but we were expecting Laura on her own, so while Laura is welcome to bring someone with her, we will be dealing only with Laura. Is that agreed?'

'Absolutely,' said Greg, secretly relieved that Mwai seemed to be saying that there would be no discussion with Greg himself. He had been worried that they might want to know all about him, and that could have raised serious complications for him.

'I will leave you to finish your drinks. I will come for you when our driver is here,' Mwai said as he left them.

Laura spent the next fifteen minutes reassuring Greg that Mwai could be trusted, as could the men that they were being brought to see – the monks in the temple. In turn, Greg emphasised to Laura that the less they told these people the better. They should simply collect the parcel, find out who it was to be delivered to, and then leave. Greg explained that he had a way out of the country that would not require any form of passport or other documentation, although he refused to say any more about it. He stressed to Laura the importance of cleanly getting the package and leaving. After a little while, Mwai returned to the table.

'Our driver is ready,' he said. 'Laura, given that you have someone with you, we ask that no names be used, is that OK?'

'Yes, absolutely.'

They left the brothel, following Mwai out through a back exit. He held open the back door of an old car, beckoning them to enter. They slid in, Mwai got into the front passenger seat and the driver accelerated away gently. The windows were blacked out, so they could not see out the side or back windows, and there was a mesh between the front and back seats. This allowed them to make out the outline of Mwai and the driver, but they could see nothing of where they were going.

The driver spoke. 'Hello, Miss Whiteland. Please relax, it is just a short drive.'

Laura recognised Kasem's voice, but, remembering Mwai's admonition not to use names, she simply thanked him without referring to him by name.

After twenty minutes, the car slowed to a brief stop, then rolled forward again. It drove for another minute or two at very low sped, with the driver seeming to negotiate a series of tight twists and turns. Eventually, the car stopped again, and Kasem cut the engine. Mwai got out and opened the back door for Laura and Greg to get out. Laura quickly realised that she was deep inside Wat Nák Tong Tieow, and she was delighted to see Chanarong standing waiting for her.

They bowed respectfully to each other, and then Chanarong wordlessly led them through a disorienting series of passages, and up and down stairwells. As they walked, Laura realised that they were going much farther and deeper into the temple than she had been previously. Finally, they came to a huge door blocking their way. Chanarong placed his hand over a glass panel to the side of the door and it swung open soundlessly. Laura heard a surprised intake of breath from Greg as they both realised that the glass panel must be a handprint scanner – it was incongruous in the extreme to see such high-tech gadgetry being used deep within the bowels of the temple. Inside was a small, plain, empty room, with a much smaller door set into the opposite wall. Again, there was a handprint scanner mounted into the wall.

Chanarong spoke gently. 'Laura, it is time for you to take possession of our secret, which we, with Mwai, have cared for and cherished as your father requested. Please – go ahead.'

Laura reached out and placed her hand flat on the glass panel as she had seen Chanarong do at the first door. To her amazement, this door too swung open. She walked in, not knowing what to expect. While she had some vague notion that she would see something like a bank vault, or at least a safe, the sheer bizarreness of what was before her took her breath away. It was a room decorated and furnished like any living room, with nothing to hint that it wasn't an ordinary room in an ordinary house.

Chanarong followed Laura into the room. 'Laura, I would like you to meet Jopl.'

Through a small door set into the opposite wall, Laura could see what looked like a simply furnished bedroom. Through that door walked a small boy. He seemed to be about ten years old, with a body that looked both delicate and sturdy at the same time. His hair was almost shoulder-length and as dark as the darkest night. His eyes were a beautiful brown, and he looked at Laura.

'Hello, Laura,' he said simply, though his gaze seemed to pierce her heart and soul.

'Hello,' said Laura uncertainly. 'Erm, I'm not sure what is going on here.' She looked from Chanarong to the boy.

'It is quite simple really,' said Jopl. 'You are collecting me, as your father requested. You now need to deliver me as your father instructed. I cannot tell you yet exactly to whom

I am to be delivered, but it is someone in the United States of America. Actually, in South Carolina, near your own home.'

Laura was literally dumbstruck, not knowing what to say. Indeed, she didn't know what to think. In her dad's video, he had referred to a package, not a person. But then as Laura replayed the video in her head, it struck her that her dad had used the word package as though in inverted commas. And she remembered that he had said, '*You will have to deliver the 'package' personally, as it is not something that you can post or courier.*'

As she replayed the video in her mind's eye, she looked at Jopl. She was not sure why, but she knew somehow that this was right, even though it was totally at odds with Greg's explanation. Laura was back to being in the dark, unsure what exactly was going on, but some inner sense told her that this was nevertheless correct. She was to collect Jopl and bring him to South Carolina in the US, and he would tell her at some point exactly who he was to be 'delivered' to.

Laura gave herself a mental shake, and went back into her commander-In-chief role. 'OK, Jopl. Are you ready to go now, or do you need time to prepare?'

'All preparations have been made. You forget that we have had a few days' forewarning of your arrival,' Jopl smiled.

'Of course, of course,' stammered Laura, thrown again by the fact that she had spent days in the temple, so close to this boy without knowing it. 'Well, if you are ready to go, I suggest we make haste.'

'Certainly. Chanarong – please lead us to the gate,' ordered Jopl. Laura was intrigued. While the boy had said it quietly and politely, there was no mistaking that he had given the monk, so much older than himself, a clear order.

Chanarong started back the way they had come, with Mwai and Jopl following, and Greg and Laura bringing up the rear.

'Now what the hell is going on?' whispered Greg furiously.

'Jopl is the package,' stated Laura without a trace of doubt. 'There are no papers Greg. I have to deliver him to someone in South Carolina.'

'OK, OK. One of two things must have happened. Either they have put the documents on microfilm and surgically inserted them into the child. Or else, and I know this will sound weird...'

Laura almost laughed – she wasn't sure that anything would ever strike her as weird again after all of this. It was like she was living in some parallel universe that she hadn't known existed – a universe very like her own, but with extra shadowy rules and happenings going on. 'Everything about this is weird, Greg,' she whispered back. 'What is the other explanation?'

You see strange things in the East,' said Greg. 'Sometimes these people can have strange abilities – you might say, strange powers. Maybe this kid has been able to somehow memorise all of those documents and will be able to spill his guts when we get to the US.'

'Well, we can worry about that when we get to the States – if we ever get back home. You said you had a way out of Thailand – can we get going immediately, and can it handle three instead of two?'

'Yes, everything is ready. Who did the kid say he had to be delivered to?'

'He didn't. He just said South Carolina. He will tell us who it is later.'

Escape

When they arrived at the entrance to the temple, Jopl wordlessly bowed to Chanarong and Mwai, before waiting to accompany Laura through the gate. Despite the fact that their farewell seemed to be so understated, Laura sensed an incredible power in the brief bow that Chanarong and Jopl exchanged. Chanarong opened the door onto the street and Laura stepped forward. As she did, the night erupted in a cacophony of light and noise, explosions and flashes detonating all around them. It was so sudden and so awesome that Laura was powerless to act, but Greg dragged her to the ground as Chanarong slammed the door shut to protect them from the gunfire.

'Someone doesn't want us to leave – that's a hell of a lot of firepower out there. Is there a back way out, one they won't have covered?' Greg shouted at Chanarong.

'Follow me.' They dashed through passages and rooms, up and down stairs, through doors and gates, finally coming to a small door in an unremarkable wall.

'This exit is three streets away from the main gate. You should be OK getting out here. But watch your backs – they know you are close by somewhere,' warned Chanarong as they slipped out the gate into the quiet street beyond.

It was now three o'clock in the morning, and this part of the city seemed quiet. There was no movement, and the metropolis seemed to slumber, or maybe it was just waiting for the next outburst of gunfire.

'Follow me,' commanded Greg. 'I need to get my bearings, so that I can see which way we need to go. And for God's sake, stay bloody close.'

Once again, Laura found herself following a man through the streets of Bangkok while other men tried to kill her. This time, though, she had a precious cargo in her safekeeping. She held Jopl's hand as they raced after Greg.

'Kid, do you know where we are? Do you know which direction Khlong Toey port is?' demanded Greg.

'I'm afraid not. I do not know these streets at all. Indeed, they are more strange to me than they are to you,' replied Jopl calmly.

'Shit! OK, let me see. That's the Baiyoke Sky Hotel over there. So Khlong Toey must be in this direction. C'mon, let's go.'

They raced down the quiet street, with Greg cautioning them to stop near the intersection at the end. He peered around the corner, hoping to see another landmark to orient himself. 'OK, I can see the Grand Hotel up there on the right. That means we are near the Royal Sports Club. So we will need to go pretty much due south. We have about five klicks to go...'

Seeing the look on confusion on Laura's face, he rephrased it. 'We have about five kilometres to go, about three miles. It's gonna be hard to get a cab this time of night, so we may need to hoof it – walk – most of the way.'

He led them off again, conscious that they were now on Thanon Ratchadamri, or Ratchadamri Road, one of the main thoroughfares in the city. If the bad guys were spreading their net wider from the main gate of the temple, then it was likely that at least some of them would be using this road. He wondered if it was worth the risk of simply trying to catch a cab in front of the Grand Hotel, and getting to the port sooner rather than later. As he paused for a moment to consider if they should continue on south, or go back up towards the Grand, he saw a jeep racing out of the

Cambodian Embassy, turning right onto Ratchadamri Road and back towards the temple. He guessed that it was no coincidence – so rogue elements from the Cambodian Embassy were now involved as well.

He thanked his lucky stars that they hadn't been walking past the gates of the embassy as the jeep had come out. Deciding to steer well clear of it, he turned back south, resigning himself to a long walk with Laura and Jopl. As he turned away, another jeep came screaming out of the embassy, this time turning left – directly towards them.

'Quick,' he yelled at Laura and Jopl. 'Into the park!'

All three of them raced into the darkness of Lumphini Park, deserted at this time of night. In the mornings, legions of Chinese would descend on the park to practice their taijiquan, or t'ai-chi. In the evenings, aerobic classes would collectively sweat to the thump of a techno soundtrack. And on the weekends, the bodybuilders would take over the weight-lifting area with one of Bangkok's few non-sex displays of bare flesh and muscle. But for the moment, the park was abandoned by the city's citizens, lying bare and quiet in the occasional moonlight filtering between the clouds.

Greg quickly explained to Laura that there were now at least two groups working together in the manhunt for them – whoever had tried to ambush them as they left the temple, and at least some of the personnel from the Cambodian Embassy, just up the road. He made sure that Laura understood the extreme danger that they were in, and that she had to place her trust in him one hundred per cent. He told her that it would be much better now if they knew how Jopl was carrying the incriminating information, and who it was to be delivered to. Greg told Laura that this would be critical knowledge if anything were to happen to any of them, or if they were to get separated.

Laura turned to Jopl as they hid in the undergrowth inside the park gate, hearing another jeep race past the entrance. She explained Greg's logic, that it would be better of they all knew what Jopl was carrying and how, and who it was to be delivered to. Jopl, however, while remaining very polite and respectful, was quite adamant – that information would only be revealed when the time was right. First, they had to get to South Carolina.

As Laura told Greg that Jopl was not yet willing to share his secrets, Greg suddenly hushed her with a finger to her lips. Laura froze, watching Greg as he seemed to listen intently. Then Greg took her hand and slowly started to back out of the bushes they were hiding in, moving away from the entrance to the park. When they were out of the bushes, Greg led them at a run across the grass, keeping off the paths. He made sure to keep the bushes between them and the entrance, so that they could not be seen. As they ran, he put Laura in the picture – he had heard a jeep quietly driving back up the main road. Greg reckoned that the Cambodians had lost track of them and so had come back to check the park.

They reached the edge of a small man-made lake, which seemed to curve away to the right in a crescent shape. Greg urged them to take their shoes in their hands and walk into the lake; but told them to shuffle their feet slowly, without lifting them out of the water, so as not to make any noise. They did as he said, and they inched along, with Laura torn between Greg's admonitions to be absolutely silent and his urging them to hurry. All this time, Jopl stayed beside Laura, with no hint of emotion on his face. He seemed to be treating this as a normal walk in the park.

After three hundred yards, they reached the other side

and climbed out of the lake, still holding their shoes in their hands. Greg told them not to put on their shoes yet, as they might make noise if they had to cross any of the paths. He led them off again, bringing them into the shelter of a low building that a sign identified as the Thai Lanna Pavilion. Greg peered around the corner, looking back in the direction they had come, to see if there was any hint of pursuit. All of a sudden, there was a short burst of automatic gunfire. The pandemonium only lasted about two seconds, but Laura couldn't count the number of shots – it was like a roll of thunder. Greg had been correct at the gate of the temple – there was a hell of a lot of firepower out there.

Greg grabbed Laura's hand, and raced southwards, towards a statue that Laura could just make out in the dim moonlight.

'They'll be both blinded and deafened for a moment after that gunfire,' he called to her. 'We need to put as much distance as we possibly can between them and us in the next few seconds.'

The three of them raced across the grass. Man, woman and child seemed to fly across the ground, although Laura felt as though they were hardly moving. She half-expected to hear another blast of shooting any moment, and wondered if she would feel the barrage of bullets ripping into her flesh or if she would die instantly. They rounded the statue and continued their run.

Greg dragged them to a halt just as they were about to emerge from one of the shaded paths onto an open area of carefully manicured lawn. 'Wait, something is wrong!'

They crouched in the shelter of the low bushes framing the lawn, waiting to see what had seemed to alert Greg's sixth sense. After only a few seconds, Greg pointed towards another clump of low structures.

'Over there, at the Food Court,' he whispered. 'See that?'

Laura strained her eyes, and was rewarded with the sudden glow of a cigarette. 'Yes, there is someone there. But it could be just an insomniac out for a walk.'

'Insomniacs don't generally carry AK-47s. Next time he takes a pull on his cigarette, look down at his waist. You'll see the glow of the cigarette reflecting off the metal of the rifle barrel.'

Laura watched, and it was exactly as Greg had said. When the man inhaled on his cigarette again, Laura watched his waist instead of the cigarette itself. She gasped as she realised that she now owed Greg her life – again! Clearly visible in the glow was the long black gleaming gun-barrel of a rifle.

Greg cautioned Laura to stay exactly where she was, to be as still and quiet as the grave, and to make sure that Jopl did the same. With a brief kiss to her forehead and a comment to the effect that it was time for the hunted to become the hunter, he crept off along the low barrier of bushes that guarded the perfectly kept grass from the semi-wilderness on the other side. Laura watched as closely as she could, but could not see him in the darkness. She wasn't sure what he was going to do, but suspected that the lookout at the Food Court was about to become the centre of the chase.

Her watchfulness was rewarded after what seemed an age. Just as the sentry was taking a deep drag on his cigarette, something flashed down in front of his face. Laura couldn't make out everything in the pale moonlight, but she could just about see the guard seeming to go stiff. She heard a gasp of breath and a splashing sound, and then he seemed to sag and was pulled back behind the corner of the wall. As

Laura watched, she heard a brief hiss, and then could just make out Greg beckoning to her from the spot where the sentry had been standing. Clutching Jopl's hand, she again raced across the grass towards her beloved protector.

As they reached the corner, Greg pulled them down beside him and looked back across the lawn they had crossed. Seeming to be satisfied that there was no immediate threat, he turned to Laura. 'I'm sorry you had to see that Laura. But that man chose to put himself directly in the path of our only way out of here. It was him or us.'

'I understand,' Laura murmured. 'Where is he? I mean it, I mean the body?'

'Don't worry about that now. I hid it in the bushes in the hope that they won't find him too quickly. I am hoping that they still think they are just searching for you on your own. They may not have seen me yet – or the boy, for that matter. I don't want to alert them that we might be capable of fighting back. We need to get out of this park – it's a death-trap for us. If we can get out of here and then across Ram Four Road, then there is every chance that we can make it to the port undetected.'

'But I thought Bangkok was miles from the sea – how is there a port here in the city?'

'The river can handle deep-sea traffic up as far as the city. Khlong Toey is the city's deep-water port. If we can get there, then I have a friend who can get us out to sea.'

Seeming satisfied that Laura knew what they had to do, Greg again led them off, keeping once more to the paths shadowed by bushes and trees. In the pale moonlight, the gloom along the sheltered paths was impenetrable to the eye. After about four hundred metres, they came to another area of clear grass, with a clock tower at the far corner. Greg held them at the edge of the lawn while he watched for any sign that their pursuers may have already staked out this area. Once satisfied that there was no sign of any observation around the lawn, he led them at a run across the open ground. They were halfway across when individual shots rang out from the top of the clock tower.

Greg shouted at Laura to keep running, while he skidded to a stop and dropped to a kneeling position. As Laura ran for the base of the tower, hanging on to Jopl's hand, she heard more shots ring out from the top of the tower and also from behind her. As she rounded the bottom of the tower, she crouched behind the wall, not knowing what to expect or what to do. She almost screamed with panic when a man swept around the corner and cannoned into her.

'It's OK, it's OK, Laura. It's me, it's Greg.'

She wept with relief, having thought it all over. 'I heard shots from behind us. I thought you had been killed,' she sobbed.

'It's OK. I'll explain later. For the moment, let's just get out of here. That gunfire will draw them like moths to a flame.'

Greg jumped into the jeep that had been left parked at the door up into the clock tower. 'Damn, no keys. Still, that shouldn't stop us. These jeeps have fairly simple wiring mechanisms.' He disappeared beneath the dashboard for a moment. Laura could hear him scrabbling amongst the wires, and then the jeep's engine roared to life. 'Quick, get in, get in.'

Laura and Jopl jumped into the jeep and Greg left a trail of burnt rubber and smoke as he sped out of the park at top speed. They hung on tight as he raced down the first road for four or five hundred metres before pulling the jeep into a screeching right-hand turn. He sped down that road for another few hundred metres and then executed a burning handbrake turn to the left just as they passed the Malaysia Hotel. He drove the jeep into a parking space and jumped out, leaving the engine running.

As Laura and Jopl joined him on the pavement, they started to run down another narrower side road. Greg led them in a series of turns and loops, so that Laura became totally disorientated.

When they stopped for breath, Greg explained what had happened back at the clock tower in Lumphini Park. The guy up in the clock tower had only had a pistol – Greg added that if he had an automatic rifle, they would all be dead. Laura shuddered with fear as Greg continued. He had kept the rifle belonging to the first sentry that he had killed and had shot back at the lookout in the clock tower, killing him. He had dumped the jeep because it had a satellite navigation system on the dashboard, which meant that the Cambodians would be able to pinpoint its position. He hoped that by leaving the engine running, some enterprising local might steal it before the embassy staff got to it. That would delay the chase, as they would keep using the GPS to track the jeep, believing their quarry to be still on board.

'We passed near to Lumphini Boxing Stadium a little way back, so we only have a little more than a kilometre to go. Hopefully we have thrown them off the track, especially if we got lucky and someone stole that jeep. We'll walk from here, quickly but not so fast as to arouse suspicion. Keep a sharp lookout all the time and let me know if you think you see anything. I still have the rifle, so at least we can defend ourselves if need be. Hopefully not though – we have been lucky so far that we have only encountered the enemy in solitary formation – if we meet of group of them, I don't fancy our chances. OK, let's go. Keep close now.'

The three of them walked along the narrow back streets,

with Greg seeming to know which way to turn at every junction. They walked as a family, with Laura and Greg on either side of Jopl, and Jopl holding a hand of each of his 'parents.' As they rounded yet another corner, and Laura was starting to despair that their desperate running would never end, Greg pushed them back into the wall.

'That's it,' he whispered triumphantly. 'There's Khlong Toey!'

Laura peered around his shoulder, and saw a row of high, wide gateways with sentry-boxes and security barriers. There was a small group of night-watchmen gathered beside one of the gates, smoking and talking. Noting the high fencing and the guards, Laura wondered how they were going to get in.

'My friend is expecting us. He should have a little 'tradesman's entrance' set up around the back. Come on.'

They moved on again, Laura desperately hoping that the end of the terrifying flight through the streets of Bangkok was nearly over. Greg led them along a deserted back street, bordered along one side by the high wall of the port. He seemed to be looking for something along the base of the wall, and exclaimed happily when he found it. He pulled at the grass and lifted up a rope ladder with small hooks at one end. He threw the ladder across the wall, and tugged at it sharply to make sure it was secure. 'Quickly now. Climb over, and hide by the warehouse just to your left.'

Laura and Jopl climbed over, and ran to the side of the warehouse. Laura saw Greg jumping down from the wall and pulling the rope ladder after him. He rolled it into a ball and ran to join them. 'Now there's nothing to show that someone might have sneaked into the port. Come on, quietly now.'

They crept along paths between containers and assorted

piles of lumber and other cargo, arriving at the water's edge. Greg counted along the jetty, stopping outside a small cargo ship, small enough to be more of a boat than a ship. Greg whistled softly a tune from 'My Way', and a light flashed on and then off again in the main cabin.

'Happy days,' whispered Greg, and led them aboard.

Out To Sea

As they climbed the gangway, a man strode to the top of the ramp to greet them. He was a bear of a man, standing six feet and four inches and weighing close to three hundred pounds. An image of the pirate Blackbeard immediately sprang to Laura's mind – the man had a mane of thick shaggy unkempt hair, with a huge beard and moustache to match. He was dressed in an oily T-shirt and ragged shorts, with a pair of thongs on his feet. A cigarette dangled from his mouth, as he looked down at the weary trio climbing onto his ship.

'Greg! By Christ, am I glad to see you! I heard gunfire a while back – that wouldn't have been you, would it?'

'Some of it was me; some of it was at me. But all's well that ends well. For a while there I wasn't sure we'd make it!'

'Just like the old days, huh? You always were a master at getting out of a tight scrape.'

'We'll have no talk of the old days, or much else for that matter. I have two passengers to take with us. This is Laura and Jopl.'

'Well, I was expecting one along with yourself, Greg, but we can manage another one easily enough. Especially one as little as him. Laura, my name is Smith, Captain John Smith,' he said to Laura, smiling as he said it to lessen the potential insult of giving her what was so obviously a false name.

'It's nice to meet you Captain Smith. Greg tells me that you are our saviour. God knows, I don't think I have ever been so relieved to step onto a boat.'

'A boat? A boat?' exclaimed the captain in mock horror. 'She's no 'boat', I'll have you know. She is an ocean-going cargo ship,' he said, smiling again as he continued, 'albeit a small one, I'll admit. Still, as long as she gets us where we're goin', that's all that counts.'

'And where exactly are we going?' asked Laura, as it suddenly occurred to her that she had not the slightest notion of what was supposed to happen next.

'Ah, now, you'd better be asking Greg that,' said the Captain. 'On this ship, we's always careful of who says what to who. Haven't you heard the old saying 'Loose lips sink ships'? Never a truer word was spoken, believe you me. Now, if you'll excuse me, I'll just be makin' the preparations for casting off with the tide. We sail in two hours – it'll be a lovely time of morning to sail, with the sun just risin' to greet us and send us on our merry way.'

With that, he disappeared back into the bridge, and Laura was left looking more than a little bemused.

'Don't worry about John,' said Greg from behind her. 'I know he can give the impression of being a bit of a dimwit, but that is just a part that he plays, even if he sometimes plays it disconcertingly well. In truth, he is a first-class seaman, as well as being exactly the kind of guy you want at your back if you run into trouble. We'll be sailing with him for the next week or two until we make land. When we do, we will need to wire 500,000 dollars into an account for him. Old friend though he may be, his services do not come cheap. Is that OK?'

'Absolutely,' said Laura, without hesitation. 'That is what dad gave me that Swiss account for – to be able to complete this mission for him. Greg, I am so happy that you are with me. I never would have been able to do this on my own.'

'I have told you before, Laura, that is why I am here, to help you. Initially, because I owed it to Ben and to myself to finish what we had started, but now mainly because I love you.'

'Oh, Greg, and I love you too. I often wondered what it would be like to fall in love – I mean, really to be in love. Now I know.'

'Laura, I'm going to have to help the captain get underway and plan for the voyage. Right now, I need you to show your love for me by helping me. I'll show you two cabins that John has set aside for us. I need you to take Jopl down below and get him settled – the poor kid must be exhausted. And you need to get some rest yourself. I'll join you in a few hours once we are well underway. Is that OK?'

With that, they went below deck. When he had left her to get Jopl settled and to catch up on some sleep herself, Laura joined Jopl in the smaller of the two cabins.

'Jopl, I'm going to share Greg's cabin. Will you be OK here in this one by yourself? It's right next to ours. If you need anything, just knock on the wall and I will come into you straight away.'

'Yes. That is fine. Do you want me to go to sleep now?'

'Well, I think that would be best. You must be very tired after being up all night?'

'Not really. I find that the human body can go for quite long periods without sleep if the need arises. I once stayed awake for a week to see what it would be like. Meditation became easier.'

'Really? Well, I think you should go to sleep now. We don't know what lies ahead of us in the coming days.'

'Laura, we never know what lies ahead of us. People often seem to think that they know what the future holds, but, in truth, there is very little, if indeed anything at all, of the future that we can be sure of. But I will go to sleep now if you feel that is best. We will have plenty of opportunity to talk about these things in the days ahead – see, I have made a prediction about the future. I wonder, will it be correct?'

Smiling, the boy climbed up on the bunk and lay down. Still smiling, he seemed to go to sleep instantly, although Laura suspected that he must be just pretending in order to please her. Feeling drained and exhausted herself, she went into the cabin next door. Stripping off her T-shirt, she lay down on top of the bunk, intending to just rest her eyes for a few minutes before going to check that Jopl really was asleep, and going up on deck to see how the preparations for departure were going and to see of she could help in any way. However, her body had other plans. Fatigued from lack of sleep and the physical exertions of the chase, and shattered emotionally by the tension and strain of the hunt, her mind and body sought refuge in deep sleep. Her head had hardly hit the pillow before she plummeted into an undreaming unconsciousness.

The next thing she knew was being woken gently, with the feel of tender fingers trailing their way along her back. She sighed and rolled over, opening her eyes to see her beloved Greg lying beside her.

'My darling. Oh, it's very bright outside! What time is it? How long did I sleep?'

'Don't worry, not too long. You've been out cold for about six hours. It's eleven in the morning. I checked on you a couple of hours ago, but you seemed to be in such a deep sleep that I didn't want to disturb you. Do you feel rested? I was thinking it would be a good idea to have breakfast – although it will be more lunch than breakfast at this stage.'

'Mmmm, that sounds good. Brunch! Although I doubt that Captain Smith's galley will be very brunch-orientated!

Oh, where are we? Did we get away from the port OK?'

'Yes, yes we did. John has a cargo for delivery to Darwin in Northern Australia. He simply sailed on out of Khlong Toey and down Mae Nam Chao Phraya – that's the river that Bangkok is built on. At this stage, we are out into the Gulf of Thailand and on our way to the South China Sea. There is nothing to connect us to this ship, so I think we can relax for now. Once we get to Australia, I will see about arranging false papers to fly us back to the US. For the moment, though, we can safely forget about it and settle down to a week or so at sea.'

'OK, that sounds like a huge relief after all we've been through. Let me go and wake Jopl and we will go and eat.'

Laura went into the cabin next door, moving quietly so as not to frighten the young boy. She looked at him sleeping – he looked like the quintessence of peace as he lay there – it was easy to believe that he had never seen hardship or fear. And yet Laura knew that he must be going through an awful time. She didn't know who he was or why she had to bring him to the US, or how exactly it all fit in with her dad's history and Greg's explanation of senior figures in government and business wanting to stop her from releasing damning information. Laura wondered if Jopl somehow had evidence of what the funds from the drugs trade had been used for – it sounded, from her very limited geo-political knowledge, that they would have been using that money to fund so-called contra-terrorism, which Laura believed was often anti-democratic terrorism funded and organised by the American government. There was no doubt that if Jopl could prove that such activities had been funded by past and maybe even the present American president, the fall-out in the American, and possibly wider Western, political landscape would be intense and brutal. Many current leaders would be broken men, with ruined careers if not jail sentences.

Looking at Jopl sleeping, Laura wondered how this little boy could hold the key to all of this. Yet the story certainly made sense – it all tied together, and indeed it confirmed her own suspicions about her leaders, distrust that she knew was shared by at the very least a significant minority, if not a clear majority, of the American people. Having travelled as widely as she had, Laura knew how the rest of the world regarded America. In the wake of September 11th and the so-called 'War on Terror' Laura knew that the majority of people in most Western democracies were opposed to the unilateral action of the American Government. People wanted the United Nations to have the lead and responsibility in these affairs, and people knew that the US Government was itself in direct contravention of a number of UN resolutions.

Laura almost groaned with the weight of duty that her dad had thrust onto her young shoulders. She could appreciate that he hadn't been able to pursue it - out of a sense of responsibility for Laura – his wife had been executed, and Laura could understand that he would not have done anything that might endanger her as a child. Now that he was dead and she was an adult, he had left the decision to her. She had taken the burden and was running with it, but right now she couldn't keep thinking about it. Resolving to be bright and cheery for Jopl's sake, she gently called his name.

The child instantly opened his eyes, seeming to undergo the transition from sleep to waking in an instant, without the gradual change from slumber to consciousness that most people experience, especially children. He swung his legs off the small bed, smiling up at Laura.

'Good morning, Laura. I have slept very well. I am quite hungry - can we eat soon?'

Laura laughed at the simplicity of the boy's thinking. Sleeping done, on to eating!

'Very well, Jopl. I am glad you slept well. So did I. And, yes, we can go and eat. Let's see where the bathroom is so that we can freshen up and then we will see what passes for breakfast or lunch on this boat – oh, no, call it a ship. Captain Smith seemed a little upset when I called it a boat.'

They found the bathroom and took turns to freshen up as best they could, considering that most of their belongings had been abandoned back at the temple. The only things Laura had managed to hold on to were her passport and money.

By trial and error, they found the galley, where Greg was waiting with Captain Smith, both of them nursing strong black coffees.

'Good morning, Laura. And hello, Boy. Ye'll be wantin' breakfast?' boomed the captain. 'Cook, yer best breakfast for our guests!'

Laura and Jopl sat down at the table with Greg and the captain, and were immediately poured a coffee each. The captain held out a grubby bottle to Laura.

'Would you be wanting a dram of whiskey in that, to warm yer bones this morning?' he enquired, with the suspicion of a leer. Laura felt that, if he was indeed playing the part of a buffoon as Greg said, then he was playing it exceedingly well.

'No thank you, Captain. Just milk and sugar.'

By the time the captain had finished asking if they had slept well and if they had any trouble finding the galley, the cook put two plates on the table in front of Laura and Jopl. The plates were piled with a greasy fry; sausages and bacon being the main ingredients, with some beans and a fried egg thrown in for good measure. While it didn't look very appetising, Laura was surprised to find that she devoured it with a will, helping herself and Jopl to bread and extra coffee as they went along. There was little talking while they ate, but when they settled back with a final coffee, the conversation resumed.

'There's a couple of rules on board this ship that you all need to understand,' the captain said. 'You will be on board for the next ten days or so, and my crew are not used to having either women or children on board ship. To make sure that we are all happy with how this voyage goes, you will have to bear a few things in mind, OK?'

'I suppose it depends on what those things are, Captain Smith,' said Laura. She was going to add that he was being well-paid for the trip, but decided not to bring that up yet, as she didn't want to antagonise the man unnecessarily.

'Well, primarily, it boils down to two things. Firstly, this is a working ship, not a cruise holiday. You will confine yourself to your own cabins or the top deck. Of course, you can use the head, and the galley for meals. You will not go into any other part of the ship. Particularly the cargo area is off-limits, as is the engine room for your own safety, and the crew's quarters – also for your own safety!

'Secondly, you will at all times obey any orders that I give, instantly and without question. I don't intend giving you any orders, you understand, since you are not part of my crew. So you need to know that if I do give an order, there is a bloody good reason for it. You do as you are told, and we can discuss the whys and wherefores of it afterwards. Is that understood?'

Greg jumped in before Laura could comment.

'Absolutely, John. We understand that this is a working

vessel. We will stay out of your way as much as possible. Isn't that correct, Laura, Jopl?'

Laura knew Greg was trying to make sure that she didn't argue with the captain about his 'rules'. In truth, she didn't have a problem with the first one – she wanted to stay out of the crew's way as much as possible. From what she had seen so far, they seemed like a rough group of men, and the less contact she had with them the better. It was the second that was prompting her to tell the captain to go to hell. She'd be damned if she would be taking orders from Captain 'Smith'. But she saw Greg's warning glance, and so she smiled and agreed.

As they finished their coffee, Laura said she was going to bring Jopl up onto the deck for some fresh air. Greg asked her to wait until the next day before going outside, as he wanted to be well away from Thailand before there was any risk of her being seen. He said that even though he was certain they had made a clean getaway, there was no point in taking unnecessary risks. He asked that she wait one day, just in case anyone had planes or boats checking the sea-lanes for them. Laura could see the logic of that, and so she brought Jopl back down to his cabin, having taken an old deck of playing cards form the captain to pass the time.

To Laura's surprise, she and Jopl managed to have fun for the rest of the day. Amazingly, he had never played cards before and they had plenty of laughs and friendly rivalry as Jopl quickly got the grasp of each game and started to challenge Laura's supremacy in each one. Laura knew that, in time, they would discuss serious issues, but, for the moment, she was content to simply indulge in a little harmless entertainment. She told herself that this was for Jopl's sake, to give him a break from the stress of the chase and the strain that he must be under, given that a stranger was bringing him to a strange place. But she also knew that she was doing it for herself as well. She needed that break every bit as much as Jopl did!

The Nature of Right and Wrong

That evening, their first full night on the ship, Laura saw Jopl to bed around ten o'clock. When she was sure he was settled, she joined Greg on deck in the moonlight. Greg opened a bottle of wine – a gift from Captain Smith's private store – and poured them each a glass.

'A toast. Here's to successful escape!'

'To successful escape,' echoed Laura.

They sat quietly for a while, each of them lost in their own thoughts. Yet the silence between them was a comfortable one. Eventually, Laura spoke. 'Greg, what is going to happen next?'

'Well, honey, it's simple really, though that doesn't mean it isn't dangerous. John is going to drop us off the north Australian coast and we will use a small powerboat to get to shore. Once there, we'll hole up somewhere quiet while I arrange false papers for us to travel under – I have a contact in Darwin who will be able to help with that. If that all works OK, then we fly you back to South Carolina. Once I get that far, I'm lost, honey. I can't plan beyond that, unless you can get Jopl to tell us who he is being sent to and how or what the hell information he is carrying.'

Laura could hear the frustration in Greg's voice, and she knew that he desperately wanted to help her and keep her safe.

'I'll ask Jopl again tomorrow, but he seems fixed on the idea that we get there first and then he will tell us what the next step is. So, what do you think are our chances of being able to get through this?'

'It's hard to say Laura. Getting to Oz should be simple.

Arranging the papers will take a couple of days and funding, but shouldn't be a problem. Flying to the States will be nerve-wracking, but once the papers stand up to scrutiny, it should be straightforward enough. It's the part that's outside my radar that worries me – what happens when we get to the States?'

'Well, like I say, I will ask him again, but I don't think he will change his mind.'

'It's strange, isn't it?', she said. 'We're going through this nightmare, and yet right now I just feel so glad to be here, with you, in the moonlight, with the ocean rocking us and the sound of the sea. It's beautiful really.'

She cuddled close to Greg, and as mouth found mouth, lips found lips and tongue found tongue, she revelled in the beauty and simplicity of true love. Arms wrapped around each other, they held each other close and pressed body against body.

Without needing to speak, they stood and made their way below deck, holding hands as they went, and found sanctuary in their cabin.

As Laura undressed Greg, she exulted in the power and beauty of his body – muscle and strength that covered his tender heart and gentle soul. As she in turn was undressed by him, she gloried in the effect that her body had on her man – his instant reaction as he stood in front of her, his manhood hard and proud, desperate to explore her body, to entwine with her, to be part of her, to become one with her. As they moved together on the simple bed, Laura took control, straddling Greg and guiding him into the inner recesses of her body and her heart. Sweating and panting with the delights of her exertions, she brought them to a plateau of delicious deliriousness that seemed to take them to another plane of existence. Laura's body wracked with spasms of pleasure again and again, until she finally brought them both to a synchronised peak that brought an existential fulfilment and happiness that Laura believed must normally be out of reach for the human condition.

Lying in each other's arms, Laura kissed Greg gently, from the top of his head to the tip of his toes. She thanked God for giving this man to her, not only in her hour of need to protect her, but simply as the love of her life, the man to whom she could truly give of herself one hundred per cent, mind, body, heart and soul. They gently whispered to each other of their love, their mutual need for each other, their commitment to each other. Drifting into a happy and peaceful sleep, Laura knew that, come what may, she had at least found one true love in her life. And for this she would be eternally grateful.

Morning brought Laura to a slow and serene awakening. Greg was gone – she knew that he would be up with Captain Smith, checking the progress of their journey. Despite Greg's insistence that the pirate-like captain was a friend and to be trusted, Laura couldn't bring herself to like the man. She found him to be crude and rude, and she was sure that he was in this just for the money. Nevertheless, given Greg's closeness to this John Smith, she would at least be civil to him, whilst trying to stay out of the way of him and the rest of his crew as much as possible.

Laura went into Jopl's cabin, and found the boy already awake, dressed and reading a book.

'What are you reading, Jopl?'

'A fascinating book, Laura. It is called *Moby Dick*. Captain Smith gave it to me to read. I think from what I have read so far, that Mr Melville knows more than a little about the dangers of over-zealousness – what can happen when commitment or dedication turns to fanaticism and extremism. Very interesting lessons for the modern world, don't you think?'

'I do indeed, Jopl. But let's chat about that over breakfast – I am absolutely starving.'

They made their way to the galley and helped themselves to a selection of bread and fruit to start the day. Laura enjoyed some strong black coffee while Jopl preferred to stick to water. After they had eaten, they went up on deck and Laura asked Jopl more about the book he was reading.

'So Jopl, what do you think are the lessons that we can learn from Captain Ahab? Anything that might be relevant in today's world? After all, that book was written quite some time ago.'

'I think it is interesting. I think you can take any person – good or evil, intelligent or not – and turn them into a terrorist if the circumstances are correct.'

'Surely not, Jopl. You mean you can take a good, honest, caring man or woman and turn them into some sort of sick evil monster that goes around murdering innocent civilians – men, women and children – in the name of some cause? I don't think I could agree with that. I don't think you could ever persuade a good person to detonate a bomb in the middle of a crowded public place!'

'No? Let me ask you this. Assume that you were driving along and suddenly the driver of your car suffers a massive heart attack and dies there at the wheel, while you are travelling along the road at one hundred kilometres per hour. The car is heading straight at a group of six schoolchildren standing at the side of the road. You only have a split second to act – the only thing you might have time to do is to grab the steering wheel and change the direction of the car. Just farther long the side of the road is a man standing by himself, who you know you will crash into if you avoid the children. That is the scenario. Your choice is simple – do you do nothing, and the six children will all die, or do you wrench the steering wheel and the man will die?'

Laura thought about it for a few minutes before giving her answer, even though she knew straight away what her answer was. 'Given the choice of many people dying versus one dying, the logical and the moral choice is to choose the lesser evil. So I would sacrifice the one man to save the six children.'

'OK,' said Jopl. 'And I think it is safe to say that a lot of people would agree with you. However, the fact of the matter is that the car was already headed towards the group of kids, so if you do nothing you have not killed the children by an act of commission, although it is true that you have killed them by an act of omission. But in this instance you acted physically, and so you killed the man by an act of commission. You made a choice – in a situation where you did have a choice – to kill the man. Isn't that so?'

'Well, yes, that's true. But I was in a no-win situation. Either way, people were going to die. But in killing that one man, I saved the six children. The net effect of my action was to save five lives. Surely that is a good thing?'

'Again, many people would agree. But what that means is that the end justifies the means, is that not so? You wanted to save all six children, but, in order to do so, you had to kill the one man. As you say, the overall effect was to save five lives. So you are saying, aren't you, that the saving of the six children justified the killing of the man?'

'Yes,' Laura stated. That she thought about it again before reiterating emphatically. 'Yes. That is correct.'

'So the end justified the means?'

'Yes. In this instance, yes, the end did justify the means.'

'OK. Now assume that it is a week later and you are

attending the man's funeral, because you regret the fact that he had to die and you want to show your respect. Do you think that you might feel that way?'

'Yes, yes I think I would.'

'So, having made a conscious decision that you were going to kill this man, and having carried it though, and still believing that you did the right thing, you feel regret for the effect that your action had on this man and his family, even though you do not regret the action itself?'

'I feel regret for the outcome of my action, but not for the action itself? Correct, yes.'

'Now the man's widow comes over to you. She berates you for killing her husband. She talks about how much she loved him and the pain and anguish that she is suffering because you killed him. She points to their four children, who are crying and distraught, and says that you have caused all of this suffering. She is of course, absolutely correct, isn't she?'

Laura was growing less and less comfortable with the direction of their conversation, but she had to stay true to her belief. 'Yes, yes it is true that I have caused all of this suffering. But in doing so, I saved the much greater suffering that would have been caused if the six children had died!'

'Granted, that is correct. Nevertheless, this woman is also correct – you have caused all of this suffering, and, if the same situation arose again, you would do the same thing again. Yes?'

'Yes, Jopl, I would. Because it is the right thing to do.'

'Well, yes, that is what you believe. But the widow disagrees. She says you could have swerved the car and hit no bystanders. She says that nobody needed to die. She says that even if you had hit the group of children, there is no guarantee that any of them would have died. She says that even if a child had died, maybe they would have been an only child, an orphan, with no one who really loved them. In that case, there would have been none of the anguish. But because of your actions, a good man is dead and five people, her and their four children, are suffering unimaginable pain. In essence, the widow casts doubt on a lot of the assumptions that you were operating on. But you still believe that it was a simple choice – the six children or the one man. What do you say to the widow?'

'I'm not sure. If I still believe that it was a choice between the lives of the six children versus the one man, then I still think I made the right choice. But I can understand how the widow would not be able to see that. She just wants her husband to be alive and she will convince herself that he should be alive. That is why she says maybe none of the kids would have been killed, even though the car was going at one hundred kilometres per hour. That is why she talks what is nonsense really – about orphans, and so on.'

'So what would you say to her?'

'I think I would explain my rationale. If she didn't accept that, and she probably wouldn't, then I would not argue the point further, there wouldn't be any point. Neither of us would be about to change our minds. I would simply state my case and leave it at that.'

'And if the situation reoccurred, you would again deliberately choose to kill a single innocent bystander in order to save the larger group of bystanders?'

'Yes, I would.'

'What this means, Laura, is that a person's perception of right and wrong is based upon their perception of the situation. For example, in the scenario we have just discussed, you believed that killing the man was good because of your perception of the situation. The widow had a different perception, and so she believed your action was wrong. Therefore it is quite possible, particularly if I had you from a young age and there were no outside influences, that I could convince you that by detonating a bomb at a bus stop full of civilians, we could force an occupying army to leave our country, thus saving hundreds or thousands of lives of innocent fellow countrymen – including women and children – of ours. Now, if I could convince you of this, then based on the rationale that you used in the scenario that we just discussed, your decision would probably be to detonate that bomb – on the logic that it is worth sacrificing a small number of lives to save a much greater number of lives. Isn't that so?'

Laura felt trapped in a cloud of conflicting logic and emotion.

'But I would never accept an argument that indiscriminate bombing will save more lives further on! You are trying to get me to say something that I fundamentally disagree with.'

'Not at all, Laura, not at all. I am simply trying to understand what it is that you do believe. You have already said that it is morally correct to sacrifice a smaller number of lives to save a greater number of lives. Do you now want to change that belief, or is it something else that is now bothering you?'

Laura paused and thought again. She carefully considered their conversation thus far, as she very much wanted to explain exactly what she was feeling and thinking. This banter had unexpectedly become a very serious discussion and Laura herself was now anxious to see where it was leading. What would her viewpoint be, by the end of the exchange?

'I think that I still believe that the lesser evil is the better choice, so it is not the justification of sacrificing a small number of lives to save many lives that is bothering me. It is the logic itself that is giving me the problem – I don't think that I would ever accept that setting off a bomb today will somehow save lives in the future. There would be too many factors involved. I couldn't be sure that the outcome would be what I wanted. And anyway, in looking around the world, I don't believe that violence solves anything. So there.'

She smiled at the boy, wondering if she was now in the clear; or were his insistent questions going to ensnare her in their implications again.

'I'm not sure that you can honestly say that you believe that violence does not solve anything. I think the widow in our scenario, whose husband you intentionally killed with a car, might describe you as a violent woman. Yet you believe that the violence of running someone down in a one-tonne motorcar at one hundred kilometres per hour, did indeed offer the best solution to that situation. So I think your assertion about violence not solving anything is more aspirational than an actual belief – it is what you would like to believe, but there are situations where you believe that violence is a good solution. To use an oft-quoted example, if someone had the chance to assassinate Hitler in 1935, do you think they have done so? It would save the lives of countless millions.'

'Well, yes. That's a pretty extreme example, but I suppose I have to say that to use violence in that situation would be justified and correct, as it would undoubtedly save the lives of millions. Yes.'

'OK, so your declaration of non-violence is not binding upon you in every situation. Agreed?'

'Yes, Jopl. But there was another reason why I would not detonate that bomb for you!'

'Indeed, Laura, indeed there was. And I was just coming to that. You maintained that you would never accept the logic that exploding a device at a bus stop containing innocent bystanders would save the lives of more people later on. Wasn't that it?'

Yes, that was it. There are simply too many factors involved. I could never be certain that a single violent action by me today would save lives in the future. Even if my country was occupied by violent foreign forces that were murdering my fellow citizens, which it isn't.'

'Luckily for you Laura, luckily for you and your countrymen. There are many people today who believe their country is occupied by a foreign force. I am interested to hear you say that you couldn't be certain that a single violent action by you today would save lives in the future. I think you are correct – it would be very difficult to convince someone that a single violent action by them today would save lives in the future. However, history shows us that it is quite possible for someone to believe that a series of violent actions by them over a period of time would indeed save lives in the future. I do not think that this is open to dispute. Through the centuries, people have fought for justice and freedom using violence as a weapon in their struggle against oppression and tyranny. Therefore, it is self-evident that given the right environment, people can be made to believe that violence is the morally correct course of action.'

Jopl stopped speaking, and Laura was left to consider his words. She had always thought of herself as non-violent, but Jopl's logic made her see that there would, indeed, be times where she believed violence to be not only justifiable, but indeed to be the only moral option. And she could see that there could be circumstances where she could be convinced that this belief applied to many different situations, where today she considered violence to be reprehensible.

'So where does that leave me, Jopl? I do believe that, sometimes, violence is the morally correct course to pursue. And I can see that given the right environment, you may be able to persuade me to apply that logic to any number of situations. Does that mean that I am a bad person – that I am evil?'

'Poor Laura,' laughed Jopl, smiling kindly so that she was not offended by his merriment at her predicament. 'No, Laura, not in the least. From what I know of you, I think you are a genuinely good person, with a good heart. You are doing this thing out of love for your father, despite the dangers that are now apparent to you. Do you often set out to intentionally hurt another person, simply for the pleasure of seeing their hurt?'

'No, of course I don't! What sort of person do you think I am?'

'Exactly! I think you are a good sort of person. Not perfect, but then who amongst us is? But certainly not evil. However, consider this Laura. If I could get you, a good person, to set off that bomb or bombs, then who are we to say that anyone who sets off a bomb is evil, is a bad person?'

'Well...' Laura was stuck for a second. She was used to making snap judgements when she read a news story – 'Whoever did that is bad.' – What was Jopl suggesting?

'Do you mean that we can never decide if someone has done something wrong? That's ridiculous. There would be anarchy – a total breakdown of law and order. Society wouldn't survive!'

'What I am suggesting, Laura, is this. Separate the action

from the agent. When asked to judge someone, refuse. Judge only the action, not the person who committed the action. You will note that in your Western system of law, a jury is never asked if a person is good or bad – the jury is merely asked to decide whether or not the accused, committed the action that they are accused of. And so it should be for you. Refuse to judge the person. Judge only the action. And, even then, bear in mind that you might be wrong. For example, if someone had assassinated Hitler in 1930, you would probably have said that their action was morally wrong. But if they knew what his plans were and explained that to you, then actually a lot of people, including I suspect yourself, would argue that the assassin was morally correct, even though you thought he was wrong. So judge the action, not the person. And always remember that, even when judging the action, there may be facts unknown to you that make the action right even if you believe it was wrong, or indeed that make it wrong when you believe it was right.'

The morning sun had rolled across the sky. Only a portion of a day had passed, but Laura felt as though she had grown immeasurably in the past few hours. She believed that she had learned something fundamentally important. She knew that she would look at the world, and especially at the people within that world, a little differently from now on. And she knew that she would be a better person because of that changed outlook. She took Jopl's face in her hands, looked deep into his eyes, and thanked him. Her thanks were sincere and heartfelt, and she saw that acknowledged in his eyes. Laura couldn't shake the feeling that she was missing something about this child – although just a boy, he seemed to have the wisdom of the ages accumulated in his very being.

Jopl laughed, transforming once again back into a young

boy. He said he was hungry, so they went and ate, and spent the rest of the day fishing from the side of the boat (without success) and chatting. While their talk ranged across many subjects, and Laura often had to stop and think about what Jopl was saying, none of their conversations were quite so fundamental to Laura's belief system as their first one had been.

Greg stopped with them now and again, chatting briefly before going back to help with the direction of the voyage. He explained to Laura that they were crossing between the Indian and Pacific oceans, threading a three-thousand mile path through the Indonesian islands. After the South China Sea, they would pass through the Java Sea and then the Banda Sea, before heading south across the Timor Sea to arrive west of Darwin. They would use a motor launch to land at Anson Bay at the mouth of the Daly River. A contact of Captain Smith's would collect them and transport them the one hundred and fifty kilometres to a town improbably called Humpty Doo. From there, Greg would make contact with some acquaintances in Darwin to arrange the false papers for them to fly back to the States.

As the days passed, the skies remained clear, the air hot, and a lovely sea breeze kept Jopl and Laura cool as they stayed on deck out of the crew's way, chatting or playing cards. At night, Laura and Greg explored their love, delving ever deeper into each other's psyche, becoming more and more part of each other. Physically and emotionally, Laura felt they were made for each other. She was a little disappointed that they didn't have more time together during the days, but Greg was busy with Captain Smith and she wanted to be sure that Jopl was safe and happy.

After ten days, the anchor was thrown overboard and the announcement was made – it was time to leave the ship and head for shore.

Coincidence?

Laura watched nervously as the motor launch was winched over the side of the ship. They were anchored off the northern coast of Australia, to the west of Darwin, but Laura couldn't see anything in the darkness. She had expected to be able to see the lights of the mainland, but all about the ship was darkness. In the small light being thrown by the ship, Laura could see what looked to her inexperienced eye like a tiny aluminium boat being lowered to the water. Clouds hid the moon, and the water looked cold and dark in the light reflected from the small ship.

Once the launch was in the water, one of the crew climbed down into it to fire up the engine and hold the tiny boat steady against the side of the ship. Then Greg helped first Laura and then Jopl down into the boat before getting in himself. He waved up to Captain Smith as the little launch powered into the open sea.

As the boat pulled away from the ship, Laura's eyes slowly adjusted to the near-total darkness. She could make out the waves looming about them, with their luminescence often seeming to shoot up over them on every side. There was a three-metre swell, which meant that when the boat was in a trough between waves, the tops of the waves all around them towered almost two metres above their heads. As the boat climbed each wave, only to hurtle down the other side, Laura started to wonder if they were going to make land at all. She drew comfort from Greg's reassuring presence. He sat beside her with his arm around her, his gentle grip letting her know that she was safe in the midst of this maelstrom of waves and wind and water.

Jopl sat just in front of Laura, seeming unconcerned by the incredible power that Mother Nature was putting on display. There was no doubt that they would be doomed if Nature were to unleash her potential fury on their little craft, insignificant in the immensity of this giant sea. Yet Jopl sat calmly, looking around with interest, seeming to enjoy and appreciate the forces arrayed about them.

After thirty minutes, Laura sensed that the height and power of the waves was dropping a little. Soon, she glimpsed a light in front of them when they topped each wave and she pointed it out to Greg.

'Don't worry, baby, we've had it in our sights for the last little while. That's our taxi to a warm soft bed.'

As the boat got closer to shore, the waves dropped further and they were able to keep the welcoming signal light in view all the time. Greg took a torch from his bag and flashed it once, twice, a third time. The light on shore flashed five times in response.

'OK, Paulo,' Greg said to the crewman piloting the launch, 'bring it in.'

Ten minutes later, they were climbing over the side of the launch as its nose rested on the sand, wading through the shallow water onto the beach.

'You are?' Greg asked the man with the signal light.

'Thomas,' he replied. 'And you are from …?'

'Captain Smith,' confirmed Greg. 'Let's go. I want to get onto the highway before dawn.'

Greg and Thomas pushed the launch back off the sand and Paulo started motoring back to his ship. Greg, Laura and Jopl followed Thomas back across the beach to where his four-wheel drive was parked.

'I'm going to follow the river back to the main road,' he said. 'It's about fifty klicks and some of it is a rough ride, so be ready to hold on tight when I tell you to.'

They climbed in - Laura and Jopl in the back, Thomas driving and Greg in the front passenger seat, and headed away from the beach. In the beginning they followed a rough dirt track through the trees, before joining a minor asphalt road and eventually driving onto the main highway into Darwin. When they were 30 miles away from Darwin, Thomas took a road to the right, signposted for Humpty Doo. They drove into a town that Laura knew from her previous travels to be typical of the Australian outback with its low buildings, hotel in the centre of the town and palm trees dotted about.

Thomas drove straight through the town on Greg's instruction, and then Greg asked Laura to pick a place to stay. Laura picked the type of slightly ramshackle hostel that backpackers liked to use. It looked cheap, but clean enough. Certainly not the type of place that would be asking too many questions of their clients as they passed through. Thomas parked outside the hostel and said goodbye to them there, explaining that he had a lift back to Darwin arranged for himself. The four-wheel drive was theirs for as long as they needed it.

After they had booked adjoining rooms, they sat out on the porch and Greg explained their next moves.

'You and Jopl will hang about here. Don't ask too many questions of anyone. Don't tell anyone anything about yourself – we are just backpackers from the States, passing through with our son. Don't wander out of the town – Australian wildlife has more poison ways of killing you than any other place. Between snakes, spiders and everything else, you wouldn't last any time if you went into the bush. I will go to Darwin tomorrow, it's only about an hour's drive away, but I might be gone overnight. Once I arrange the identity papers for the three of us, I will come back and let you know that we are on track. When the papers are ready, which will take a few days, I will collect them from Darwin. Then we fly to the States.'

Laura nodded that she understood.

'The key question for me now is what happens when we get to the States. Jopl, you are putting us in a very dangerous situation here. We will fly into the States and make our way to South Carolina, but I have no idea what dangers and threats wait for us there. Please, you've got to tell me what you are carrying and how you are carrying it, and who you are delivering it to.'

'I am sorry that this disturbs you, Greg,' Jopl answered calmly. 'I understand why you want to know this. But the time is not yet right. These things can only be revealed when the correct circumstances are in place. Part of those circumstances is that Laura and I must be in South Carolina in the United States of America. Until that is so, I cannot discuss the records that I am carrying. Nor can I discuss to whom I and those records are to be delivered.'

When Jopl finished speaking there was an air of finality to his tone that brooked no further discussion. Again, Laura was struck by how mature, how grown-up, this child seemed to be.

Greg was clearly annoyed that Jopl would not tell him what he wanted to know, but he bit back a sharp retort. As he climbed off the porch and rolled a cigarette, Laura turned to Jopl. 'Don't worry. You do what is right, and I am sure it will all work out just fine.'

'I am glad that you are sure of that. For myself, I am sure of nothing. Yet I do what I must do. I do what seems most right to do.'

They spent that day alternating between chatting, playing

cards and reading on the porch, and eating and drinking in one of the typical Aussie pubs in Humpty Doo. By nightfall, early though it was, they were ready for bed. Laura was ravenous for Greg's body that night, knowing that the next day he would leave her side for the first time in almost two weeks. She drew him to her and celebrated their love and their passion again and again through the hours of darkness.

At dawn, Greg gave Laura a final kiss as he left her dozing in their bed, exhausted from the expression of their love throughout the night. She implored him to be careful, and he promised that he would be back by evening of the next day at the latest. After sleeping deeply for a couple of hours, Laura roused herself and went in search of Jopl. They wandered the quiet streets of Humpty Doo together, looking in the souvenir shops and chatting about the wonders of this Aussie world.

In the afternoon, they went into the pub nearest to their hostel, and ordered lunch. This involved a bit of searching the menu, as Jopl was unfamiliar with a lot of the dishes, but once Laura explained what was in each, he settled for scrambled eggs on toast. They were starting their meals when there was a cry from behind Laura.

'Laura, is that really you?'

Laura nearly choked on her food, and had to cough and splutter before being able to turn around. Standing behind her, with a smile as wide as a Cheshire cat, was a young man her own age. He was dressed casually in old but neat shorts and T-shirt, with thongs on his feet. His hair was jet black and fashionably short and spiky. Laura racked her memory – he looked familiar, but she could not place where she had met him before.

'You don't remember me – oh Laura, I'm hurt, deeply hurt,' he said, his wide grin belying his words. 'I can't believe you have forgotten me – did our time together in the Madre de Dios mean nothing to you?'

That was the memory prompt that Laura needed – Rob, although she couldn't remember his second name. They had met by chance two years previously when Laura was exploring the Inca ruins in the Andes Mountains. He was American like herself, and they had travelled together for two or three weeks after meeting at Mount Ampato. It had been a brief though pleasant encounter she thought, as she remembered busy days trekking to various Incan ruins, and lazy evenings eating and drinking. She remembered that Rob played harmonica fantastically well, there had been some great singsongs at their camps with a mixture of traditional Peruvian song and dance, and with her singing along to Rob's harmonica as they performed mostly songs from the sixties. And the sex, although casual, had been very enjoyable. But what was he doing here?

With a shock, Laura brought herself back into the present.

'Rob, it's so great to see you!' She thought fast, anxiety and suspicion jostling for supremacy in her mind. 'My God, what a coincidence! What brings you to Humpty Doo?'

'Oh, you know me, Laura – the eternal traveller. Still searching for something, although I'm not sure what it is. How about you, what are you doing here?'

Laura could see that Rob was wondering who Jopl was, although he hadn't asked the question directly. She knew he must be curious, as they had shared a bed in the Andes and she hadn't mentioned anything about being a mother of a young child. Again, Laura's mind raced, needing to think of an innocent explanation to stop Rob asking too many more questions. 'Oh, like yourself, I'm still travelling. I'm with my boyfriend Greg on this trip. This is his son, Joe. Say hello to Rob, Joe.'

Laura prayed that Jopl would have enough sense to play along with her and not question his sudden change of name.

'Hello Rob,' Jopl said, thankfully understanding the subterfuge.

'Hello yourself, Joe. It's nice to meet you. Well, that's great, Laura. Although I have to say...' Rob leaned a little closer to Laura so that Jopl couldn't overhear '...I am a little disappointed that you are travelling with a boyfriend this time around. The last time we met like this, it was pretty spectacular.'

'I know, Rob. But that's the way it is this time around, OK?'

'Sure, sure, Laura. I am disappointed, but I play fair. If you are with someone else now, then that's your prerogative. So where is loverboy anyway?'

'He had to go into Darwin today. He'll be back this evening or tomorrow.'

Laura wondered how she could try to find out a little more about Rob and why he was here, of all places. She remembered that when she had met him in the Andes, he had struck her as a bit of a mystery man. He hadn't talked about himself very much, but had encouraged Laura to talk about herself and her past, present and future as much as she liked.

'This really is an amazing coincidence, Rob, meeting you again like this. Are you travelling on your own?'

'Yes, I'm afraid I am. Sad isn't it? But you sure are right – it is one hell of a coincidence. That's why I couldn't believe it when you walked in – I had just finished my dinner, but I nearly choked on my coffee.' He pointed disparagingly at the front of his T-shirt, which had some coffee stains on it. 'I thought to myself that you must be stalking me, following me into this place like this. I'm not going to be here much longer. I got in a few days ago, and just needed somewhere to rest up awhile before moving on. How about yourself – will you be here long?'

'Only for a few days,' said Laura, answering slowly as she thought about what Rob had said. So he had arrived in Humpty Doo while they were still out at sea, and he had come into this pub before herself and Jopl – it seemed that it must really be a coincidental meeting then. She relaxed a little, while still making sure to weave a story that would stand up to scrutiny.

'Greg, my boyfriend, has gone into Darwin to attend to a few matters that he couldn't do here. He'll be back today or tomorrow, and then we'll probably rest here for a couple of days and then head on again.'

'Yeah, same as myself, then. And where are you going on to from here?'

Laura had to think again quickly. 'Well, Greg is in touch with his office from Darwin, so it partly depends on that. We might have to head straight back to the States, but I would love to go on as far as the North Queensland coast if we can. I have never been there, and I am told that the Great Barrier Reef is incredible. I would love to do some scuba diving, maybe around Cairns.'

'I would definitely recommend that Laura. It is absolutely fantastic – incredible experience to dive the reef. I spent a month on Fitzroy Island, just off the coast from Cairns, and it is unbelievable. If you do decide to head across that way, I'll give you the names of the hostel and the dive shop that I used.'

Laura relaxed a bit more – it seemed fairly certain to her at this stage that this meeting was coincidental. Nevertheless, she thought that one more question might put the issue beyond doubt.

'What about yourself, Rob? Where are you going to after Humpty Doo?'

'South for me next Laura. I am going to ride 'The Legendary Ghan.' It's a train that that runs across the oldest, flattest, hottest, driest, dustiest, most deserted bit of earth on earth, going all the way from Darwin to Adelaide – it is the only practical way I can think of crossing Australia north to south – I'm certainly not going to walk it – too many men have died trying! I really want to see what the middle of this amazing continent looks like – can you imagine what it must be like to look all around you, three hundred and sixty degrees, knowing that the nearest human habitation is hundreds, maybe thousands of kilometres away? Imagine looking as far as the eye can see in every direction, and seeing nothing but flat, unending bush.'

The enthusiasm in his voice assured Laura that Rob was genuinely looking forward to this trip. While she no longer looked on him as an immediate threat, Greg's warnings still rang in her ears.

'It sounds pretty amazing all right, Rob. And after that, what are you doing?'

'Well, that will bring me to Adelaide. Then I'll take about three weeks to go from there to Sydney via Melbourne – I fly from Sydney to New Zealand next month. I spend two months there, and then head home.'

'Wow, you really are travelling the long road this time. Remind me, whereabouts in the States is home?'

'Oh you know what they say, 'Home is where the heart is.' If that's true, then I'm not too sure where exactly I would call home. But for the moment it's the Big Apple – good old NY itself. You are a South Carolina girl if I remember correctly?'

'That's right,' Laura confirmed, before steering the conversation back to Australia. She mentioned the Great Barrier Reef again and Rob happily prattled on about the amazing fish, the incredible coral, the beautiful beaches.

She spent another hour or so chatting to Rob before saying that she wanted to get Joe back to the hostel for a while. She explained that he had gotten a bit too much heat the previous day, and she wanted him to take a bit of a rest in the afternoon so that he wouldn't overdo it again. Promising to meet up for a drink the next evening when her boyfriend was back from Darwin, Laura and Jopl left Rob to his beer and went back to their hostel. Taking heed of Greg's warnings, they lay low for the rest of that day.

The Meaning Of Life

Laura and Jopl were sitting on the porch at the back of the hostel the next afternoon when Greg appeared around the corner. Laura ran into his arms, so relieved to see him back. If there had been any doubt in her mind about the strength of her feelings for this amazing man, the loss that she had felt for the day and night that he was away had removed those doubts instantly and absolutely. She had felt bereft of a part of herself when lying in their bed on her own. She had worried about him incessantly, hoping that nothing would go wrong in Darwin, hoping that he would come back to her safely.

Greg updated Laura on what had happened in Darwin. He had obtained travel papers for all three of them, using his and Laura's passports as templates; and using a photo of Jopl that they had taken with a camera belonging to Captain Smith while on the ship. He had used two hundred thousand dollars from Laura's Swiss bank account to pay for the false passports; but then illegality at this level did not come cheap. In two days, the three passports would be ready for them and they would go to Darwin to collect them. When they had the passports, they would be able to use Laura's funds to buy tickets to fly from Darwin to the States, probably via Perth. This meant that their initial point of departure was on an internal flight, which would help to minimise the number of checks that their paperwork would undergo when leaving the country. They would have to buy luggage and a full wardrobe of clothes for them all in Darwin, as it would be very unusual to have a family of three travelling from Australia to the United States with no luggage.

Greg declined to discuss anything about whom he had dealt with, as he said it was safer for Laura to know as little as possible about some of the people that Greg had to deal with in order to expedite their safe arrival in the States. He told her a little about Darwin, whetting the ever-present curiosity that Laura felt for new places. Greg asked Jopl again if he would tell them what he was carrying and how he was carrying it, but Jopl once again refused, politely but firmly. Greg tried again, asking him if he would tell them who the information had to be delivered to, but again Jopl refused.

Laura then told Greg how she and Jopl had spent their time while he was gone. She explained that they had spent the first morning wandering around Humpty Doo, and that thereafter they had stayed in or around the hostel, using Jopl's supposed heatstroke to explain to the landlady why they were staying there instead of looking around the town and its environs. Greg was looking pleased with that, until Laura started to tell him about her chance meeting with Rob.

'The only strange thing that happened, and it really was a strange one, was when we were having lunch yesterday. We were in the pub just down the road there, when I actually ran into someone that I know! Isn't that a coincidence that beats all coincidences?'

'What? That's impossible! Who the hell was it? What are they doing here? Did you tell them anything about us?'

'Whoa, Greg, slow down. I thought at first that it couldn't be a coincidence either, but having spoken to him, I am certain that it is just one of those one-in-a-million flukes. Let me tell you what happened.'

Laura explained how she had met Rob two years earlier in the Andes, though she neglected to tell him that she and

Rob had been lovers. She explained that Rob had been in that pub before Laura and Jopl had walked in; and indeed that Rob had been in Humpty Doo for days before they had arrived. Greg still wasn't convinced, and asked Laura to tell him everything that Rob had said. She told him about their discussion of the Great Barrier Reef and how Rob had offered to give her details of places he had used while there. Surely, she argued, that meant he must be telling the truth about being in Cairns for a month before coming to Humpty Doo. She described how Rob had spoken about the trip he was going to take in a few days on the Ghan, and how enthusiastic he was about crossing the interior of Australia. She said that he was then going to spend a few weeks in south eastern Australia before flying to New Zealand for two months before going home to New York.

Greg admitted that the whole story sounded convincing, and might even be true. But he told Laura that the people who were searching for her clearly had huge resources at their disposal. If they had somehow been able to track her to Humpty Doo, then it would not be beyond them to come up with a cover story that would sound convincing and that would stand up to close questioning or examination. Nevertheless, it did all seem too much of a coincidence to be true, and he wondered if they should make a break for Darwin without delay. He had hoped to wait in Humpty Doo until their passports were ready – he felt that it was so remote, it would be safer than waiting in Darwin. But now, maybe it was best to go immediately.

Laura argued that since she believed Rob was above suspicion in terms of being involved in the hunt for them, it was pointless to deviate from their plans at this stage. If Humpty Doo was safer than Darwin, then that was where they should stay. Also, it was now over a day since she had met Rob – surely if he was chasing her, he would have tried to capture her or something before now? In addition, Laura had told the landlady that they would be staying with her for a day or two after Greg returned from Darwin – going now would only create more questions. Finally, Laura explained how she had tentatively arranged that they might meet Rob for dinner in the same pub if Greg was back from Darwin.

'If you still think he is part of the hunt for us, why not meet him for yourself? Then you can make your own judgement on his involvement.'

Eventually Greg relented, agreeing that it might be hasty to run for it immediately, which could create more questions and problems than it would solve. But he insisted that if they were going to stay, then he would need to meet this Rob to check him out for himself. Laura said that all they had to do was to be in the pub that evening. Greg agreed to that, but warned Laura and Jopl that they were to follow his lead in the conversation at all times. Then he got Laura to recall the conversation as closely as she could, so that they could be sure that they would not unwittingly contradict any part of the story that Laura had already established. Any time that Laura wasn't sure what had been said next, Jopl would prompt her – he seemed to recall the entire conversation that he had heard word for word. When Greg was satisfied that he knew everything that had been said, he again warned Laura and Jopl that they were to let him steer the conversation and they were to make sure that they didn't say anything to contradict him.

Greg told them that he had bought a mobile phone in Darwin, and that he needed to make a few phone calls. Laura and Jopl were to stay on the porch while Greg made his calls in their room. When he was finished, they could all go down to the pub for dinner, and Greg would check out

Rob's story and see if he was as innocent as he seemed.

When Greg had left the porch, Laura turned to Jopl. Despite the fact that he was a child, he was the wisest person she had ever met, and he always seemed to be able to answer her questions. 'Jopl, you know sometimes I wonder why I am doing this at all. It just seems to be causing trouble at every turn. Do you think I should stick with it, or should we just run away and forget about all this? Why are we here?'

'Why do you ask me, Laura?'

'Because you always seem to understand what I need to know, and you always have the answers.'

'I wish that were so, Laura. But truly it is not. When we have discussed various matters, I have usually asked the questions, and you have supplied the answers. For example, if you think of our first day on Captain Smith's ship when we discussed the nature of right and wrong, I simply asked questions. You supplied most of the answers. Isn't that so?' he asked, ending with a question.

Laura laughed. 'I think you are making fun of me, little man. But really, what do you think I should do?'

'Well, I suppose that depends on what exactly it is that you are asking. If you mean what you should do at this particular time in this specific situation, well I'm afraid that only you can answer that. If you mean why are we here in a more general sense – what is the purpose of our existence, what is the meaning of life – well that is a question that has exercised some of the greatest minds in history, from Socrates to Descartes, from Augustine to Chomsky.'

'OK, then, I will try to decide what I should so at this particular time, in this specific situation,' Laura said, a little sarcastically. 'But do talk to me about the bigger question – it will help to take my mind off my immediate worries. Why are we here?'

'Yes, indeed, a very interesting question. Many say the most interesting, and the most important, question of them all. I wonder how much difference it would make to our lives if we truly understood the answer to that question. I really feel sympathy for the people who don't even believe that there is some central purpose to their lives. I would hate to live like that – believing that my life was simply the random result of a lottery of physics and genetics. Believing that there is no guiding principle by which all men should be directed, a central principle that joins all of mankind in a unified endeavour.'

'So, are you saying that there is some such central 'principle'?'

'I would never be so arrogant. Who am I to make such a grand declaration? All I can say is that I believe it is possible. Maybe, given my limited understanding of the universe about me, I might even say that I believe it to be probable. If you read Einstein and Bohr, Schrödinger and Hawking, it seems to me that this is the direction that we are being pushed in. Through the Renaissance in Europe in the sixteenth and seventeenth centuries, science seemed to be providing answers that religions had failed, or refused, to provide. Accordingly, through the eighteenth and nineteenth centuries, there was a growing secularism, which in many ways may have been a good thing. Science became the new religion, the new font of all knowledge, the new repository of all the answers. People believed that as scientific knowledge and understanding grew, eventually all of our questions would be answered. And all of this negated the proposition of some underlying entity that either created or was guiding the universe – who needs any of the many versions of the Gods, when you have science?'

'Yes, I know,' said Laura, wanting to check that she was following Jopl's line of reasoning. 'For example, when we found out about the Big Bang, then there was no need to have a God who created the world in seven days. And when we found fossilised animals millions of years old that supported Darwin's theory of evolution, then that meant that the world couldn't have been created from scratch six thousand years ago.'

'Indeed, so it seemed,' confirmed Jopl. 'And no matter which of the major religions you look at – Buddhism, Hinduism, Islam, Judaism, Christianity – it seemed to be the same. Science apparently disproved the possibility of reincarnation, negated the need for an afterlife – science said, "Who needs these gods anyway? We don't." And yet, as I said a moment ago, if you read the published works of some of the leading scientists of the last century, including the most recent, there seems to be a problem. As the scientists work at the astrophysical level, the atomic level and the quantum level; it appears that science may not be able to provide all of the answers after all.

'As you have mentioned it, let's look at the Big Bang. As a theory, I like the Big Bang. And all of the evidence, as we currently understand it, seems to support the theory. There is just one problem. The Big Bang theory can explain the entire universe from about 10 million trillion trillion trillionths of a second after it's formation to the present day. It can even predict the eventual demise of our universe many billions of years hence. But, and this is the key point, it cannot explain that first 10 million trillion trillion trillionths of a second. Yet that is where it all started. That 10 million trillion trillion trillionths of a second is the key to explaining, and therefore understanding our universe. Yet the physical sciences seem baffled on that one. So it seems to me that there may very well be more to this universe than the purely physical – there may be something metaphysical, something literally 'beyond the physical' or 'other than the physical.'

'Now what form that takes is an entirely different question, and that is a question that I am even less qualified to comment on. Is it some sort of omnipotent monotheistic 'God' as many religions suggest? Is it the powerful gods of the Greeks? Is it the animist gods of the American Indians? Is it the Brahman of the Hindi or the Nam-Myoho-Renge-Kyo of the Buddhists?'

Laura waited. Jopl had just asked the 60 million dollar question. This was it, this was the big one. But he seemed to have finished speaking.

'Well, Jopl? Don't stop there! Tell me. What is the answer? Which of these belief systems, these religions, has it right? Do any of them? Tell me!'

'But, Laura, I cannot tell you. I do not know. And in any case, it is not important.'

'Not important? How can you say that? Wars have been fought over this question. More people have died in religious wars than any other type of war. Look at the Inquisition in the Middle Ages. People tortured and put to death because of their religious belief. Look at the Crusades. Of course it's important!'

'Well, I think many of the so-called religious wars that you refer to had more to do with human politics and power struggles than they had to do with religious beliefs. But anyway, the reason it is not important is that the answer to your original question is the same, regardless of what metaphysical philosophy you choose to believe in.'

Laura had to think back and try to remember what her original question had been. In her mind it had been supplanted by a more important question of whether or not there was a God; and if there was one, who or what was he, or it or she? 'What was the question again?'

'The question was what many say is the most important question ever asked – 'Why are we here?', 'What is the meaning of life?', 'What is the purpose of my existence?' – all variations on the same question, and all with the same answer.

And the answer to this question is the same, regardless of what belief system you have. Whether you are Christian, Buddhist, Jewish, Hindu, Muslim; the answer is the same. A lot of philosophical traditions, even agnostic ones that choose to believe that there may or may not be a God as such, have also arrived at the same answer to this question. The answer is out there, it is known, it is discussed in learned philosophical journals, it is preached in churches and mosques. And yet, people still ask the same question. To my mind, that is a more interesting question. Not 'What is the meaning of life?', but 'Why are people still asking, when the answer is already so widely known and indeed so widely taught'?'

Laura found herself hanging on every word that exploded from this young boy's lips. He reminded her of the biblical story of Jesus in the Temple as a child – talking to the elders as an equal, displaying superior knowledge and understanding of the scriptures than his learned seniors. If we all know why we are on this earth she wondered, then why do so many of us flounder through life without direction?

'It doesn't actually matter how the world was created or by whom. All that matters is why. The reason, which is in itself the 'The Meaning of Life', is simply this – to give us all an opportunity to be divine. Whether in the Buddhist

The Meaning of Life

belief of reincarnation leading to Nirvana, the Christian belief of death leading to Paradise, or any of the other religions and philosophies that propose existence after death, the objective of all life should be to make the world a better place. Our impact does not have to be famed or big, it merely has to be good. We are judged by a simple weighing of the effort we put into making the world better, and the absence of that effort. If two people put in the same effort, and one achieves world peace while the other simply makes a neighbour happy for a moment, the same effort and desire to do good existed, so they are valued the same. Does this make sense to you?'

'Yes, I suppose it makes sense. But you said that we all know this answer – that our purpose in life is to make the world a better place. How can you say that? How can you say that, when so many people have no sense of purpose in their lives?'

'I often think that the greatest tragedy of the modern world is that so many people no longer believe in this purpose. I can unequivocally say that the answer is known – go to a priest or elder in any religion and you will get the same answer, though maybe in different words. Ask any great philosopher and again you will get the same answer, though maybe in different words. So the answer is known. The difficulty is that today, many people, knowing the answer, refuse to believe the answer. They hear from their parents that they should be 'good', they hear it from their community leaders, their political leaders, their religious leaders. But they are seduced by another voice, a voice that tells them that this is not so. A voice that tells them that the purpose of life is to amass possessions. A voice that tells them that their self-worth is defined by their material worth. A voice of poison and pain that is slowly killing the appreciation of the intangible, which is fundamental to a sense of community. Feeling isolated, people turn more and more to the voice of materialism, becoming more and more lost. A tragedy.'

Laura thought about it for a while before speaking – something she often found herself having to do when having a conversation with Jopl. There was no doubt that for one so young, he seemed more learned and wise than anyone she had ever met before, of any age. 'Well, it makes sense, yes. But you are the very one who usually declines to be too definite about anything. You always say that one can't be certain of the answer to these big questions. Yet you state this as a fact – as something beyond doubt. "The objective of all life should be to make the world a better place." How do you know?'

'That is a very good point. I am glad that you do not simply accept what I say. It is always good to question. In truth, I do not know for a fact that this is correct. However, I have looked at life from all angles, from all beliefs, from across the ages of Man's understanding. And it seems to me that this is the best hypothesis that I can derive at this time. Maybe as I learn more, I will change my mind. Maybe, in the future, mankind will learn and understand more, and thus disprove my theory on the 'Meaning of Life'. However, in the absence of any definitive evidence to the contrary, this theory seems to me to best fit the bill. I believe that there is a metaphysical component to our universe. I believe that our purpose in life, the reason we are here, the meaning to our existence, is to make the world a better place. And I can only suggest some reasons why this might be correct.'

'OK, go ahead. I am with you so far, and I certainly cannot prove you wrong. But I would be very interested to hear why I should agree with you, even if I cannot put forward any concrete reasons for disagreeing with you.'

'Aha, you are challenging me,' said Jopl, with a gleam in his eye. 'OK. Let me see now. In no particular order. Firstly, as I have already said, science cannot explain the physical universe to my satisfaction – certainly not its creation in the first place, and I think not its development since; although I am aware that there are arguments which claim to explain how the incredibly complex universe that we have today could have evolved from the Big Bang by random chance. But science certainly cannot explain the creation of this universe to my satisfaction.

'Secondly, my theory that there is some sort of a metaphysical constituent in our universe is a fairly close fit in general terms with all of the world's major religions, and indeed with many of its major non-religious or agnostic philosophies. I think that, in itself, is important – it seems unlikely to me that all of these competing philosophies would have arrived at what is effectively the same answer since the dawn of mankind, and that this answer should be wrong.

'Finally, I think that believing that the purpose of our existence is to make the world a better place is probably the most practical way to live life. For example, people – particularly in your Western culture – often make the mistake of thinking that they will get happiness from possessions. They say, "If only I had a bigger car, or a better house, or more money, I would be happy." But if they get more, then they generally will want more again. So they are in a pretty permanent state of wanting something – a permanent state of dissatisfaction – a permanent state of unhappiness. But if you even think back across your own life – when have you experienced the most satisfaction and happiness? Is it possible that the happiest and most satisfying times of your life have been when you have given something, or when you have done something for someone else? Would that be true?'

Again, Laura thought carefully before answering. She was more surprised than Jopl when she answered the question honestly. 'You know, I think you are right! Yes, that is true. But now I am confused. I always believed that happiness came from loving relationships more than possessions. Am I wrong?'

'Let us talk of happiness, and how to be happy, another time. Greg is coming, so I will finish this discussion. For these three reasons, I believe there is something other than the physical in our universe, and that the 'Meaning of Life' is to make the world a better place. Firstly, science cannot explain the creation of the universe to me. Secondly, it fits with all major religions and most non-religious philosophies. Thirdly, from a practical point of view, living this way gives the best results and the happiest most satisfying life, both for yourself and for the rest of humanity.'

Just as Jopl finished speaking, Greg came out onto the porch. 'Hi, Darling,' he said to Laura. 'You guys ready to go?'

The three of them went down to the pub where Laura had met Rob, playing their roles as girlfriend with boyfriend and his son. When they walked in, Laura saw Rob at the bar straightaway. They got a table and, when Rob saw Laura, he walked over. Laura did the introductions and Greg invited Rob to join them for dinner. As they ate and talked, Laura was aware of Greg pumping Rob for information, testing his story, asking about the same thing on a number of occasions during the meal to check for any inconsistencies in the answers he was given. She was sure that Rob was totally unaware of this and thought that if anything he might think that Greg was a little forgetful, as he sometimes seemed to ask Rob a question that has already been answered. By the time they left the pub two hours later, Laura was exhausted from concentrating on maintaining a consistent storyline all the time, and worrying that Jopl might say something to undermine the subterfuge.

As the three of them walked back to the hostel, Greg announced himself satisfied that Rob was the genuine article. Indeed, he suggested that they have a beer with Rob each evening until they left for Darwin. Greg felt that it would provide an even better cover, just on the one in a million chance that anyone would come around asking questions about them. When they got back to the hostel, Laura settled Jopl to sleep before she and Greg retired to the porch to savour a glass of wine. Discussing their situation, Greg assured Laura that everything was looking good. There was every reason to believe that they were totally off their pursuers' radar, and he was confident that the quality of their false passports would get them into the States without any trouble. He did ask that Laura continue to press Jopl for details on what he was carrying and who he was going to deliver it to.

Reassured by Greg's strong presence, and thankful that he had agreed with her about Rob's non-involvement in the whole perplexing affair; Laura was happy to sit with Greg and talk about normal things – the funny name of the town, the vastness of the Australian continent and the incredible landscape. And later that night they brought each other to bed and spoke of love and fulfilment and joy and ecstasy.

The Secret of Happiness

Laura rose to the edge of consciousness, groaned, went back down under.

Seconds or minutes or hours later, she again became vaguely aware of her surroundings for a moment, before sinking back into a deep sleep.

For a third time, Laura almost awoke. Just as she was about to sleep again, a thought struck her – it was bright, very bright. She forced her eyes open, having to battle a terrible weight that insisted she should just go back to sleep. Looking around the room, it took her a moment to recall where she was. As memories flooded back, she sat up sharply, before subsiding with another groan. A headache was pounding at her temples, making it difficult to think properly.

Resting her head back on the pillow, Laura tried to think. For some reason, she felt like panicking. There was something wrong, but she couldn't put her finger on it. Then it struck her. Greg! Where was Greg? As soon as the fear became conscious, it subsided. She was being silly. He had probably just gone to the bathroom for a moment. Her head hurt. She thought it must have been that wine last night – it must have disagreed with her somehow.

She lay on the bed for a while, and the headache gradually subsided to a dull pounding. After a while, when Greg had still not appeared, she thought he must have gone out for an early morning walk. She decided to get up herself and check on Jopl. Judging by how bright the sunshine was, it must already be mid-morning, and it wasn't like her to sleep so late. She and Jopl could get breakfast – she really needed a drink of water. Today was their last day in Humpty Doo - tomorrow they were going to Darwin to get their passports and fly back to the US. She had to be alert, be ready to help Greg to get them through the trip back to the US successfully.

Laura forced her body out of the bed and stood under the shower for much longer than usual, alternating the water from scalding hot to as cold as she could get it – tepid in this climate. She was hoping that the water would wash away some of her lethargy. Eventually, she got out, towelled herself dry and dressed. Brushing her long hair was an exercise in endurance, as each stroke seemed to aggravate the headache, but she persevered. Eventually she was presentable, and if not ready, she was at least capable of meeting the day.

Laura knocked before going into Jopl's room. Usually, he was awake when she came to get him – Laura sometimes wondered just how long he slept each night – but this morning his angelic head was beautiful in a deep repose – the sleep of the truly innocent, Laura thought. She called his name softly, and gave his shoulder a gentle shake. Not getting any response, she called and shook a little louder. This elicited a moan from the boy, but no more. Surprised that he was so hard to rouse, Laura called and shook again, more forcefully this time. He stirred in the bed, giving a little whimper as he opened his eyes for a second before closing them again.

'My head. There is something wrong with my head.'

'What do you mean, Jopl? What is it? What's wrong?'

'Inside my head. It is like … like someone is banging on my head from the inside. It hurts. I don't like it. Make it stop.'

'Oh, poor Jopl. You just have a headache, I do too. It

must be this heat and humidity that is getting to us – it never stops. Don't worry, it will ease off soon. And when you drink some water and have something to eat, I am sure that will help. If it still hurts after that, I'll get something in the pharmacy to make it better, OK?'

'You mean this is … normal? I have never felt anything like this before!'

'You've never had a headache before? Well, you should consider yourself lucky, young man. Haven't you ever had a headache when you've had the flu or an upset tummy?'

'I've never had those things.'

'What? Have you ever been sick?'

'No. If you look after your body, mind, heart and soul properly, and keep them in balance, why would you get sick?'

'Jopl, everyone gets sick sometimes. Now, enough of this nonsense for the moment. I want you to get up and get ready, and join me for breakfast as soon as you can, OK?'

'OK, Laura. I'll be there in a moment.'

Laura made her way to the hostel cafe, surprised to find herself a little unsteady on her feet. She felt that her legs might give way underneath her. Seating herself gingerly at a table, she poured herself a glass of chilled water, and sipped gently. In between sips, she held the cool glass to her forehead, easing the headache. She thought to herself that she would have to tell Jopl to do the same, as he had seemed quite distressed by his discomfort. She wondered where Greg was, and thought that if the heat was affecting him the same way, he might have gone for a walk to shake off the lassitude and prepare for the day. She knew he would want to be both physically and mentally alert. She smiled as she thought about him and how much he had come to mean to her, so quickly. She knew that she meant the world to him, and that he would do anything for her to help her and keep her safe.

As Jopl arrived and took a seat beside her, they were asked what they would like to eat. Laura ordered scrambled eggs on toast and more chilled water and orange juice for them both, and strong black coffee for herself.

'How do you feel now, Jopl?'

'My head still hurts. And I feel that I have no energy. It is a very strange feeling. I do not like to feel like this. My body is not healthy, not in balance.'

'Don't worry, it will pass quickly enough. We probably haven't been getting enough salt to make up for the amount of saline we are losing through sweating in this heat and humidity. Take plenty of salt on your eggs, it will help. And be sure to drink lots and lots of water – we are probably both a little dehydrated.'

Laura showed Jopl how to roll the cool glass against his forehead between drinks of his orange juice. Gradually, he too, like Laura, started to feel a little better.

Feeling a little more refreshed as they finished their breakfast, Laura suggested that they go out on the porch to wait for Greg. There they would be able to take stay in the shade while taking advantage of any slight breeze that might be blowing. In addition, they would have the ceiling fan going at full speed, and they could continue to sip chilled water.

They talked desultorily for a while about nothing much at all. Remembering what Greg had asked of her the night before, while they drank their wine on this very porch, Laura asked Jopl if he could tell her what exactly he was carrying and how he was carrying it. This time, instead of a point-blank refusal, Jopl told her that he was 'carrying the records', but then refused to elaborate any further on what the records were, or how, exactly, he was carrying them. Laura thought of Greg's theory of microfilm surgically inserted under the boy's skin, and shuddered on Jopl's behalf. When she asked him who he was bringing these records to, he again politely but firmly said that the time was not yet right for him to share that information with her.

Wanting to change the subject, Laura thought back to the conversation that she had with Jopl on the porch the previous evening. 'Jopl, when we were talking yesterday evening, we mentioned happiness. Do you remember?'

'Yes, Laura. I always remember – haven't you realised that?'

'Well, yes, you do seem to have a bloody good memory. Anyway, you know you spoke about a God, or some kind of 'metaphysical constituent in our universe'; I think is how you described it?'

'That is correct.'

'OK. And I get your argument on that, I think I understand it. And you said that our purpose in this short life of ours – 'The Meaning of Life' you said – is to make the world a better place.'

'That was my proposition, yes.'

'But then you said something about happiness – something about how to be happy. What was that again?'

'I said that one of the reasons why I believe that 'The Meaning of Life' might be to make the world a better place is that, in doing so, or at least in trying to do so, we make ourselves happy as a consequence. We are at our happiest when we are giving, not when we are receiving.'

'Yes, yes, that was it. Can you explain that to me a little more? I guess I have always associated happiness with either getting something that I wanted, or with having loved ones around me – effectively, I suppose, getting love as well as getting material things. I am not a material person you know. At least, I don't think I am. But I think that to really know, and I mean to actually *know*, how to be happy – I think that that might be the greatest knowledge of all. Tell me more about that, Jopl, please.'

'Certainly, we can discuss it, Laura. Whether or not I can 'tell' you anything, I am not so sure. I often think that we need to discover these things for ourselves, through reflection and meditation. I am not sure that anyone else can ever 'tell' us something like how to be happy. Although I think it is true that, if we reflect on the words of the wise through the ages, then that can help us to find the path to our own truth. And you have to remember that the truth may be different for different people, which of course complicates the picture. Every person is unique, both physically and psychologically from a genetic point of view, and also from the point of view of their own culture and their own personal history. Every one of us has had different experiences.

'I suppose the other point that I would make before we discuss your question on how to be happy is this. I am not sure that anyone can ever know these things as an absolute fact. You said to actually *know* how to be happy might be the greatest knowledge of all. But I am not sure that I would ever be confident in claiming that level of certainty about anything in life. There is always a margin of error, always some room for doubt, no matter how tiny.'

'Oh, Jopl! Not always. There are some things that we know as indisputable facts.'

'Oh really? Let us test that proposition. For example, we are in Australia, just outside Darwin, aren't we?'

'Yes,' said Laura, happy that for once she could answer one of Jopl's questions during these discussions without hesitation, without doubt.

'How do you know?'

'What? How do I know? Look around you Jopl! Believe me, this is Australia.'

'But how do you know, Laura? How do you know beyond any possibility of doubt that this is Australia? How can you be one hundred per cent certain, instead of just ninety-nine point nine nine nine per cent certain?'

'But, Jopl, it is a silly question. There is the climate, the vegetation, the fact that Captain Smith sailed us here, the fact that we have spoken to people here in the hostel, in the pub and around the town, spoken to Rob. I think if we thought we were in northern Australia and we were actually in, I don't know, India or something; we would have realised our mistake by now! Don't you?'

Laura looked at Jopl, wondering what point he was trying to make. The reality is, she thought, that actually some things are one hundred per cent certain.

'Let me give you a scenario,' said Jopl.

'Oh no,' groaned Laura. 'Your scenarios always land me in trouble! OK, go on.'

'We know that you are being pursued across the world by some very powerful and sinister forces. Now, let's say they did not want to hurt you, but simply wanted to study you for some reason, maybe they want to find out more about your motives or want to understand how you think so that they can predict your next move. With me so far?'

'So far, so good.'

'So they want to study you – ideally in a laboratory if they could. But if you were in a laboratory, you would not act in your normal fashion. So they need to study you without you knowing that you are being studied. So they hire all of these actors, and create a huge open-air controlled environment in the desert in Somalia on the east African coast. Actor Greg meets you and gains your trust. You are successfully introduced to more actors, such as myself, Captain Smith and Rob. There are actors with non-speaking parts as well, such as most of the supposed residents of Humpty Doo. Captain Smith's ship actually dropped you off the African coast in Somalia. The climate and vegetation are the same as northern Australia. The actors all play their roles. Now I know that this scenario is very improbable, that it is almost impossible for that to have happened. But my question is this. Can you state with one hundred per cent certainty that my scenario is false?'

'Bloody hell! Just to put my mind at ease, before I even think about – you don't actually think that's what has happened, do you?' asked Laura, with a nervous laugh.

'No, Laura, no. Don't worry, it is not true. I believe we are in northern Australia just outside Darwin, in the funnily named Humpty Doo. But back to my question – is my scenario impossible, or is it just extremely unlikely?'

'Well, I suppose in theory it is possible. It's ridiculous, but, theoretically, yes it is possible.'

'OK, back to my earlier question. Do you know for definite that we are in Australia, just outside Darwin? And I mean beyond *any* possibility of doubt or error.'

'Well, I certainly believe that we are. And I am happy to say that I know we are, I know for definite. Is there a one in a quadrillion chance that I am wrong? Yes, I suppose there is. But the possibility of error is so small as to be meaningless.'

'Well, I think I would have to challenge that, Laura. You have just said that there is a possibility that you are wrong, albeit a tiny, tiny possibility. Nevertheless, it is a possibility. Therefore, all you can honestly say is that you believe you are in northern Australia; and so your actions will be based on that belief. But you should always be prepared for the possibility that you are wrong. Being open to that possibility is what stops people from becoming zealots or fanatics. Being open to your own limitations, believing that you might be wrong, that someone else might one day change your mind – this is a fantastic device to keep yourself open to new possibilities.'

'OK, OK, I get it. I mean, I accept that what you say makes sense. So, I should never be too absolute in my opinions or beliefs. I should always keep in the back of my mind that I may be wrong, is that it?'

'That is it exactly. It is not saying that you are not committed to your beliefs. It is not saying that your actions are any less fervent. It simply means that you are more likely to avoid the excesses of fanaticism, because you are conscious of the possibility of error on your part.'

'OK. I get that now. But I am lost again! How did we get onto that?'

'We got on to it when you asked if we could discuss the issue of how to attain happiness and you said you wanted to know how to be happy – that you wanted to know with absolute certainty. I am suggesting to you that we can discuss it, and that doing so might give us some insights. But I am saying we can never be absolutely certain that we know anything beyond all possibility of doubt or error. Particularly because every person is unique, and so the answer to any question such as this might be different for different people.'

'Oh, yes, I'm back on track now. OK, so we can discuss how to be happy, and we might even feel that we have a few answers, but we can never assume that our answer is right and everyone else is wrong. Is that it?'

'Laura, you gladden my heart! That is it exactly. So, let

us discuss happiness.'

They each took a sip of water and paused for a moment. Laura felt as though she was getting ready to do battle. These conversations with the boy who sometimes seemed to be as old as the stars were fascinating, invigorating, and she enjoyed them hugely – but they were not easy. They demanded thought and introspection and concentration. Laura wanted to be ready as they launched into a new topic.

Jopl kicked things off with a question, as he was wont to do. 'What makes you happy, Laura?'

'Well, I have always associated happiness with one of two different things. I suppose one is the material, the consumer side, and one is the abstract. On the material side, getting something that you have always wanted. For example, when I was younger, I really, really wanted to get a new album that my favourite singer had released, but my dad said that I had to buy it with my own money, and I had none. It took me two weeks to save the money by doing chores for him around the house. Then I went off and bought the album and I was so happy when I was listening to it in my room. On the abstract side, I have been happy in relationships – especially with my dad. When he hugged me or told me I was a good girl, that always made me happy.'

'I see. So whether something material or something abstract, you are happy when you get something that you want. Is that what you are saying?'

'Erm, well, when you put it like that, it doesn't sound very nice. But, yes, I guess that's it in a nutshell.'

'Well, you know, I think that most people would give an answer similar to yours. They might phrase it differently, but essentially it would be that they are happy when they get something. I have a couple of difficulties with that explanation of happiness, however. Firstly, I suspect that the evidence shows us that people are actually happy when they give, not when they get. And, secondly, I think that happiness may be fundamentally dependant on internal choices, not external circumstances. Shall we discuss the first of these?'

'Yes, absolutely. I remember you saying something about this yesterday. It certainly runs contrary to our typical thinking.'

'Well, contrary to the typical thinking of someone raised in a materialistic society. Especially one like yours where capitalism has reached such extraordinary extremes.'

'Well, I'm sorry, but I happen to think that capitalism is a good thing,' Laura retorted.

'And a good thing it may well be. But remember that old adage 'Moderation in all things'. I have no argument with a degree of capitalism per se. But I think when it goes to the extreme that it has in many Western societies, most especially your own, then it is not a good thing. But, anyway, back to the first of my problems with your assumption on what makes you happy. You say that you are happy when you get something that you wanted, be it a physical object, be it affection, whatever, yes?'

Laura thought about this for a moment. 'Well, that is what I would usually say. But I remember you asking me about this yesterday evening, and I suppose some of my happiest times have been when I have done something for someone else, or given something to somebody else.'

'Indeed. One of your Western writers, William Shakespeare, had what I think was a very good observation on this. He said that, "A gift is twice blest – it blesseth him that gives and him that takes." He is a writer for whom I have a lot of admiration – I think he had some quite brilliant insights into human nature. Anyway, what he was saying is

The Secret of Happiness

that there is as much to be gained from giving a gift as there is from receiving a gift. I actually believe that there is much more happiness to be derived from the giving than from the getting. And I think experience bears this out. You can experiment yourself if you like.'

'Oh? How so?'

'Well, simply decide to consciously do things for other people. Do things for other people without any hope or expectation of reward – you do not want them to then do something for you in return, you do not want the recognition that you did something for them, you do not even want them to thank you. The easiest way to do that is to do things for other people without them knowing about it. I know experiments and trials have been done on this type of thing, and there is no doubt in my mind – I'll correct that, there is as little doubt as possible in my mind – that this is true. Happiness actually comes more from giving than from getting. One of the greatest misconceptions ever to exist about the human condition is that happiness comes from getting.'

Laura considered what Jopl had said and, thinking about her own life, realised that what he had said was indeed true. Even when she was in bed with Greg – she loved when he made her feel good, but she truly expressed her love by doing things for him. She felt happiest when she gave pleasure to him. The same was true in many other examples that flitted through her mind.

'OK, Jopl. So my assumption that I am happy when I get things is wrong – indeed it is the exact opposite that is true. Yes, I can see how that might well be a more accurate reflection of the root of happiness. You said you had a second problem with my assumption. Remind me – what was that?'

'Ah yes. My second problem applies every bit as much as much to my assertion that happiness comes from giving, as it does to your assumption that happiness came from getting. You see, both assume that happiness is dependant on the external world. Whether you assume that happiness comes from giving or getting, you are by definition tying the opportunity for happiness to other people or objects. But what if there was nobody, nothing to give to or get from? Would it still be possible to be happy? What do you think?'

'What, you mean if I was the only person left in the world or something?'

Jopl nodded, then hesitated. 'Not necessarily. Let's say you are just on your own. For example, if you are locked in solitary confinement for an extended period.'

'OK. Well, it would be incredibly lonely, which I guess would make me sad, or upset – depressed or whatever. But would it be possible to be happy? I guess it would, yes. For example, if I believed that I had done something really worthwhile, and that was why I had been locked up. Then, yes, I think it would be possible to be happy even though I had nobody else to get anything from or give anything to. Is that what you mean?'

'Yes, that is what I mean. So therefore, it follows QED, that happiness cannot be solely dependant on either giving or getting. There has to be at least some element of happiness that is internal. Again, I think the evidence suggests that this is truly the case.'

'And what evidence are we talking about this time?' Laura asked with a smile. It truly was stimulating and energising to talk with Jopl like this.

'Simply this. You can often see two people in the same situation, yet one is happy and the other is not. I think it is best illustrated with another old adage – 'Every cloud has a silver lining'. There are very few situations, very few events, very few things that happen to us, that are either one hundred per cent positive or one hundred per cent negative. Everything has positives and negatives, advantages and disadvantages, pros and cons. Our happiness depends on looking at the positives, focusing on the advantages, fixing our attention on the pros. That is not to say that we ignore the negatives – to do so would be to delude ourselves, to live in a world that was not real. But we can be conscious of the negatives, take them into account and plan for them, while still focusing on the positives.'

'Hmmm. So what exactly are you saying? That if we focus on the positives, we will always be happy? I'm not sure that sounds very realistic.'

'No? Well, pick any example you like. Any event or occurrence. If you like, think of something that made you unhappy.'

'Unfortunately, that is easy. My dad died only a few weeks ago. That made me desperately sad. I loved him to bits. I miss him awfully. I wish he was still here.' A tear rolled down her cheek, as she momentarily relived the terrible loss of the one person in the world whom she loved so deeply.

'The loss of a loved one is always a sad event. That is natural, that is only human. So I am not saying that you should be happy when your dear father died. However, what I am saying is that there is a time for grieving, and a time for being happy. And, believe it or not, I am sure there are positives about your father's death, whether you like to admit it or not.'

'What!' Laura was outraged. She liked Jopl, and she respected him, but this was too much. 'What are you saying, Jopl? That it was actually a good thing that my dad died?'

'All I am saying, Laura, is that any event has positives and negatives. In this case, the negatives are mostly on your side, not your father's – your loss, your loneliness, your pain.'

He paused, before asking gently 'Do you believe in an afterlife?'

The concern with which he asked the question calmed Laura, as she realised that he hadn't been belittling her loss as she had first felt. 'Well, I didn't until recently. But having talked to you, I think there might be some form of life after death.'

'Well, for anyone who believes in life after death, death isn't actually such a terrible thing. It is merely changing one's form from this earthly corporeal body to life in some other form. Tell me, Laura, your father was ill before he died, wasn't he? In pain?'

'Yes, he was. Poor dad.'

'Well then, death was in a way, a happy release for him.'

'I suppose that's true.'

'And you wouldn't have met Greg if your father was still alive, would you?'

'That's true.' Laura almost smiled at that thought. 'I wonder what is keeping him.'

'And your father didn't feel he could ask you to undertake this task for him while he was still alive, did he? So you couldn't be doing this good deed if he hadn't died, isn't that true?'

'Yes, Jopl, yes. Everything that you say is true. But you will never get me to say that I am happy that my dad has died and left me!'

'And I would never ever try to get you to say that, Laura. All I am saying is that everything in this life, even your father's death, has negatives and positives. So while it is right and proper that you should grieve for your dad, there is a time for the grieving to end. At that time, you should be able to think of your dad and be happy. Be happy for all the good times you had with him. Be happy because you had such a loving father. Be happy because he lives on forever in your heart, in your memories.'

'Yes, I suppose that is true. I know that is what he would want. He wouldn't want to see me crying for him for the rest of my life. He would want me to be happy and enjoy life.'

'Exactly. So that is my second problem with your suggestion about what makes us happy. I am not sure that it is anything to do with our external situation – what we have or what we do or even the people around us. I think it may have much, much more to do with an internal decision that we make – do I want to be happy? If I do, then I need to look at this positively, and then go on.'

Laura lay back in her chair on the porch, sipping her cold water again. She thought that Jopl might very well be correct. Maybe happiness is more to do with simply deciding to be happy, and less to do with what we have or do not have. She resolved to bear that in mind in future, and that she would always try to think of the positives, no matter what happened.

Pondering that, her mind wandered again to Greg. It was now early afternoon and there was still no sign of him. Where was he? Had something happened to him?

The Guide

Laura rested on the porch, pondering Jopl's suggestions, enjoying the breeze created by the ceiling fan. As another hour passed, she became increasingly restless, wondering where Greg could be. They had talked as they drank their wine the previous evening, had made passionate love during the night. Yet Greg had made no mention of going anywhere this morning.

But still there was no sign of him, and it was now approaching mid-afternoon. Laura wished that she had thought of asking Greg for the number of his new mobile phone, so that she could have rung him to see where he was and check that he was OK. As she became more agitated, Rob appeared around the corner.

Hi, Laura. Hi, Joe,' he called out cheerily.

'Hi Rob,' Laura answered, a little wearily.

'How are you guys doing?'

'Not too bad. Trying to cope with the heat. Joe and I both had headaches this morning – I think the heat and humidity are getting to us. I have kept Joe quiet here today and had him drinking plenty of water to get him back to himself.'

'Yeah, that heat can be a bit of a killer all right. Do you know that Darwin has Australia's highest suicide rate? And it's highest incidence of alcoholism? The experts reckon it's the damned heat and humidity. There's no escape from it – winter or summer, day or night, it's always the same!'

'You are full of good news, you are! Talk about cheering us up!'

'Sorry, Laura, didn't mean to be the bearer of bad

tidings. Say, where's your Greg?'

'Actually, I'm not too sure. I'm a bit worried about him to be honest. He was gone when I got up this morning and there's been no sign of him since.'

'Oh! Really? Well, didn't you say he was in Darwin the other day? Maybe he had to run in again and didn't want to wake you.'

'Oh, I'm sure its something simple like that. I just wish he had left me a note or something.'

'No chance that … Sorry, nothing.'

'What, Rob? You might as well say it as think it. What were you going to say?'

'Nah, it was stupid. I had forgotten that Joe is Greg's son, and I was going to ask if there was any chance that he might have done a runner. Not that any guy who ran away from you would have to be crazy. But, anyway, a stupid idea. Forget I said it.'

'That's OK, Rob. I'm just getting a bit worried about him, that's all. The four-wheel-drive is gone, so he must have driven somewhere. I suppose he must have gone into Darwin. That's the only explanation.'

'Yeah, he could have broken down on the road. The coverage for the mobile networks is hopeless, so he wouldn't be able to ring. And it might take a while for a car to pass him. But that road is busy enough, not like some of the roads in the remote outback. Don't worry, I'm sure he'll turn up in a while. Probably a bit sheepishly, no doubt.'

Laura was reassured by Rob's commonsense explanation. She relaxed a little and she asked him what he was up to for the rest of the day.

'Actually, I was going to take a drive over to the beach at the estuary of the Adelaide River. It's not too far and I have been told it's beautiful around there. Say, why don't you come along for the ride – the sea air will do young Joe good as well. It's bound to be a bit cooler on the coast than it is here.'

'Oh, it sounds lovely, Rob, but I think we had better wait here for Greg. I wouldn't want him to worry about where we were or what had happened to us if he came back and we weren't here.'

'Well, I can understand that, but I do think the kid would benefit from a bit of sea air. Why don't you leave a note for Greg saying where we've gone? I'll have you back in time for dinner.'

Laura knew that Greg would say that under no circumstances should she go off to some unknown remote place with Rob. He would say it was too risky, that maybe Rob was with the enemy after all, that anything could happen. He would say that she should lay low with Jopl, waiting for Greg, right here on this porch. But, right now, she was mad at Greg. He had disappeared without any explanation or warning, and she was spending her entire day worrying about him. To hell with it! She would leave him a note and she would bring Jopl for the drive with Rob. If Greg did come back before they got back, it might teach him a lesson, to let her know what was going on in future.

'OK, Rob. Give me a minute to write a note for Greg and leave it in our room. Jo—Joe, will you get those bottles of water from the cooler please?'

Laura left a note for Greg, checked she had sunhats and cream for herself and Jopl, and met Rob back on the porch. They walked around the front of the hostel to a four-wheel drive that Rob had rented, and set off with Laura in the passenger seat beside Rob, and Jopl safely ensconced in the back seat.

As they neared the beach, Rob dropped into four-wheel

drive and the vehicle clambered across the last piece of rough ground and onto the sand. They all got out, and Laura and Jopl revelled in the cool sea breeze blowing in from the Van Diemen Gulf as they started to stroll across the sand. Laura held Jopl's hand for the first few metres, but then he ran across the sand to the dunes. Laura again marvelled at the contradiction he presented – one moment he was the wisest person she had ever met, the next he was an ordinary little boy, taking delight in running up and down the dunes, falling, rolling, and then doing it all over again.

'Nice kid,' Rob commented.

'Yeah, he is pretty incredible,' Laura said.

'So, are you and Greg … I mean, is it … I guess what I am trying to say is, are you two, like …' Rob trailed off into an embarrassed silence.

'You mean, are we permanent? Is it serious? Are we likely to break up soon? I'm happy to say, Rob, that, yes, it's very serious. I think this is it. I think this is the real thing.'

'Ah,' sighed Rob with a look of regret.

'Oh, I'm sorry, Rob! I didn't mean to, to rub it in or anything. And what we had back in the Andes was beautiful, and I will always treasure that memory. And I am glad that we met here, like this, just to see you again, but, with Greg, it's the real thing. I hope to grow old with that man.'

'Well, I am glad you're happy, Laura. That is the important thing. Although, I guess I am just surprised that you would be with someone so much older than you – the guy must be twice your age. He is literally old enough to be your father.'

'I know, Rob. Believe me, nobody is more surprised than I am. But I guess you just can't pick when or where, or with whom, true love will strike. If it is OK with you, I think maybe we should change the subject.'

'Yeah, yeah, I guess you're right. I'm sorry, Laura, I hope I haven't upset you. I guess I'm just jealous – Greg is one lucky guy.'

Laura frowned. She wasn't annoyed, but the conversation couldn't really go anywhere or do either of them any good. Seeing her frown, Rob apologised again. 'Tell you what, I'll run back to the truck and get us a beer each. I have water in the cooler as well – I'll get one of those for Joe. While I am gone, you think of another topic of conversation, OK?'

Laura smiled. 'Yeah, a beer would be good. And Joe could certainly do with a water. He is running around like a greyhound, up and down those dunes.'

Rob turned and walked back towards the four-wheel drive which was now out of sight around a bend in the coastline. Laura called to Jopl, telling him to slow down a little and to come and get the water when Rob came back. Jopl ran over to her side, and fell into step beside her. She told him that Rob was going to get water for him, and that he was to take it easy. He would be even more dehydrated and ill the next morning if he kept racing around like a jackrabbit.

Laura walked away from the water's edge, intending to sit in the shade of the trees at the edge of the beach and wait for Rob there. Jopl sat with her and they rested together in companionable silence, as Laura looked out across the white sand and deep blue sea, admiring the beauty of the vista that Nature laid out in front of her. Suddenly, she heard a rustling in the bushes behind her. She turned, expecting to see a bird flying through the branches, but there was nothing. As she looked back out to the sea, she heard the rustling again. Laura's heart almost stopped with the fright – this was altogether too similar to what had happened in Koh

Samui. Then she wondered if it could possibly be Greg, as it had been on the island paradise.

Laura was determined not to frighten Jopl, so she tried to say Greg's name sufficiently loudly that, if he were there, he would be able to hear her. At the same time, she tried to say it conversationally, so that Jopl would not be alarmed. 'Oh Greg, Greg, Greg, where have you gotten to today. Oh, I wish you would just step out of the trees now and surprise us.'

Laura waited, but Greg didn't appear out of the foliage as she had hoped – a silly hope, she knew. Meanwhile, Jopl looked at her with a slightly amused look on his face, as though he knew exactly what she was doing, but didn't want to dishearten her by telling her that he too had heard the rustling.

Laura heard the rustling again. It was definitely closer this time. She decided to get up slowly and walk with Jopl back towards Rob. She would be ready to make a run for it if she had to and she knew that, if it came right down to it, she would try to stop any attacker so that Jopl could make it back to Rob. At least then he would get back to Humpty Doo and be reunited with Greg. Laura cursed herself for agreeing to come out here with Rob. She had really only done it to get back at Greg for disappearing, now she knew that it might turn out to have been a very serious error of judgement on her part - a very costly mistake.

Slowly, she stood up and put her hand out to Jopl to pull him up off the ground. Jopl reached up, took her hand, and stood beside her. She tried to turn and walk back the way they had come, but Jopl stood where he was, ignoring the pull of her hand.

'Jopl, come on, we need to go.'

No movement from the boy.

'Jopl. Now! We need to go right now. Come on, Jopl, walk with me.'

Laura pulled harder, but Jopl refuse to budge. He had his feet planted on the ground, and he looked as though it would take something an awful lot more powerful than Laura to make him move an inch.

'Jopl,' she whispered in a fierce undertone. 'What are you doing? There is something – or someone – in there. You must have heard it as well. We need to get out of here, back to Rob, back to the truck, now. Move it, Mister, right this second.'

Jopl looked at her, with that look of forbearance that parents reserve for their children when they know that the child is simply too young to understand - when they know that the child is not being intentionally naughty, but that their undesirable action is simply the result of an inevitable lack of understanding on the part of the child, in a situation that is beyond a child's comprehension.

'Laura. It is OK. You have no reason to be afraid.'

'What? Jopl, what are you talking about? Do you know who is in there – or what is in there? What is it, Jopl? What is going on?'

'Sometimes, Fate takes a hand Laura. You should understand that by now. She has come to help us.'

'Who, Jopl? Who has come to help us?'

'Her.'

Jopl pointed, and a young Aboriginal girl walked out of the bushes. She looked about twelve years old, though a small twelve. Her hair was shoulder length and wavy, almost dark enough to be black. Her skin was dark, much darker than the Aboriginals that Laura had seen around Humpty Doo. She wore only a pair of shorts – no top and no shoes. Her eyes were large and round, with irises that seemed to be as black as the pupils. She was a beautiful child, and Laura felt she could relax a little – this little girl could not be a threat.

Laura wondered what the girl wanted, and waited for her to speak, but, for a moment, the girl simply stood and watched them both, not moving. Laura knew very little about the Aboriginals and she wondered if the girl spoke English. 'Hello,' Laura said tentatively, not wanting to startle the young girl.

The girl walked over to Laura and took her hand. Laura jumped a little – she didn't want to frighten the girl, but she wasn't comfortable with physical contact either. She didn't know anything about this girl. She wasn't sure what was safe and what was not. She gently tried to disengage her hand, but the girl held onto her. Finally, she spoke.

'Come, the spirits have sent me to bring you home.'

Now, Laura was worried, very worried. Was the kid crazy or something? What was she talking about? Laura didn't know whether to be scared that the child was mentally unstable, or suspicious that this might be the preamble to some scam that the local people ran on unsuspecting tourists. While Laura tried to think of how best to manage the situation, Jopl took the initiative away from her. He kneeled in front of the girl and spoke to her. 'Thank you, Sister. I knew you when you watched us in Humpty Doo. The time is right.' With that, he stood in front of the girl.

Laura was dumbstruck. What was going on? Jopl seemed to be saying that the girl had been watching them in Humpty Doo, and that, somehow, he knew her. Laura gathered from the way he said it that he didn't mean that he had met the girl previously, or that he knew her personally. Something about the way he spoke conveyed a feeling that he knew her in the sense that one might recognise a kindred spirit.

This time the girl addressed Jopl, seeming to decide that he was the authority figure, not Laura. 'I have come to be your guide. You need assistance. You are moving in the wrong direction. You must change your path, for danger awaits you.'

'Thank you, Sister. I appreciate and accept your offer to be our guide. I have felt uneasy about our path, but I did not know what course to change to. If you will do us the honour of showing us the way, we will gratefully follow in your footsteps.'

The girl turned and walked off with her back to the sea, heading straight into the undergrowth and was almost immediately lost to view. Jopl followed, while Laura stood rooted to the spot with surprise, or shock. She couldn't believe what was happening. A strange girl appears from nowhere, Jopl says he knows her, and then they have a cryptic conversation about what is the best path to be on. And now the girl was disappearing into God knows where and, even more unbelievably, Jopl seemed prepared to follow her. Craziness! Madness! Insanity!

With a start, Laura realised that Jopl was about to disappear as well. In a daze, she ran after him. She would grab him, get back to the beach, find Rob and get the hell out of there back to Humpty Doo where Greg would be waiting for them. He would be mad at her for sure, and right now she couldn't blame him. She would apologise, admit that she had been wrong to go with Rob, and the next day they would go to Darwin, get their new passports and fly home.

A Different World

A Different World

Laura ran after Jopl, who was following the girl. She had the weirdest sensation. She was racing through the undergrowth after Jopl, and he simply walked on steadily; yet she was unable to catch up on him. The distance between them seemed to be decreasing, yet she remained a constant distance behind him. Strangest of all was that Laura was vaguely aware of this anomaly, and yet seemed unable to focus sufficiently on the incongruity of it to be able to worry about it properly.

She continued to race after Jopl as fast as she could, and yet she felt as though she was walking at the same pace as he was. Again, she was conscious of the abnormality of this sensation in an indistinct kind of way, but whenever she tried to think about it or concentrate on it; the feeling would slip away like a dream. Occasionally, she could get a glimpse of the girl walking a few metres in front of him, while at other times she would be totally lost to view. Jopl had obviously put his trust and faith in this girl for some unknown reason, and he was clearly determined to follow her wherever she might lead them. Laura wasn't sure if he was unconcerned about whether or not she followed as well; or whether he was working on the assumption that she would stay with him.

Suddenly, Laura realised that they had been walking for many minutes, and she looked back to check that she could still hold her bearings back to the beach. With a shock, she realised that she could see nothing but the low bushes in all directions. There was no sign of the sea, no indication of which direction it lay in. Laura knew that her sense of direction was unreliable – she wasn't even sure if she was walking or running, let alone what direction they had come from. She listened carefully, hoping to be able to hear the noise of the surf so that she could get a fix on where the beach was.

She could hear nothing at all at first. Gradually, she became aware of a sound, made faint by distance. She knew that she should be able to recognise it, she knew that it was familiar, but she couldn't place it. Concentrating took a supreme effort of will power, but Laura was determined not to fail. She set herself the task of recognising this sound. She engaged every sense, focused every fibre of her being, directed all of her thought towards the sound. Then, she remembered.

Again, Laura was conscious that there was something very surreal going on, that she should have been able to place that sound immediately, but she just couldn't hold onto the fact that she was undergoing a bizarre experience. The thought crossed her mind that maybe she was hallucinating, and then the thought evaporated, leaving no trace behind. At least she had been able to identify the sound – it was a human voice. A man's voice. Rob's voice. He was shouting. Shouting, 'Joe.' Shouting her name. Why was he calling for her? Why was his voice so angry, so distressed, so desperate?

He seemed to be very upset that he could not find her. More than that, he seemed to be focusing his calling on Joe. Laura had told Rob that Jopl's name was actually Joe for a reason – to stop Rob from asking questions about Jopl. Because she did not want Rob to know who Jopl was. She had to protect Jopl from Rob. As this thought clicked into place, Laura clamped her mouth shut. She had been about to call out, to try to get Rob to find her so that together they could get Jopl and escape from this peculiar nightmare. But she knew now that she could not call Rob, that to do so would put Jopl in danger.

Listening to the anger in Rob's voice, she suddenly knew that Rob must have had his own plans, his own agenda. He was not as innocent as he had appeared! His presence here was not a coincidence! His voice was not the worried voice of someone who is concerned for a friend who seems to have gone missing. His was the angry voice of someone who has had some great prize taken from his reach, just as he was about to grasp it. It had to be Jopl. Rob had to be after Jopl. Once that realisation hit Laura, she knew that the last thing she could do was to draw Rob's attention. Instead of shouting to him to attract his notice, she crept away from the sound of his far-off voice, following after Jopl, who she could still see in the distance in front of her.

As she continued to chase Jopl, trying not to make noise so that Rob wouldn't be able to hear her, she became conscious that Rob's voice was fading into the distance. After another few minutes, she could no longer hear him at all. She moved into a steady pace to try to catch Jopl. As before, she felt she was closing the distance all of the time, yet the distance stayed constant. She could still catch an occasional glimpse of the girl in front of Jopl, though such brief sightings were rare and short-lived. She lost track of time, not sure if they had been on the move for minutes or hours. Thoughts would occur to her at times, sometimes thoughts that should have worried her, such as the lack of water. But each time the thought occurred, it would as quickly dissipate into an insubstantial mist and fade, leaving not even the faintest impression on her mind.

Eventually, an idea did occur to her, which seemed more solid. She was able to hold on to this idea, give it attention, consider it carefully, albeit slowly. The thought was that they were now a long distance into some very inhospitable terrain. She had read the stories of the early convicts who escaped into the bush, only to die and have their remains discovered years later. She had heard the stories of the early explorers, many of whose lives had been claimed by the unforgiving character and personality of the continent's environment. Not only her life, but, much more importantly Jopl's life, might well be at the mercy of this Aboriginal girl. They would have to follow her and rely on her for survival. If they were left without the girl, they might well die in this harsh and inhospitable landscape.

As Laura was considering this frightening possibility, and wondering what she should do about it, she noticed that Jopl had stopped walking. Looking ahead, Laura could see that the girl had stopped too, and was now standing beside Jopl. Both of them were standing still, looking back at Laura. She was almost afraid to approach them, which struck her as a bit ridiculous, given that she had spent all of this time trying to catch up with them. Strengthened and encouraged by this thought, Laura walked up to the two children, prepared to lay down the law and insist that the girl take them back to the beach.

Before she could speak, the girl addressed her, as though they were in the middle of a conversation. 'No, it is not. You are wrong. This is not a "harsh and inhospitable landscape". Unlike you in your world, my world loves me and supports me and will always provide for me. Do not assume that just because your world does not care for you that my world will not care for me. It does. It loves me and will always protect me and try to save me from harm.'

The girl spoke fiercely, as though Laura had ridiculed and belittled something very close to the girl's heart. She seemed hurt and shocked that Laura had called her world into question, bewildered as though Laura had committed some unimaginable blasphemy. Moved by the girl's obvious upset, Laura tried to explain that she had not meant any harm.

'I'm sorry, I didn't mean to insult you. Please, if I have said something wrong ...' the thought briefly crossed Laura's mind that she hadn't actually said anything – she had been thinking to herself about dying in this harsh land, but the thought failed to gain any traction in her mind and disappeared as quickly as it had arisen '... I didn't mean to offend you. If you say that this land, your land, cares for you, then I am sure it does. It's just that I am not familiar with this land. I am not sure that it would be able to protect me, even if it wanted to.'

The girl appeared somewhat mollified by Laura's concern and contrition.

'I am sorry, Miss. I should not have been angry. You are correct. It is simply that you do not know this land. But I tell you, this land, while unforgiving of fools and demanding hard effort of its peoples, this land will provide. This land will care for us and nurture us as we travel. Please do not worry. No harm will come to you while you travel with me.'

The girl paused, apparently trying to gauge Laura's reaction. Not sure what to say, Laura muttered a reply. 'It's OK. Don't worry about it.'

Laura looked around, thinking again that this was the first time they had stopped in ... she wasn't sure. How long they had been travelling? The girl seemed more amenable to conversation now, and didn't seem in any great rush to move off again, so Laura decided to try to find out what was going on.

'How far have we walked?'

'We have walked many cycles. You would call it almost five hundred kilometres.'

'Five hundred kilometres! That's impossible!'

'We have walked almost five hundred kilometres. We have walked at a constant pace for three days. When you needed it, I gave you garliwirri to chew on. Garliwirri gives us the ability to go for a long time without stopping, without sleeping. You do not feel the tiredness, you do not feel the pain. But now it is time to stop and rest, to sleep and to eat.'

With that, the girl instructed Laura and Jopl to sit, saying that she was going to get food for them, and she disappeared. With the girl gone, Laura turned on Jopl.

'Jopl, what the hell is going on? Who is that girl? What did you mean when you said that you knew her? And did you say that she had been watching us, spying on us, in Humpty Doo? Where the hell are we? What's going on?'

Distraught, Laura buried her head in her arms and the floodgates opened. All of the stress and worry and anxiety, all of the exhaustion and pain and hunger and thirst; all of it came rolling out in an upheaval of sobbing. Remarkably quickly, the torrent subsided, and Laura straightened, wiping her nose on the back of her hand like a child herself. Through all of this, Jopl had looked at her with compassion and love, with sympathy and understanding, and waited for her to be ready before he spoke.

'Laura. I have told you that I believe that there is more to our world than just the physical universe. I believe that this girl's arrival is part of that. I am not sure who she is, where she has come from, or where she is taking us. But I have felt since I joined you that there was something wrong. I was unable to gain sufficient understanding of my new environment and the people in it to be able to identify what the problem was. However, my feeling is that this girl is the solution to that problem. I believe that we need to place our trust in her and join with her. I sense that if we do, that this is the best course for us to follow.'

'Jopl, it just all seems so, so outlandish. I mean, it's bloody weird. But I do have to accept that Greg seemed to disappear – I'm wondering now if Rob did something to him. And when we were leaving the beach I heard Rob hunting us and he sounded desperate – I think he was chasing us, or chasing you, after all.'

'I have to tell you Laura that this is certainly possible, but I do not get the feeling that what you have said is correct. I do not know why this is, and I cannot say for definite that it is not correct. I can only caution you to be careful and not to put too much emphasis on that possibility.'

'At this stage, I don't know what to think. But I have to accept that everything seems to have gone wrong – Greg has vanished, Rob 'may be' chasing us. So if you feel that this is what we should do, then I am willing to put my faith in your judgement. We probably don't have much choice in any case, because there is no way we can get out of here without her help anyway.'

They talked about what was happening, but Laura was at a total loss, and Jopl couldn't be specific about why he felt that this was the right thing to do. As they mulled it over, the only conclusion they could draw was that while Jopl felt they should stay with the girl because it was the right thing to do, and Laura felt that they had to stay with her because they could die out here without her; in either case, for whichever reason, they had to stick with her. As they reached this conclusion, and decided that they would just have to trust the girl to lead them to safety, the girl herself returned.

She was laden down, both her arms piled high with sticks and food. Not speaking to Laura or Jopl, the girl placed her load on the ground and proceeded to build a little tower of dried kangaroo dung. Then she took a long stick, splitting the end of it with a knife she took from the waistband of her shorts. She used small sticks to hold the crack open, and stuffed it with the kangaroo dung. Then she proceeded to briskly rub another stick across the first one, just at the top of the crack and at the edge of the dung. Her hand whipped back and forth, a blur of movement. After only thirty seconds or so, as if by magic, a little smoke started to curl upwards. The girl knelt forward, blew gently, and a small flame materialised. She added dry grass to the flickering flame, and then twigs and small branches. Within a few minutes, there was a blazing fire jumping skywards.

The girl then produced a surprising quantity of food, although some of it was not what Laura would normally have considered to be food. There were nuts and berries, which the girl said were riberries, and leaves, which the girl called warrigal. In addition, there were ants with swollen golden abdomens that the girl said were the sweetest food on earth, and three-inch long white grubs that the girl proudly said were witchetty grubs. She roasted the grubs on the fire, and everything else was eaten raw. They ate heartily, Laura amazing herself by eating food that previously would have left her retching. But now she savoured every morsel, from the tasty nuts to the luscious grubs. When they had eaten, the girl asked them to lie down and rest. Dusk was coming on, and Laura now started to feel the after-effects of the three days of continuous walking. She felt the exhaustion starting to roll in on top of her in waves, and she could see that Jopl was dropping into a deep slumber as well. Laura surrendered to the warm embrace of sleep, and slid into an ocean of peace and quiet, where the waves gently whispered soothing sounds to her as they rocked her tenderly in their soft lullaby. She fell into a dreamless gathering, where worlds crossed and all that she had known was taken apart and put back together again.

As Laura awoke, she savoured the fabulous sensation of waking from a deep sleep, knowing that she was well rested. The girl sat beside them, and the sun was high in the sky.

'How long have we slept?'

'The sun has crossed the sky and is now on its homeward journey. You have slept three-fourths of a day.'

It took Laura a moment to work that out in her head – eighteen hours! No wonder she felt so refreshed, and also so hungry and thirsty. She leaned forward to a stream running past her feet, with the thought occurring to her that the stream hadn't been there the previous evening. She decided that she was simply going to have to accept some things in this world that she would not have previously thought possible, and she drank deeply. It was the most delicious drink she had ever tasted – cold, clear and sharp, with a slight tingling as though the water was ever so slightly effervescent.

As Jopl woke and drank from the stream, the girl held out broad palm leaves to them, with food for them to eat, mostly nuts and berries. As they ate, Laura questioned the girl. 'Do you mind if I ask you your name?'

'My name is Imno.'

'Imno. Thank you for the food.' Laura decided to start the conversation gently, casually, trying not to offend or frighten this young girl, on whom their lives now depended.

'You need to eat. We have a long way to walk.'

'Ah. Yes. Erm, where exactly are we, Imno?'

'We are three days walk from where we started, towards

the heart of my country.'

Laura wondered what exactly the girl meant. She had said they had walked five hundred kilometres in that first three days. If that were true, what did 'towards the heart of my country' mean?

'The heart of your country. I'm sorry, Imno, I am not sure what that means.'

'You will see. When we reach the heart, you will see.'

'But what is the heart, Imno? Or where is it?'

'The heart is the heart. The ...' Laura could see that Imno was struggling, before continuing '... where everything began, where all things have their root. That is the heart.'

Laura realised the girl's frame of reference was so different to her own that Imno was not going to be able to explain this heart in any sense that Laura could understand.

'OK, Imno, OK. How long will it take us to reach the, the heart?'

'It will take a number of days, but not as much as one cycle of the moon.'

Laura assumed 'cycle of the moon' meant a month. So they were going to be more than a day and less than a month. Laura was not reassured.

'Imno, I am not sure that Jopl and I will be able to walk for that long. I am not used to walking long distances.'

This was not strictly true, as Laura had mountain-walked and hiked some very long distances during her travels around the globe. However, she suspected that this was going to be much more than anything she had done previously. Even more than herself, she was worried about Jopl. He seemed healthy so far, but Laura wasn't sure how long he would be able to keep going if Imno expected them to walk continuously day after day.

Imno however laughed gently at the idea, seeming to find it amusing that someone might not be able to walk as far and as long as she did. 'You will be able to walk all the walking that is needed,' she smiled. 'I told you that my world will look after you. The paste on your feet has already healed and hardened them.'

Laura looked down at her feet, and wondered how she had not noticed the paste on them before. Imno must have put it on as she slept. It was a thick whitish paste with green streaks through it. Laura had to admit to herself that her feet felt better than they had in a long time. She allowed herself the first glimmer of hope that maybe Jopl was right – maybe this was all for the best - and maybe the girl was saving them, rather than possibly leaving them to die somewhere in this formidable country as Laura feared.

Before long, Imno had them on their feet and moving once more. Laura was now conscious of time and distance, and marvelled at how they seemed to cover the ground. They walked all the time, alternating between a brisk power-walking pace and a slower walk, just a bit quicker than a stroll. Occasionally, at what Laura guessed were intervals of maybe an hour or so, they would stop and Imno would give them a drink from a hide bag that she carried. Every fourth stop or so they would have something small to eat – usually nuts, berries or more of the warrigal leaves - a green succulent plant that reminded Laura of a leathery spinach. At night, Imno would make a fire, disappear, and return with a selection of food. She would then feed Jopl and Laura as though they were guests in her home. Then they would lie down and fall quickly into a dreamless sleep before awaking and repeating the process the next day.

As the days passed, Laura started to understand that she had entered a world different to her own. A world into which so-called civilisation had made no intrusion, had no impact. Laura observed the girl apparently divining food and drink from nowhere, and indeed sometimes the land itself seemed to mould and shape itself to the girl's needs. At one time, she was describing kangaroos to Jopl, who, for once, seemed at a loss. She said 'watch', and a herd of kangaroo seemed to rise from the ground in front of them, bounce past, and disappear into the ground behind them.

As they walked and as they ate their evening meals, Imno spoke to Laura and Jopl of the beliefs and practices of her people. Through these conversations, Laura learned that the Aboriginals had a fundamentally different view of reality than the 'civilised' societies of the modern world. For the Aboriginals, life was merely an interruption of their eternal existence, they believed that each person had a part of their internal nature that was eternal, and that this eternal being pre-existed the life of the individual here on earth, and at death melted back into the eternal life. This concept was closely related to the concept of Dreamtime – the single rock of belief upon which all Aboriginal tribes agreed and depended. In Dreamtime, four aspects of life co-existed simultaneously and unendingly, these being the beginning of life, their ancestors, life and death and the sources of power in life.

It was through this belief that Imno explained how she came to help Laura and Jopl – she saw nothing unusual in appearing just when they needed her and knowing how to help them. For Imno, she had entered Dreamtime, where past, present and future co-existed simultaneously. In Dreamtime, all things could be known if one was sufficiently aware. In seeing the past, present and future; in communing with ones ancestors, answers came unbidden. In Dreamtime, the limitations of space and time were overcome, as reality moved from Laura's perception of a discrete passage of events in time, to past, present and future being accessible simultaneously.

Homeward Once More

As the days passed, the landscape became ever more barren and desert-like. Laura lost exact count of the days, but she thought they had been walking for about ten or eleven days, plus the initial three, when they saw the first sign of civilisation other than the roads they had crossed. Imno said that they were walking about one hundred kilometres a day, so Laura thought they must have walked about one and a half thousand kilometres since leaving the beach two weeks previously. She knew that they must have crossed roads and perhaps even seen other signs of civilisation during the first three days, but she hadn't been conscious of them while under the effects of the garliwirri. But in the ten or eleven days since then, even roads had been scarce. They hadn't seen a road other than an occasional track in the dust for the first five or six days. Then they had crossed a deserted blacktop road, and two days after that had crossed a dirt track that showed signs of wheeled traffic, even though it too was deserted when they crossed it.

Since morning they had been able to see a reddish bump on the horizon growing steadily larger, as they walked towards it on a course as direct as a flying arrow. With a shock of recognition, Laura realised that she knew this mountain – it was one of the most iconic images of Australia! 'Imno. Is that Ayer's Rock?'

'No!' Imno's answer was sharp and curt. But there was something about the response that made Laura think that maybe it was not a simple negative. She knew that Ayers Rock had another name that the Aboriginal peoples used and she was racking her brain, trying to think of what it was.

'Imno, is that the heart of your country?'

'Yes.' Anther short answer, but this time bursting with pride and love and anticipation.

'Imno, is it called Uluru?'

'That is one of its names.'

Laura gasped. So it was Ayers Rock, but Imno obviously denied that name for this most sacred of Aboriginal sites. Laura knew from her conversations with Imno that the Aboriginal people believed that there was a hollow space beneath Uluru containing an energy source which they called Tjukurpa. Many of the geographical features on and around Uluru were believed by the Aboriginals to be the remnants of events in the past where people or animals formed the present-day landscape.

As they get closer, Laura could see glinting sparks moving along the horizon. With another shock of recognition, she realised that what she was seeing was the sunlight reflecting off car windows as they sped to and from Uluru.

'Imno, where exactly are you taking us?'

'There' the girl said, pointing into the distance. Laura shaded her eyes from the sun, and could make out what looked like some sort of tower and a couple of low buildings. As they walked, now at a slight angle from the straight line they had been following to Uluru, Laura saw a small aeroplane lift off from the place that they were walking towards and realised that it was an airfield. As they got closer, she could make out the fence and the runway, and could see that what she had thought was some sort of tower was the air traffic control tower.

They came to the edge of a paved road that went straight on to the airfield, and Imno stopped. Laura got quite a shock at the break from routine, as it was only twenty or thirty minutes since they last stopped to drink.

'This is as far as I can bring you. You must go there,' Imno said, pointing to the airfield, 'and fly away. Everything you need is in locker thirty-two.' She stumbled over the unfamiliar word 'locker', but it was clear to Laura that she and Jopl were to go to the airfield without her, and apparently there was something for them in a locker.

'But … but, Imno. Will we see you again? Where will you go?'

'We may meet again. I do not know. That is in the future. The future is an illusion. Only the present exists. I go home now. I am tired.'

With that, she simply turned, and started walking back into the desert in the direction that they had come from. Jopl bowed as Imno waked away, and then turned to face the airfield, waiting for Laura. Laura was shaken by Imno's abrupt departure, and turned to Jopl.

'So that's it? Just like that, she's gone? Don't you care?'

'The time has passed for Imno to be with us. This is a new time. It is as it should be.'

And with that, Laura knew that a chapter of her life had closed. She felt she understood the Aboriginal people so much better. She knew of their beliefs, she marvelled at their incredible connection to nature, she understood the challenges they faced in a so-called civilised society. And now the girl who had taught her these things, who had appeared into her life in an instant on the northern coastline, was disappearing almost as instantly into the heart of the continent.

As Imno seemed to evaporate into the desert air, slowly vanishing from sight, Laura started to cry a little from the sadness of parting. But then she felt Imno inside her head, telling her not to be afraid of the future, nor regret the past –

that both are illusions, and have no impact on your life unless you give them that power. We need to live in the present. Somehow, Laura knew that Imno was right. It was as it should be. Feeling that all was right with the world, while understanding that new challenges lay ahead, Laura turned to face the airfield with Jopl and together, hand in hand, they walked the final leg of this marathon.

Laura and Jopl walked the final mile or two into the airfield, and paused while considering their next move. Imno had said that everything they needed was in locker thirty-two. Laura wondered what kind of locker she was referring to; or had the girl meant hanger thirty-two, although there were only three hangers that Laura could see, so that seemed unlikely. Thinking that the most likely place to start was the area that the general public had access to, Laura headed for the arrivals and departures terminal with Jopl in tow, and they walked into the cool interior.

While Laura wondered where to start, and indeed what she was looking for, Jopl simply spoke to a security guard inside the door. 'Excuse me, Sir. Where are the lockers?'

Laura shrank back from the guard, horrified that Jopl had called attention to himself so blatantly, and with a security guard of all people. But the guard just answered disinterestedly, 'Over there', waving towards the far left-hand corner of the austere terminal. Laura looked in the direction of the wave, and saw a 'Left Luggage' sign. She and Jopl walked over, to find three banks of lockers. The lockers were large, each one big enough to hold a bulky suitcase and more. Laura found number thirty-two and stood in front of the locker, wondering how she was going to open it. Jopl reached up, grabbed the handle, and opened it - it hadn't been locked!

Inside were two medium-size suitcases and a handbag.

Laura pulled out the suitcases and opened them. One was obviously for her and the other for Jopl. Each one contained a couple of changes of clothes, and it looked as though the sizes were about right for herself and Jopl. There was also a bag of toiletries in each, with all of the essentials, and a pair of shoes. Laura stared into the two bags, flabbergasted that all of this should be here. Things had been very weird and outlandish while they were with Imno, but this was getting curiouser and curiouser, to quote a favourite book of Laura's childhood. And indeed, at the moment, she felt like Alice, in a world where the old rules no longer applied.

Laura next opened the handbag, only to find what looked like two perfect passports for herself and Jopl, in the names of Mary and John Carney – they were obviously to travel as mother and child. There was also a printout of an itinerary with the heading 'eTicket' – apparently a valid ticket for air flights. Laura scanned it – they were due to fly to Kalgoorlie later that night, then straight on to Perth before changing planes to fly to New York via Hawaii, with a final leg from New York to South Carolina. The only other contents of the bag were a driver's licence, a credit card and a social security card, all in the name of Mary Carney; and some Australian and American cash.

She was stunned by the contents of the bags, wondering who had put them there, and why, and how they had been able to get passports that looked perfectly genuine and valid. When she thought about it, she realised that this was probably no stranger than everything that had happened to her in the past two weeks. She resolved to use what they had as best they could. She gave Jopl his suitcase, instructing him to go into the bathroom and wash and change his clothes. She told him to dump the clothes that he had on into the bin in the bathroom, as they were ragged and dirty after their two-week hike across the desolate outback. Laura went into the ladies bathroom and did the same, emerging like a different woman. She laughed when she saw Jopl, as he had undergone a similar transformation, from wild bush-boy to elegant young gentleman.

They went to the café and had a meal, while Laura watched the check-in and security procedures at the small airfield, which seemed quite relaxed. When a group of noisy travellers came into the terminal to catch their flight, Laura decided to move while the boisterous crowd could provide something of a distraction. Taking Jopl's hand and their suitcases, she walked up to the check-in desk and handed over her ticket and the two passports. The process was as monotonous and unexciting as always, much to Laura's relief. With their bags checked in, and boarding passes in hand, they moved to the next hurdle – the security check. Laura put her handbag through the x-ray scanning machine, and she and Jopl walked through the x-ray portal. Laura half-expected alarm sirens to start screaming, and an army of guards to descend on them, but, again, it was just another tedious security check, no different from any other check she had been through at other airports around the world.

They moved into the Departures area with an hour to spare before their flight. Laura found a payphone and rang Directory Enquiries to get the number of the hostel that they had stayed at in Humpty Doo. When she got through to them, she asked if she could speak to Greg, only to be told that the American family had checked out two weeks previously. Laura put down the phone, unsure what this could mean. Greg had disappeared for most of the day before she went off with Rob, and it was now weeks since she and Jopl had followed Imno in to the bush. Who could have checked them out? Had Greg reappeared, and if so, where was he now? She had no way of contacting him – she kicked herself for not agreeing some strategy for being able to find each other if they got split up.

Knowing that there was nothing she could do about her lover right now, Laura rejoined Jopl. They sat near the gate that their flight was leaving from and watched as more people joined them. When the call came to board, Laura again became tense, wondering if this was when they were going to be captured. But, again, it was a normal boarding routine and, before they knew it, they were seated on the aircraft waiting for take-off. Twenty minutes later, they were in the air and Laura felt that she could relax for a while at least. At Kalgoorlie, the plane landed, some people left, others joined, and they were quickly airborne again and headed for Perth.

Laura woke to the smell of food, and realised she was hungry again as the cabin crew came around with a hot meal. She woke Jopl, and they started to eat. 'I'm afraid it's not up to the standard that you were used to in the temple, Jopl' Laura said with a smile.

'It is not up to the standard of the grubs and shoots that Imno cooked in the fire for us,' Jopl said, laughing.

Laura chuckled with him, happy that he could still joke and laugh. They ate the bland food and Laura thought about all that had happened, and what was going to happen next.

'So Jopl, when we get to Columbia tomorrow, are you at last going to tell me who I am supposed to deliver you to?'

'You are to bring me safely to Professor Symington of Columbia University.'

Laura stared at him.

'You know, I don't know what I was expecting. I think part of me somehow hoped that once we got home, it would all be over. So there really is someone that you have to go to, huh?'

'Yes.'

'And who is this Professor Symington?'

'He was a very close friend of your father, and he is working with a group of people to try to correct a blight that has been visited upon the world for decades. For the moment, I can tell you no more than that.'

'Oh, OK. And what is this information that you are bringing to him?'

'For the moment, I can tell you no more than that.'

'Oh! Right.'

Laura thought that Jopl was almost automaton-like in the way he responded to queries about this dammed information. Whatever it was, thought Laura, it had better be worth everything that she had gone through. Thinking of that, Laura started to think about how she would make contact with the professor once they got to Columbia. Given everything that had happened, an open move was probably out of the question. She would have to find some clandestine way of approaching the man. As she tried to think ahead and plan what she would do, the parting words of Imno popped into her head. Puzzled, Laura turned to Jopl. 'Jopl, do you remember the last thing that Imno said when she was leaving us?'

'She said "We may meet again. I do not know. That is in the future. The future is an illusion. Only the present exists. I go home now. I am tired", and then she walked away.'

'Yes, that was it. What do you think she meant when she said that the future is an illusion, and that only the present exists? What was she talking about?'

'Ah, yes. She was simply stating a fact. The past and the future are illusions, they do not exist. The only thing that exists is the present – the present is all that matters. People should not worry about the past or the future, because they are no more substantial than myth and legend. Do not be afraid of the past or the future, for they have no power over you, unless of course you grant them power over you. The present is the only reality. Therefore you must live in the present, not in the past or the future.'

'Now hold on a minute! I know that you say some very strange things, often that turn out to be correct; but this is a really crazy one. Of course the past and the future are real. We really did make that walk with Imno, and I really am going to bring you to see this professor guy.'

'Yes, we did walk with Imno, but, right now, at this moment in time, we are not. And we never will relive that walk, even if we meet Imno again. This is what I mean, what Imno meant. The problem is that people live in the past, or they live in the future. But you can only ever really live in the present. The present is the only tense that can ever be truly real – it is the only time that you can actually experience, and the only time that you can actually affect or impact or change. What Imno meant was that when you have something to do, then do it. There is no point yearning for the past, or worrying about the future. If you live truly in the present, then the future will look after itself.'

'But how can that be? For example, I have to decide how to get you to Professor Symington, which is in the future. Surely, I have to think about that and plan for it. Doesn't that mean that I am living in the future while I make those plans?'

'No, it does not have to. When you have to make a decision, gather as much knowledge as you can, apply a mix of heart and reason, and make your decision. Then go forward, continuing to live in the present, and the future will take care of itself.'

As he spoke, the captain addressed his passengers over the intercom, telling them that the plane would shortly be starting its descent towards Hawaii. Laura told Jopl about Hawaii, which she had visited a number of times. He was a little disappointed that they would not get to even leave the plane as it refuelled and moved on to New York. As they left Hawaii, Laura showed Jopl how to use the controls to view a movie, and left him engrossed in the antics of a group of animated penguins. Eventually, they landed at New York.

As she had on a number of occasions before, Laura approached Immigration in the airport, although this time with Jopl beside her. However, as she got closer to the wall of immigration desks, she started to notice that there were some differences compared to previous times. The first thing that she noticed was the length of the queues – she had seen them getting very long on other visits, but nothing as bad as this. She heard a group of businessman in the queue next to her grumbling about the delays, and one of them mentioned something about 'extra security checks' because of some unspecified 'security alert'. She started to worry when she realised that there two immigration officers at each desk instead of the normal one per desk. There must be something very serious going on, for the Office of Homeland Security to double its staffing.

Laura started to panic started when she glimpsed a photo on the desk in front of her when she was standing at the yellow line with Jopl, waiting to be called forward. It was her! Laura nearly fainted, and was brought to attention by a quick squeeze of her hand from Jopl. Looking at the photo while trying to appear as though she was idly looking around, Laura read 'Travelling with unidentified man and child', in big bold writing, but she was unable to make out the text below that.

She knew now that all of this extra security was in place in order to net her as she came back into the country. The photo was an old one of her with her long blonde hair; which was now dark and tied up in a bun. Laura wondered if the combination of her disguise, and the passports for herself and Jopl, would be enough to prevent her from being recognised. She thought it was a good thing that they were looking for a party of three – again, that should help to deflect attention away from her. And in any event, she thought, she was next in line to be called, so there was no going back now – no escape from the scrutiny.

Thinking quickly, Laura told Jopl to untie the lace on one of his sneakers, which he did with a puzzled face. When she was called up to the desk, Laura handed over the two passports, and immediately turned to Jopl, saying to him in an exasperated voice 'Oh, John, how many times do I have to tell you? Tie your lace before you trip over and hurt yourself. Come on now – dad is waiting to see his little man. You want to impress him with how much you've grown during your holiday, don't you?'

She turned back to the lady who was looking at her passport, with an apologetic smile as if to say 'Kids!' The lady smiled back sympathetically, before handing the passports over to the officer beside her.

'Never a moment's peace with them, eh?' the female officer said to Laura with a smile, nodding in Jopl's direction.

'You've got that right! I just can't wait until I can hand him to his dad, so that I can put my feet up and get a few minutes peace,' Laura replied, seeming to share, as all parents do, the occasional frustrations that are an inevitable part of parenting.

As their little exchange continued, the male immigration officer stamped the two passports and handed them back to Laura with a casual, 'Thank You, Mrs Carney.' Laura could see that he was already looking behind her at the next person to be called forward. Laura smiled at the lady one last time, and then went through the gate with Jopl in tow, his hand firmly captured in hers.

Within a few hours they were safely on board the flight to Columbia, on the last leg of their journey. Still Laura wondered and worried about Greg, but taking Jopl's advice about living in the present, she resolved to focus first on keeping Jopl safe and getting him to the professor. Then she would try to find some way to make contact with the man who now meant so much to her.

The Professor

As the plane landed, Laura and Jopl gathered their few belongings and prepared to disembark. As the passengers started to file off the plane wearily, Laura and Jopl walked with the crowd, through the sky-ramp and into the arrivals hall. Having been through the airport many times, Laura started walking towards the baggage reclaim area. As she walked along with Jopl, she could see that even this smaller airport had an increased security presence. Laura kicked herself for not having thought of it before – if they were searching for her as she entered the country, they would also be watching for her here, at her home airport.

As they entered the baggage reclaim area, Laura made a snap decision. She remembered a piece of advice that her darling Greg had given her when they had travelled from Koh Samui back up to Bangkok. He said that you should always try to guess what the enemy will expect you to do, and then do the opposite. Thinking of this, and thinking of where she was standing, Laura thought that they would certainly expect her to have baggage if she arrived in to Columbia airport, since they had last seen her in Bangkok, or possibly Australia if Rob had worked for them. She thought about the two suitcases – all that was in them were some clothes – there was nothing that could identify her or Jopl, either under their real names or their assumed names. All of the paperwork that they needed was in her handbag. Taking all of that into account, Laura decided on impulse to leave the bags and not collect them. The less time she spent in the airport, the better.

As they walked out of the airport, Laura was acutely

aware that she was now entering what might be the most perilous part of this whole operation. She had enjoyed periods of relative calm in the last month, both on Captain Smith's cargo ship and walking through the Outback with Imno. The increased security presence at the airports indicated the lengths to which her pursuers were willing to go. They couldn't possibly know that she was heading home to South Carolina, as only she, Greg and Jopl had known that. Yet they had vastly increased the resources dedicated to watching travellers coming into the United States, just on the chance that she might turn up.

Laura caught a taxi to Heathwood, then changed to another taxi which she asked to drive to Winchester, before finally switching to a third taxi. She asked the final driver to bring them to the Columbia Place Mall, one of South Carolina's largest shopping malls. She told the driver that her husband was a mean drunk and that she was leaving him, and asked him to see if he could detect anyone following them. The driver drove a circuitous route to the mall, taking a lot of unnecessary turns and sometimes doubling back on his tracks. Declaring himself satisfied that 'that no-good husband of yours' was not following them, he left them safely outside the mall, and refused to accept a fare from her.

Laura brought Jopl around the shops in Columbia Place Mall, using Mary Carney's credit card to buy clothes, shoes and toiletries for them both. Packing the whole lot into a new suitcase, she then took a cab to Hollywood-Rose Hill and booked into the Mountain View Motel. They rested there for the evening, and Laura planned how she would go about finding and approaching Professor Symington the next day.

The next morning, Laura left Jopl watching television,

with strict instructions that he was not to make any noise or open the door to anyone. She went to a pharmacy and bought more hair dye, and to a children's' clothes store where she picked up some more clothes before returning to the motel. She asked Jopl to listen to her, not sure how he was going to react to what she wanted to do.

'Jopl, we have to find your Professor Symington. I am back in my hometown, so it is quite dangerous. As you know from the airport, they are watching out for us here. We have to change our appearance as much as possible. Can you understand that?'

'Yes.' Spoken softly, simply. No drama.

'OK then. I am going to cut my hair and make it short. And I am going to dye it again, this time to black instead of brown. Now, I want to dye your hair as well. Is that OK?'

'Yes. But there is more.'

Laura wondered if the kid was a mind-reader.

'Yes, Jopl, there is more. I want to disguise you as much as I can. They believe that I am travelling with a man and a boy. Even though Greg is not with us, I still think we should change your appearance as much as we possibly can. I think the most effective disguise would be to make it look as though you are a girl. I could style your hair and put you in a dress. I know you might feel silly or embarrassed, but it is the safest disguise that I can think of.'

'If you truly believe that we should do this, then we will do it.'

Laura was relieved. She hadn't been sure if Jopl would agree to her plan. She went into the bathroom herself and started to work on her hair, cutting off most of the length to leave it a little shorter than shoulder length. She shed tears as she shed her hair. She loved her hair the way she usually wore it, the long, golden silky-soft cascade of it, the feel of it, the look of it. But she wanted to be transformed, transfigured. She wanted to be able to stand in front of her closest friend without them being able to recognise her. When she was finished cutting, she got to work with the dye. She eventually emerged from the bathroom, and was thrilled by the look of surprise on Jopl's face. Her disguise must have made her look radically different. She now sported a boyish bob cut of black hair.

Next, Laura got to work on Jopl. She applied the dye thoroughly, changing his hair from jet-black to dusty blond. She then washed and blow-dried it, putting a few curls into it and giving it more bounce and body than it would normally have. When she was finished, Jopl too looked drastically different, with the change in hair colour also seeming to change the tone of his skin. She dressed him in a simple summer dress and light shoes that she had bought, and asked him to stand in front of the full-length mirror. Jopl's jaw dropped, as he stood there, open-mouthed with surprise. 'Is that really me?'

He moved one arm, and then the other, turned this way and that, checking that when he moved, the reflection moved with him. 'It is me. Well, not me, me. But me.'

As he looked at his reflection, Laura stood beside him, and he looked at both reflections. 'I think there is a lesson here, which I shall have to give some thought to. Looking at us, we are different people. Yet we are the same. I think these reflections are telling us something.'

Laura left him to his musings as she got ready to go out again. 'Jopl, I am going to do a bit of scouting around the university to see if I can find this Professor Symington. I want you to stay here again, just like this morning. No noise, no opening the door. OK?'

Jopl nodded his agreement and, happy that he was settled

and leaving him in his dress so that he could get used to the feel of it, Laura set out for the university.

Following the signs to the Caroliniana Library, Laura found an impressive building fronted with columns gleaming white in the evening sun. She went into the on-line area, and turned on one of the computers. As she had hoped, the university had an intranet site. She browsed it for a time, before coming across a section called 'Student Resources'. Clicking on it, the screen asked her for her username and password. Laura frowned. There was a young man, about twenty years old, working on the computer beside her. Laura turned to him.

'Excuse me.'

He looked around, his face brightening when he saw how attractive Laura was.

'Yes?'

'I have to use the resource centre, but I left my username at home, and I can't remember my password. Ditzy of me, I know.' She fluttered her eyelids, doing her best impression of a clueless bimbo. 'Is there any way you could sign me on using your credentials?'

'Well, we're not supposed to. What happens if you're looking at something you shouldn't, or something? The IT guys will be on my case!'

'Oh, I wouldn't so anything like that. Do I look as though I would be looking up something dodgy? It will only take me a few minutes. You can log me off again before you go. Please? Just for lil' ole me?'

He looked at her appreciatively, before muttering to himself and pushing his chair close. Leaving over her, he entered his username and password while Laura looked on admiringly. Once he returned to his own screen, Laura started searching.

She looked for tutors, and got a list. Sure enough, there was a listing for a Professor Symington – he taught Political Science and was also heavily involved in the Philosophical Society. Laura looked for his tutorial schedule and hit the Print button. Under contact details, she got his home, office and mobile phone numbers, the address of his office on the campus and his home address, which was very close to the university. It seemed that the professor was one of the old-fashioned university dons, who believed in being highly accessible to his students.

According to the tutorial schedule, the professor should be just about to finish a lecture. Laura walked to the James F Byrnes Building, and waited within sight of the doors of the lecture hall. Before long, the doors were pushed open and a host of noisy university students piled out. After them came an elderly gentleman, who Laura assumed must be the professor. He looked like the stereotype of an old university professor – dressed a bit untidily, bow-tie askew, hair sticking out wildly. He had a pile of papers under his arm, and he shuffled off down the hall. Laura wanted to be certain that the old man was indeed the professor before she approached him, but was unsure how to check. On impulse, she looked into the lecture theatre, only to see a group of four cheerful young students arguing heatedly. From what she could gather, they were discussing the merits of applying market forces to the Chinese economy.

Laura walked over to them, looking a bit flushed. 'Excuse me guys. I was hoping to catch Professor Symington before he left. Has he gone?'

The four looked around the room in an exaggerated fashion, poking a gentle bit of fun at Laura. 'Well, unless he's hiding under a desk, I don't think he's here,' one finally replied.

Laura managed to look embarrassed, annoyed and worried all at the same time.

'Shut up, Mark,' another said, admonishing his comrade. 'Don't mind him. You just missed the Prof. But if you need him, you'll probably find him in the library. He usually goes there mid-afternoon. He says it's to do research for a book he's writing, but he actually goes for a bit of a mid-afternoon snooze. You can bet your life's savings that right about now, he'll be settling into that big wing-backed armchair for forty winks.'

Laura thanked the young man and retraced her footsteps to the library. Entering the hushed building, Laura browsed around and quickly saw the armchair that the young man had been referring to. And, just as predicted, the old man that she had seen leaving the lecture hall was settling down, a book in his lap, his eyelids already drooping. Within another few minutes he would be dozing, not researching.

Laura left the library and returned to the motel. She had identified the Professor. Now she had to bring Jopl to him. She decided that the safest way to take Jopl to the professor was to approach the professor off the campus. She decided to bring Jopl to the professor's home. When she got back to the motel, she proudly explained to Jopl how she had identified Professor Symington, that he did exist and that he was only a couple of miles away. She told Jopl that they would go to the professor's house that very evening, and that within a couple of hours, they would have accomplished their mission.

They ate in the motel, and played cards to pass the time and ease the tension while they waited. At eight o'clock, Laura decided that the professor would surely be home and, checking her and Jopl's disguises, flouncing his hair up a little, they set off. Using a free tourist map that she had picked up at the motel, Laura checked the directions to the professor's house, which was only a few hundred metres from the university. As they approached his house, they saw that the professor lived on a grand old street with imposing trees along each sidewalk and expanses of lawns carpeting the front gardens.

As they strolled past the professor's house, it looked just like all the others. Two big trees grew in the front lawn, one on each side of the driveway that led up to the front door, ending in a small turning circle. There were two bushes framing the entrance to the driveway, neatly manicured into perfectly round outlines. Like the other houses on the street, there was no fence separating the lawn from the road, and the closely mowed grass was picture perfect. Everything seemed quiet and normal, and Laura started to relax in anticipation of the end of her saga. They walked past the professor's house and down to the end of the street before turning back. Laura intended to simply go to the front door and ring the bell when they reached the professor's house for the second time.

As they approached the house again, Laura knew the end of the mission was in sight. Happy that she had successfully done as her dad had asked, in spite of all the dangers and the obstacles, Laura breathed deeply and felt happier and more relaxed than she had in a long time. As she relaxed, it felt as though Imno was walking alongside her. 'Blend into your world Laura. Feel your world.'

'What?' Laura jumped. 'Jopl, did you hear someone say something?'

'What did you hear, Laura?'

'I almost thought I heard Imno speaking!'

'And what did she say?'

'Something about blending into my world, feeling my

world.'

'Then, may I suggest that you do just that?'

Laura paused, undecided. She was not sure what was going on. She had been anticipating the end of the nightmare, and wasn't ready for more strange happenings. Nevertheless, feeling guided by Jopl's comment – and just possibly feeling guided by Imno as well – Laura tried to relax as much as she possibly could. As she eased her mind, forgot her worries, wiped her thoughts clean, she started to feel as though she were entering some kind of trance. Internally she was perfectly still, perfectly calm, observing, while externally she was strolling and chatting with the little girl at her side.

Her senses seemed to sharpen, become more acute, more intense. She could feel the vitality and growth in the trees and shrubs, and the movement and activity of the wildlife. She could sense the birds even when she could not see them in the foliage, she could almost taste the sap flowing in the tree trunks. She gradually became aware of disturbances in the flow of nature and started to pick out the sources. The two bushes framing the driveway were actually artificial, lifeless, and Laura could sense the electronic equipment within. She could sense more and more electronic equipment expertly hidden around the house, and she knew it had to be surveillance equipment. Was it home security measures put in place by the professor, or was it spying apparatus put there by somebody who wanted to keep an eye on who visited him? As she continued to probe around the house, she was able to sense electronic pads under the lawn – they had to be weight-activated.

Continuing to walk along the footpath, Laura knew that she could not risk approaching the professor here. Until she knew whether the surveillance equipment was spying for the professor or on him, the risk would simply be too great. They were so close to the end, they could not afford to make a mistake at this late stage. As they turned onto the next street, Laura decided that she would have to make contact with the professor on her own at first, leaving Jopl at the motel for safety. Thinking back to her morning at the university, and the large number of people milling about, she decided that the university itself now presented the safest opportunity for making that initial contact.

With the new plan in place, Laura and Jopl returned to the motel. Laura explained to Jopl about the spy gear around the professor's house, and told him that she would make the first contact with the professor on her own the next day.

Delivery

The next day, Laura went again to some clothing stores, this time dressing herself in what she thought of as old woman's clothes. She chose garments that were plain in cut, dull brown in colour and a little too big for her. She had applied foundation to her face, neck and hands to make her skin look darker than it was. She topped off the ensemble with a shapeless black beret. Satisfied that she had changed her appearance as much as she could from the previous day, she made her way back to the university.

As she approached the main entrance, Laura tried to sink back into the trance-like state she had been in the previous evening. When she felt that she was sufficiently aware of the ebb and flow of the intangible life forces about her, she scanned the area but could not detect anything out of place. She kept searching for anomalies as she walked towards the library, but everything seemed to be as it should. She could feel the maze of electricity that she was walking through, with wires criss-crossing the ground beneath her feet and each building alive with the power. She could sense the security cameras that were mounted at intervals as part of the campus security, but they seemed to be part of the routine safety measures taken by the university to protect their students rather than any threat specifically aimed at her.

Nervously, Laura entered the library for the third time. Today, she felt as though she was bearding the lion in its own den. As she pretended to browse among the bookshelves, she found that she could sense the emotional state of the people around her. Some were worrying, some were bored, one or two were excited. But none seemed to be in a state of watching, observing. Her new senses seemed to be telling her the same as her senses of sight and sound – these people were the usual eclectic grouping that you might come across in any university library. There did not seem to be any intruders here, anyone here who should not be here.

As he had done the previous day, Professor Symington entered the library as three o'clock drew near. He shuffled around to the Philosophy section and rummaged amongst some of the books, withdrawing and replacing a number before choosing one. Retiring to his armchair, he sat and opened the book, seemingly at a random page, and started to read. Laura watched him and kept her antennae working overtime on all of the other people in the library. Everything still appeared normal, although her new senses were a little confused by the professor. It was not that he appeared ill-intentioned towards her – indeed he was most definitely not aware of her presence. Nor was it that he appeared out of place – he seemed the most natural element within the library. Rather it was that he seemed partially closed. Laura felt that there was apart of the professor that she could not reach, could not sense.

As she watched, the old man's eyes began to close, just as they had the previous day. His head dipped forward a little, and he jerked it back up. He laid his head back against the winged arm of the chair and again started to doze. With his head supported this time, there was nothing to stop him from gently drifting into sleep and, after another minute or two, he was indeed asleep.

All of Laura's senses told her that he was asleep. She circled the room again, looking at the professor, the librarian, all the users of the library. Still everything appeared normal. No out-of-place equipment. No out-of-place people. Laura sat and pretended to read for thirty minutes and still all seemed well. She knew that she was going to have to make her move before the professor left the library. She decided not to approach while he slept, as waking the sleeping man might draw attention. Instead, she would wait until he woke, and then approach him just before he left his armchair refuge. Another few minutes passed, and the professor began to stir slightly. He shifted a little in his seat and drew his head down a fraction. As Laura watched, the old eyes opened and then shut again. The next time, they opened fully and the man reached up and scratched his face, rubbing his eyes. Sitting up straighter in the armchair, the professor yawned quietly and stretched his arms. Now or never, Laura thought.

She rose from the table where she had been reading, and carried the book as she walked over to the professor. 'Professor Symington?'

'Yes, dear?'

'I wonder if you could help me with this passage I have been reading?'

Laura leaned over the professor, holding the book up as though they were looking at a page together. As he started to look at the book, Laura whispered to him. 'Professor. My name is Laura Whiteland. My dad was Ben Whiteland. He asked me to deliver something to you.'

There was no doubting the Professor's reaction. He jerked upright, and looked at Laura speechless for a moment, a mixture of fright and excitement in his eyes. 'We thought you were dead! We have heard nothing since you disappeared. Do you have him with you?'

The professor looked around, clearly searching for Jopl.

'No. I thought it might be dangerous. He is nearby, but safe. I can bring him to you, but I saw all the surveillance equipment around your house and I didn't know if you had put it there or if someone is spying on you.'

'No, no. That's mine. For my protection. Can you bring him to me tonight?'

'Yes. Just tell me when and where.'

'My house. Midnight. Here, use this to let yourself in.' He handed her a key before continuing, 'Come in the side door. Make it exactly midnight – I will deactivate the alarms for precisely one minute. Sixty seconds, no more and no less. Bring him. Can you do that?'

'See you at midnight, Professor.' Laura straightened up, and spoke clearly. 'Thanks for explaining that to me, Professor. It's much clearer to me now.'

With that she closed the book and casually sauntered back to the section she had taken it from and put it back on its shelf. She then left the library, looking at her watch as though she was late for a lecture. As she left the campus grounds, she breathed a huge sigh of relief. Now, hopefully, she would be able to deliver Jopl, and rest in the knowledge that she had accomplished everything that her dad had asked her to do. She would be able to think of her dad, and be proud that as his only child, she had secured his legacy as he had so desperately needed.

Back at the motel, Laura excitedly updated Jopl on what had happened. She showed him the key, telling him that it was the key to the side door of Professor Symington's house. Jopl too looked excited for the first time.

'This is good Laura. This is why I Am. This is my purpose. All people have a purpose in life. For most, it is a general purpose, as we have discussed. It is simply to make the world a better place. This is my purpose also, to make the world a better place. But I am to fulfil my purpose in a very specific way. Once I am with Professor Symington, I will be able to fulfil my purpose. You might say, my Destiny.'

Jopl was more animated than Laura had ever seen him, clearly keyed up and eager to complete is mission. 'Laura, I am sorry that I have not been able to tell you more before now. But that is the way it has to be. Once you deliver me to Professor Symington, you will see what this has all been leading up to. Tonight, you will be the witness as I start to deliver justice.'

Laura was warmed by Jopl's apology. It seemed that he wanted to share everything with her, but had been indoctrinated with the belief that some things had to be kept secret from anyone and everyone including her - at least until she delivered him to the professor. It seemed that she would then, finally, find out what exactly all of this was about.

Again they spent the evening resting, ate a meal, played cards and chatted to pass the time. As the evening wore on, Laura found herself almost wishing it did not have to end. She still didn't now what was going to happen when she delivered Jopl to the old man, but she suspected that she would not have Jopl with her thereafter. She was going to miss the child. She would miss both his childish presence and his ancient wisdom. She would miss the calming aura that seemed to surround him and the occasional words that he would utter, dropping like oil onto stormy waters, calming and quietening and soothing her mind and heart.

To stop herself from dwelling on these things, and remembering Jopl's advice to always think of the positive, Laura reflected on how much she had learned from this ancient child in the past few weeks. Thinking of that prompted another train of thought – something Jopl had said, that had puzzled her at the time, but that she hadn't been able to query with him there and then. 'Jopl?'

'Yes, Laura.'

'Do you remember when we were in Humpty Doo, sitting on the porch in the hostel, when we spoke about our purpose in life? You said that our purpose is to make the world a better place – to do good for the world and for each other, and you also said that this is well known, that every major religion teaches it in one form or another, and that parents and community leaders generally give the same sort of message. I remember I asked you how so few people are aware of this purpose, given that it is so widely preached. You said something about a voice that gives a different message. Do you remember?'

'Certainly, Laura. I said, "So the answer is known. The difficulty is that nowadays many people, knowing the answer, refuse to believe the answer. They hear from their parents that they should be 'good', they hear it from their community leaders, their political leaders, their religious leaders. But they are seduced by another voice, a voice that tells them that this is not so. A voice that tells them that the purpose of life is to amass possessions. A voice that tells them that their self-worth is defined by their material worth. A voice of poison and pain that is slowly killing off the appreciation of the intangible, which is fundamental to a sense of community. Feeling isolated, people turn more and more to the voice of materialism, becoming more and more lost. A tragedy." Is that what you are referring to?'

'Yes, that is it. What did you mean when you said that? What voice are you talking about?'

'I am talking about the voice of materialism, the shout of consumerism, the roar of extreme capitalism. The voice that is poisoning society, alienating individuals, dismembering community. As mass communication becomes easier and cheaper, as mass production becomes more and more mechanised, as distribution becomes global, so this voice becomes more powerful. Don't you see it?'

'See what? I still don't understand what you are talking about.'

'We have hypothesised in our discussions that our purpose on earth is to do good. We have suggested that there may be some form of a god. We have thought that true happiness comes from giving, more than it comes from receiving. All of these things are under attack. Commercial interests fight these suggestions. Big business argues that the opposite is true.

'For-profit enterprises say that our purpose on earth is not to do good for others, our purpose is to gather material possessions to ourselves. Market organisations that that there is no God; there is only 'Brand'. Retail brands say that true happiness comes not from giving; but from getting and having.'

Jopl paused, giving Laura a moment to let his words sink in. 'The problem is this, Laura. Human beings naturally know that what we have suggested is true. Our purpose is to do good for others, to make the world a better place for all. There is more to our universe than the physical world. Happiness comes from giving and from doing good.

'But, there is no profit to be had from these sentiments. So you do not have a marketplace that proclaims these things from the rooftops. No, the profit in the modern capitalist economy lies in consumption. You must get people to buy. That, more than anything else, drives the capitalist economy. Because this is the belief system that will drive consumption, it pays these companies to market the message – billions upon billions are spent, hammering out this message. For example, when did you last see an advert for a car that used a marketing message to the effect that the vehicle will get you from A to B? No, the marketing message is that buying this car will make you happy. So, the average Western citizen is subjected to a barrage, a veritable torrent of messages all day every day, telling him that if he consumes, he will be happy.

'So what happens? There was a time in the average Western capitalist society, when a family with one wage earner could live a comfortable, in material terms, life. Today, though, in most of these economies, both adults in a family have to be bringing in a wage, if they are to have what they consider a comfortable, in material terms, life. Why is this? Because now they consume more. Years ago, if they had a car that worked, that was all that mattered. It could be old, the paintwork could be damaged, it didn't matter. As long as the car functioned, then that was all they needed. Today, however, having been subjected to the marketing deluge all of their lives, the young parents feel that they must have a new, or newish, car. They would be horrified at the thought that they might drive around in a twenty year old wreck, that had bumps and scratches. What would their friends say? No, they must have a better car than that. And what's more, they must have two.

'And so it is with all of their possessions. In the past, if the family had a television, they were happy. But the marketing message tells us that that is not enough now. No, if you want to have a happy family, you must have many televisions, as well as lots of other entertainment systems in the house. Seduced by the marketing, people try to buy this happiness. Of course, it is a vicious circle, because the more entertainment systems they buy, the more they are assaulted with marketing, so the more seduced they become.'

Laura listened, fascinated. It was as though Jopl was

describing some horrific *1984*-type of world. He seemed to be suggesting that there was some sort of global conspiracy to trick people into doing what they would not otherwise do, living a life that they would not otherwise lead, following a belief system that they would not otherwise follow.

'Jopl, are you saying that there is a world-wide conspiracy on this? That marketing companies get together and plan how to trick the population into buying things they do not need, into being led?'

'No, Laura, not in that overt way. There doesn't need to be a conspiracy, because it is inherent in the capitalist philosophy. If capitalism is allowed free rein, and is not tempered with any degree of social conscience, then the pattern of increasing consumerism and an increasing personal philosophy of self over community is inevitable. For example, do you know that under the legal system of most capitalist economies, the directors of a company are legally bound to do whatever best serves the financial interests of the shareholders of that company? This to me is an incredible impulsion to have built into the legal and economic system of a country. It means that if the directors of a company decide to divert some company profits into helping a local community where they have a factory, and there is no reciprocal benefit for the company, then the shareholders could technically have the directors found guilty of illegality. That is why most companies, if they do any kind of community funding, insist on accompanying advertising so that they can say that the good work of helping the community is in fact just another marketing function. Unfortunately, I think that when they say this, it is often true. I think that a lot of companies who put company resources into supposedly charitable or community concerns, are in fact simply using alternative marketing channels to complement the traditional mainstream channels of television and other media.'

'So, you are saying that capitalism is a bad thing?'

'No, no I am not saying that. I am saying that unbridled capitalism is a bad thing. Remember what I said before – "moderation in all things". Socialism can be spoken of as though it were a utopian solution – where the state provides for every individual. To allow for this, you remove the concept of personal ownership – after all, if everyone has enough provided by the state, then why would anyone need to own anything in their own name? However, the problem with this form of extreme socialism is that there does not seem to be any true way to accurately reflect the value of the effort that people put in. If one person works extremely hard and another does very little, and there is no personal ownership, how do you reward the person who works harder? So no, I am not saying that capitalism per se is a bad thing. I am suggesting that any ideology taken to extreme may be a bad thing. Do you remember what we said about always bearing in mind that you may be wrong – that doing so will help you to avoid the excesses of the zealot, of the fanatic?'

Laura nodded. She felt that this child's tongue was revealing the world to her in a different light. As he spoke, she felt the filters being removed from her eyes – now she saw her society as it truly was. And it was disheartening. Was her society really the mass of huddled sheep that Jopl seemed to suggest? Doing what they were told to do, thinking what they were told to think, believing what they were told to believe?

'Jopl, it's a frightening thought - to think that what you say may be true. I think it is scary because I cannot see an end to it. If it is a vicious circle as you say, then the more successful the marketing message is, the more consumerism will grow and the more people will think of themselves in terms of their material possessions and ignore their neighbour and their community. And the more that happens, then the more successful will the message of self over others be. If that is so, then what can we do? Where will it all end?'

'Well, Laura, every society has its day. I have no doubt that, in time, this model that the Western world is now so infatuated with, will eventually be replaced with something different. And I have no doubt that in the long-term, if not the short-term, it will be replaced with something better. If you look across the aeons of history, you can see a gradual improvement in the type of society that humans establish. Sometimes, there is an interregnum, an interruption in the progress. So for example, the Western world went from the ancient Greeks to the Romans, only to fall into the desolation of the Dark Ages before being lifted again by the Renaissance. But if you look at a broad enough timeline, there is gradual improvement. And in many ways, we are living in a Golden Age. There is much about the modern world that is good. For the first time, most societies generally accept that one person cannot own another – this is a relatively recent phenomenon, yet we now take it for granted.

'So while your modern Western societies have the curse of extreme capitalism, with your own country being the worst afflicted, there is also much to celebrate. And, in time, the current model will be replaced with another. One hopes that this will happen through discourse and thought, through well-managed development. The fear, of course, is that it will be violent, sporadic, with a period of two steps backward for every one step forward.'

'So, is there anything that I can do? Anything that the

ordinary person in the street can do?'

'Oh yes, most certainly. Be conscious of the effect on society of the message that is being pushed. Resolve not to be seduced by the call of marketing. Be ready to accept that objects have a functional value, sometimes an aesthetic value, but they cannot bring you happiness. Reject the message that tells you that "Brand Matters" – it does not. Do good – for others, for your community, for your world. Remember that all you need to do is your best. All else will follow.'

Laura nodded, thinking that, as always, Jopl was leaving her with a lot to ponder. She needed to mull over what he had said, but more immediately, she needed to be getting ready for what to happen this evening. She looked at the clock, and seeing that it was now eight, she told Jopl that they would be leaving soon, and that he should start getting ready. She wanted to deliver, not just the child, but a happy, healthy, clean child. She told him to shower and wash his hair. When he was finished, she blow-dried his hair, again curling and fluffing to make it as feminine as possible. She was taking no chances tonight – every possible measure that she could think of would be employed to ensure the boy's safety. She told him to put on the dress and the girl's shoes again, and to call her when he was ready. When he was dressed, Laura applied just a touch of rouge to his cheeks to redden them slightly, making him look more feminine than ever. When Jopl protested that this was really too much, she assured him that they would carry a change of clothes for him so that he could get back into boy's clothes as soon as he was safely ensconced in Professor Symington's house.

At eleven o'clock, Laura called for a cab, and asked the driver to bring them to Dutch Square Mall, where they wandered aimlessly as Laura let time pass and constantly tried to see if anyone could be following them. Eventually she was satisfied that no-one was paying them undue attention, and she hailed another cab and giving an address in Earlewood, a neighbourhood close to the university. From there they walked to the university and she and Jopl started to stroll back towards the professor's street, conscious of the time left before they needed to be at his house. They entered his road at two minutes before midnight, and stood in front of his house just before the hour.

Laura could sense the moment the security system was deactivated. Cameras and microphones in the bush and tree, the weight-activated pads under the lawn, the alarms on the windows and doors – all of them went abruptly dead at the same time. She had sixty seconds to get into the house. She walked across the lawn with Jopl, feeling like sprinting, but not wanting to run in case they might draw the attention of an inquisitive neighbour. Walking around the side of the house, she looked for a side door. But this was a blank wall – there was no door! Stifling a curse, Laura realised that the door must be on the other side of the house. Feeling the seconds tick past, she walked back around to the front of the house, across the front lawn and down the other side. She saw the door and could not stop herself from breaking into a run. Fumbling the key into the lock, it seemed to take forever to make it slide home. But, eventually, it was in, though Laura thought that her sixty seconds must surely be over by now. Swinging the door open, she pulled Jopl inside and closed the door again, remembering only at the last moment to grab the key from the outside lock.

Laura leaned back against the wall, panting from the stress rather than from any exertion. Her heart hammered in her chest. As she steadied herself, she could sense the security system flicking back into life, back on guard, protecting the property and its occupants. She held Jopl close to her, wondering what to do next. She tried to feel her way through the rooms of the house with her new sixth sense, but found that it would not function inside the house. Even though she could sense the security equipment outside, she could not seem to penetrate anything within.

Relying on her traditional senses, she looked around her. Judging by the small amount of light filtering in from the internal doorway, they were standing in what looked like a small utility room, with a door ajar into what she assumed was a hall. Gently pulling the door open, Laura leaned out and confirmed for herself that she was looking out into the main hallway. To her right, she could see the front door and a staircase leading up to the first floor. Between her and the front door was another door leading into a room that had to be beside the utility room, with the door closed. To her left, the hall ended in another doorway. This door was partly open, and light spilled into the hall. It seemed to be the only light on in the house, so Laura assumed that this was the room she should head towards.

As she stepped into the hall, Laura gesticulated to Jopl to indicate that he should stay as close as he could, immediately behind her. They started to inch their way down the hall, and Laura immediately noticed that this was certainly a man's house. There were no feminine touches about it, with hardwood predominating, and a complete lack of ornaments or decoration. She approached the partly open door as if it could be the gateway to either heaven or hell, though she wasn't sure which one. Coming to a stop just in front of the door, she drew in a deep breath and slowly released it, tensed the muscles of her body and relaxed them, and gently pushed the door open.

The room inside was a combination living room and kitchen. There was a fire blazing in the wall opposite, throwing heat and warmth into the room, its flickering light softening the functional surfaces of the kitchen. Standing in front of the fire was Professor Symington, back half-turned to Laura, rubbing his hands together over the fire as if to warm them. Hearing the door open, he turned and smiled heartily, and exclaimed, 'Come in, come in.' Relieved that the nightmare was at an end, Laura ran to the professor, and gave him a desperate hug. The man was quite astonished, as it didn't seem that getting hugs from beautiful young ladies was an everyday occurrence for him.

'There, there,' he murmured, apparently at a loss for what else to say. 'There, there, you're here now. Everything is going to be OK. You are both safe and that is all that matters. You have made the delivery successfully.'

All Together Again

Laura relaxed, pulling Jopl to her side as she gently disengaged from the professor, becoming aware of his discomfort. Just as she was about to speak, a familiar voice spoke from behind her. 'No hug for me?'

Laura whirled around and a short scream escape from her lips. It was Rob.

'How did you get here?' she gasped, before swinging back to Professor Symington. 'Why is he here? He wants to hurt Jopl! You were supposed to help me finish this for my dad.'

'Laura, Laura,' said the professor. 'Rob told me that you disappeared on him, so I thought you might for some reason think he was your enemy. But I can assure you that he is in fact one of your closest allies. Rob believes fundamentally in completing the chain of events that your father set in motion when he sent you to get Jopl and deliver him to me.'

The professor walked over to Rob and put his hand on his shoulder. 'Rob is as anxious as I am to do what needs to be done to fulfil the legacy that your father left you. Ben had a mission, a mission that he could not act on because he knew that if he did, you would be murdered. However, once he died he left the decision to you. He told you that it was dangerous, that you could walk away, but that it was up to you. You are your father's daughter, Laura – Ben would have been very proud of you.'

Laura looked at them both, trying to understand how she was supposed to reconcile the professor's words with what she had seen. The old man clearly believed that Rob was on her side. Yet she was sure that she could trust the old man and that he would not lie to her. But she knew Rob was the enemy – she had heard the desperation in his voice when he thought he had lost Jopl as they followed Imno into the bush. The only possible explanation was that Rob had tricked the professor. He had somehow made Symington believe that he wanted to fulfil Ben Whiteland's legacy as much as the professor did.

Laura wondered how she could get them out of this. She had to somehow get the professor and Jopl on their own, away from Rob. Then she could explain to the old man, make him understand that Rob was their enemy. As Laura was wondering how she could do this, another door into the room eased open. This door was behind Rob and the professor, and they hadn't seen it opening. As Laura thought about shouting a warning to the professor, she saw a figure take shape in the opening, and she drew in a quick breath. It couldn't be! Surely, she couldn't be that lucky? Then, as the door opened a bit wider, she saw that she was indeed blessed with good fortune.

'Hands on your heads, boys!' barked Greg, coming around the side to enter Rob and Symington's peripheral vision. Rob went to reach under his jacket, but Greg warned him. 'Tut tut, Rob. I wouldn't do that if I were you. I can guarantee you an early grave if you make a move.'

Rob took his hand away from his jacket and clasped both hands on top of his head, as Symington had already done.

'Laura, get over here beside me. Bring the boy.'

Laura rushed to Greg's side, sobbing with relief. 'Oh, Greg, thank God you're here. Rob had convinced Professor Symington that he is on our side. We have to explain to the professor that Rob followed us to Humpty Doo.'

The professor pleaded with Laura. 'Please, Laura. You don't understand. You have it the wrong way around. I sent

Rob to help you because I knew someone had joined you and I wanted to be sure that you were safe. If anyone here is trying to hurt you and Jopl, it is him,' he said, shaking a little as he pointed at Greg.

'Shut up, old man' snapped Greg. 'When I want you to talk, I'll let you know. And when I want you to talk, you will talk,' he warned, before turning to Laura. 'Laura, have you been able to find out what the boy is carrying? Do you know how he is carrying it?'

'Not yet, my darling. We have to make the professor understand what is going on here.'

Jopl was still standing beside Laura, not having spoken since he entered the house. He did not speak now either, at least not out loud. But Laura could hear him in her head, could hear the echoes of conversations that they had had, could hear Imno's discussion of her people's beliefs and other things that she had said. Laura looked down at Jopl. He looked back at her, still not speaking out loud, but delivering a message that Laura could hear as clearly as if he had shouted it at her. He was telling her to remember how to make a decision at any given time. She knew what she had to do – gather all the facts, apply a mixture of heart and reason, and then make a clean decision and proceed on that basis.

Laura thought back over all that had happened. Greg had come to her in Koh Samui, having previously trailed her from the States and losing her in Bangkok. He said that he was a friend of her dad's, and he certainly knew a lot about him. That meant he had been closely involved with her dad, but didn't warrant a conclusion about whether he had been his friend or foe. He had helped her and Jopl at every turn, getting them out of Bangkok and to safety, but he was always interested in knowing what Jopl was carrying, and how. Even now, that seemed to be his overriding concern. Laura wasn't so sure now that she was the most important thing in his world. It seemed that Jopl might be even more important to him.

She thought about Rob. He had turned up in Humpty Doo, and the professor was saying that he had sent Rob to help and protect her. Yet, there had been undoubted desperation in his voice when he was losing them into the bush. She had assumed that was because he wanted to hurt Jopl – but it could as easily because he was afraid for them. Jopl had said that they should follow Imno away from danger, but had the threat come from Rob or from Greg?

Laura reviewed all the facts, replayed conversations that she had had with all three men in the room over the past minutes, days and weeks. It felt like a long, long process, but Laura could sense that it was in fact happening in the blink of an eye. She considered all that she knew, went over everything from her dad's video, through Thailand, Australia and back to her home here in Columbia. She knew what she had to do. She wasn't at all certain that it was correct, but it seemed the course of action most likely to be correct; especially when she applied heart to the equation as well as reason.

Laura swung into action. It felt like slow-motion as she watched herself launch into battle, but she knew that in reality she was moving blindingly fast. She ripped the gun out of Greg's hand, throwing it to Rob. 'Hands up,' shouted Rob, catching the gun expertly and turning it on Greg in the blink of an eye.

Now it was Greg's turn to clasp his hands on top of his head. 'What the hell have you done? Have you gone crazy?' Greg screamed at Laura, who flinched under the verbal onslaught from the man she loved, each word a dagger in her heart of hearts.

'I don't know,' she cried. 'I don't know. I have believed in you, Greg. Believed in you and loved you. God, I love you so much!' she sobbed, falling against his chest. Greg kept an eye on the gun that Rob had trained on him. Afraid to lower his hands, he let Laura rest against his chest.

'So why the hell have you given that bastard the gun?'

'Because I thought back. I reviewed all that I knew. And one thing stood out for me, when I looked back dispassionately. You have always seemed more interested in what Jopl was carrying than you were in the child himself. More interested in how he was carrying it, than you were in me.'

Greg snorted, as if to say that Laura was talking rubbish.

'I can tell you why that would be,' Rob said

At the same moment, Professor Symington said, 'I know why he needed to know what Jopl was carrying, and how he was carrying it.'

Laura looked over at them. 'Well?'

The professor spoke before Rob had time to answer. 'Because he must be working for the enemy – the people your father swore to hold to account. His job would have to be to find the records that will pull down their whole rotten empire. Find them and destroy them. Once you collected Jopl, he knew it must involve the boy in some way. But he couldn't take any action until he found out what records there were, and how and where they were stored. Well, Greg, if that really is your name. You lost. You had the prize in your grip the whole time. All you had to do was make Jopl disappear and your masters would have been safe. There are no written records, at least not yet. It is all in Jopl's head, every bit of information that we need to make your masters' criminal empire implode. Once Jopl dictates all of the information to us, we will destroy the whole putrid design. We will root out every member of your filthy brotherhood and a new age will dawn.'

The professor's face lit up as he spoke, an almost messianic zeal manifesting itself in his features. Laura looked up at Greg and saw the truth in his face. He looked crushed, a man who had failed in his mission. 'It's all in his head? If I had just thrown him overboard in the middle of the Pacific, then the sharks could have finished it for me? I'm a dead man!'

'It doesn't have to be that way, Greg. If you turn evidence for us, then we can help to get you a fair deal. If you work with us, I'm sure that something can be arranged – that we will take account of your assistance' the professor said.

'You don't understand. They are everywhere. They know everything. You cannot stop them. You'll never stop them,' Greg was almost sobbing.

'What are we going to do with him?' the professor asked Rob, seeming to defer to the younger man on the topic of security.

'Well, we can't hand him over to the authorities. Not yet, not until we have gotten all the information that Jopl can give us. We need to document everything Jopl tells us, get into position and then go to war. For the moment, we will have to lock him up here – that is the only thing I can think of. I am going to have to interrogate him. We need to know how he found us here – I thought I had gotten rid of him in Australia. We need to know if he got here on his own – if anyone else in his organisation knows where we are.'

'OK, then. I can't say I enjoy the prospect of keeping him here, but I can see that we do not have much choice. As for your interrogation, there is a sound-proofed room in the basement. You can use that when you want to question him. I suspect you may need to use force. He is too terrified of his masters to speak freely.'

Laura felt her world spin out of control. She had loved this man, worshipped him. She had given herself to him, completely and without reservation. She had subsumed his body into the depths of her own. And now she was betrayed. 'Greg, was it all an act? Didn't I mean anything to you?'

'At first, of course it was an act. I had a job to do. And I knew that I might have to kill you, as part of that job. But … was it all an act? No. No, Laura, it wasn't. Not once I got to know you. You came to mean a lot to me, an awful lot. I think that's why I made such a huge mistake. I should have killed that bastard as soon as he showed up. But I wanted to spare him if he was innocent, because he was your friend. That was a mistake.'

Greg glowered at Rob, clearly regretting his decision to stay his hand. 'Then he came after me. He ambushed me on the road to Darwin. My four-wheel drive went into a ravine and burst into flames. Luckily for me, I had been able to jump clear just as it left the road. I heard him making a phone call, talking to Professor Symington. The rest was easy.

'Anyway, it's all academic now. I have failed. I failed in the forests of Stung Teng, and I have failed here. My life will be forfeit. But I am sorry Laura, sorry for us. In a different life, in different circumstances, I could have allowed myself to love you. Properly. Fully.'

Greg hung his head, defeated, a beaten man.

Rob kept the gun trained on Greg, while asking the professor if there was a secure lock on the sound-proofed room.

'Yes, yes, the room is fully secure. It was built as a

nuclear shelter by the previous owner. It's as safe as Alcatraz.'

'Good. Is it out this way?' Rob asked, nodding towards the door that Laura had used to enter the room.

As Rob nodded towards the door, Greg made his last desperate roll of the dice – the desperate act of a desperate man. Whipping his hands from behind his head, he held a short vicious looking dagger that he had had concealed between his shoulder blades. He swung Laura around, the knife to her throat, before anyone realised what was happening.

Rob started to squeeze the trigger, then hesitated.

'That's right, hero' taunted Greg. 'You had better think twice before you pull that trigger. You would want to be confident, very, very confident, in your marksmanship skills. You need to get a perfect headshot first time, or she's dead.'

He moved the blade a fraction to emphasise his point, and a single drop of blood flowed from Laura's neck, trailing its way into the hollow of her collarbone and resting there.

Rob glanced at the professor, seeking support or guidance.

'Greg, you know we can't let you leave. We must protect Jopl at all costs. At any cost,' the professor said, looking at Laura sadly. His look spoke a thousand words, every one of those thousand words asking her for her forgiveness for what was about to happen. Greg and Rob saw the look as well, and they all knew what had been decided. Laura's life was expendable.

Laura again experienced the strange time dilation that had been so strong when she was with Imno. She thought ironically – hoisted by thine own petard. She had argued so passionately with Jopl that the lesser evil was the moral choice when faced with two evils. The professor was obviously applying the same logic to this situation. It was her life on one side of the scales, and the undoing of the evil empire that the professor had referred to, on the other. It looked as though all three men knew that the assessment was that the loss of her life was the lesser evil, and therefore the correct moral choice to be made in this situation. As she watched events unfold around her, a supernatural clarity threw every colour, every shape, every contour into sharp relief and allowed every minute detail to register with her. She thought how beautiful the world was, when one knew one was about to die.

She felt the push from Greg, a huge shove that propelled her across the floor at Rob. She realised that Greg was hoping to shake Rob's aim, distract him, so that Greg could make good his escape. Even as this thought crystallised in her mind, she realised that she was mistaken. She thought of Jopl's advice – always remember that you might be wrong – and she thought how correct, how wise, the little child was. Greg was not trying to escape – he was moving towards the centre of the room, away from the doors. He was moving towards Jopl. Laura realised the truth with horror. The professor had told Greg that if he had killed Jopl, then he would have fulfilled his mission. Greg had no thought of escape, no thought of his own safety. Driven by fear of his masters, he had one thought and one thought only burning in his brain. And that thought was to complete his mission – to destroy the records that Jopl was carrying.

Laura watched in horror as Greg's arm rose into the air. The dagger glinted in the light as it began its downward swing. Everything was happening incredibly fast, but looked to Laura as though it was happening in slow motion. The problem was that while her mind was racing at full speed, her body too was moving in slow motion. She was still hurtling across the room at Rob, unable to stop her forward momentum. She desperately tried to twist sideways, to get back and stop the dagger as it swung towards the child who she had come to love and respect, who she now cherished so dearly. But it was impossible. She couldn't halt her forward rush. She couldn't save Jopl.

She saw the dagger swing down, Jopl standing, looking up, making no attempt to save himself. She knew it would have been pointless anyway. Jopl was a small child. There was no way he could have defended himself against this big burly man. Laura marvelled at the calm look on Jopl's face as the knife fell. She remembered that he had said you must learn to accept the inevitable. He was putting that into practice, right there in front of her eyes, with a bravery and a courageousness that she wouldn't have thought possible. His eyes tracked the downward path as the blade moved to complete the killing swing.

Just as the blade was about to slice into flesh, through flesh, through life; just as the blade was about to extinguish life, a drum-roll tattoo of shots rang out. In her hyper-observant state Laura was able to hear each shot as a distinct sound, was able to see the impact of every bullet, was able to see the effect of each collision of bullet into flesh. The first bullet hit Greg in the shoulder, knocking his hand from its path, deflecting the blade away from Jopl's throat. The tip of the blade nicked the shoulder of Jopl's shirt as it passed, tearing and ripping at the material, slicing through it effortlessly. But it missed his body. Laura mentally shuddered to see how easily the blade destroyed the fabric. It had almost destroyed the fabric of the boy's existence.

The second and third shots hit Greg in the chest,

throwing his body back across the room. Laura was astonished at the force that each bullet carried. A small piece of lead could propel the body of a grown man so effortlessly. As Greg fell backwards, he connected with the wall and rebounded. With an animal roar, he again attacked the child, but he knew himself that he had lost. He made his final frantic effort, reaching for the boy, but he was weak. Another shot rang out, and another. Both hit him in the chest, throwing him back across the room again. His body crashed into the wall but, this time, there was no rebound. Greg no longer had command of his limbs, and he fell to the floor in a heap. His body shook for a moment, there was a rattle from his throat, and he stopped moving. As Laura watched, she thought she could see the life force leave his body – an insubstantial invisible mist that looked to have the strength to endure all eternity rose from his body and moved into a different plane of existence.

Laura cried out, not knowing who to rush to first. She ran to Jopl, hugged him to herself, reassuring herself that he was all right. He looked up at her, sadness and understanding in his eyes. He mouthed, 'I'm sorry,' at her and a tear ran down his cheek. Laura wasn't sure if he cried for Greg, because he loved all living things, or if he cried for her because she had lost someone she loved. She released the boy and moved across the room to Greg's body. She knelt, stroked his face.

'Oh, Greg, now I have lost two men. Two men that I loved. Rightly or wrongly, I loved you, Greg. I loved you so much. And now you too are gone.'

She leaned down, kissed his cheek gently, and straightened.

'I need to understand. Please.'

Her short plea had all the force of someone is lost in

grief, who is trying to find an anchor to steady themselves. The professor knew that she needed to get an understanding of all that had happened so that she could appreciate her own place in the sequence of events – in what had happened thus far and what had to happen now. He poured her a stiff brandy to counteract the shock, and Rob covered the grisly sight of the corpse lying helpless on the floor.

Global Conspiracy

'It all began in the 1960s, although I did not meet your father until relatively recently,' the professor said, as he started the long task of explaining how they all came to be here, in this quiet room in a quiet suburb in Columbia City, South Carolina, USA.

'In the 1970s, Ben was working with the CIA in Vietnam. His assignment was to work on the 'Hearts And Minds' program, designed to whip up support for the American action among the Vietnamese population. As time went by, Ben started to wonder at the direction of some of the orders he was receiving from his organisation, wondering at some of the information he was being asked to collect. Initially, he had to concentrate on getting an understanding of the alliances and affiliations among the local power-brokers, partly to know who might be supporting the North Vietnamese and partly to see who the Americans could count on for support. Over time, however, the emphasis of his intelligence gathering seemed to focus more and more on the drug smuggling organisations throughout Vietnam and the Golden Triangle – Thailand, Laos and Burma, which of course is now called Myanmar.

'Ben started to get worried about why his CIA bosses were so interested in the drug manufacturing and distribution networks. In the beginning, he assumed that the CIA must be working against the drug trade, as the drug scene was just taking a real hold at home in the US, and it had priority at national level for the first time. But more and more information was gathered and reported, and yet no action was taken against the local drug lords.

'Then Ben started to hear rumours. Rumours about American support for the drug chiefs. Rumours about finance and equipment being made available to them, but no one knew who the mysterious American benefactors were. Ben's life started to become intolerable, his work becoming more and more risky. Each time he was with his contacts in the drugs business, there were more and more questions being asked of him. Was he involved with the American suppliers? Why were Americans supporting the trade – did they want to take it over? Were the Americans supporting one drug chief over and above the others? Ben began to get very nervous. Whoever these Americans were, the questions they were generating as a result of their involvement were going to get him killed.'

The professor paused, and took a sip of the glass of brandy that Rob had given him. He looked around wearily, his eyes pausing for a moment at the sheet that Rob had laid over Greg's corpse.

'Jopl, please correct me if I get anything wrong or omit anything important,' he asked the child.

'Yes, Professor,' Jopl answered.

Laura wondered how the child might be able to know more about what happened in Vietnam in the 1960s and 1970s than the professor, who she assumed got all of this information from her dad. She knew that, for the moment all she could do was listen as the professor picked up the story again.

'Ben didn't even know if these Americans existed, or if they were just a rumour that had grown on the back of his own work in trying to drum up support among the local communities for the American war effort. Then one day, he was in Koh Nheak and was invited to meet a local chief. It transpired that these Americans did actually exist and had supplied this particular chief with some very sophisticated laboratory equipment that speeded up the processing of opium into heroin. The chief thought that Ben was connected to his American backers and wanted to thank him, proudly showing Ben around the laboratory, not realising that this was a top CIA operative that he had in his operation.

'Ben was shocked. At first, he was shocked by the scale of the support that the drug organisations were receiving. Some of the equipment was state of the art, ultra-expensive and extremely hard to get. However, his shock turned to dread – he told me that the blood turned to ice in his veins – when he saw a crate that had been discarded outside the lab as he left. There was a sticker on the crate, with a shipping reference. Ben knew that reference. It told him that regardless of how the equipment had entered Vietnam, it had left the USA as a CIA shipment.

'Ben got out of there as quickly as he could and spent two days hiding out in the jungle, trying to make sense of what he had seen. Then he returned to his unit, saying that enemy forces had been on his tail, which is why he had hidden in the jungle and was days late returning from his last mission. When he was debriefed, he made no mention of seeing the equipment in the laboratory. At that stage, he wasn't sure why he omitted that information, as it was critical to his report, but he felt he couldn't say anything until he figured out what was going on.

'For the next few weeks, he asked around quietly, both among American operatives in the CIA and the regular army. He grilled his local contacts, and a picture started to emerge. At first Ben thought he was adding two and two, and getting five – or maybe fifty-five – but as the picture became clearer, he knew he wasn't mistaken. As he pieced together the pieces of the puzzle, Ben knew that if anyone suspected that he knew what he knew, his life wouldn't be worth a plugged nickel.

'What Ben had uncovered was this. In the 1960s, the CIA was under pressure from the political establishment at home. The FBI's McCarthyism had fallen apart, with the courts making significant judgments that put an end to Hoover's demagoguery. The peaceniks were marching, the Kennedy's were gaining profile and power. There were a lot of elements in society that were starting to ask questions about CIA dirty deeds. People wanted accountability. People wanted control over the CIA. The CIA mandarins knew that, in time, they would be subjected to much closer scrutiny. They needed some way of being able to operate without having to report on some of their activities.

'In some ways, this was relatively simple – all they had to do was to omit certain operations entirely from any of their reports to Congress. However, the difficulty lay in funding. If they didn't report entire operations, then they couldn't spend money on those operations. The CIA realised that what they needed was a source of funding that would be completely separate from and invisible to the political arm of the state.'

Jopl interrupted. 'Not separate from the entire political arm, Professor. Only separate from Congress and the Senate. The president was fully aware of what was going on. Indeed, it took presidential authority to launch Operation Separation.'

'Yes, yes indeed,' confirmed the professor. 'Of course, that is why the whole scenario became so terrifying for Ben, and indeed for us today. Ben didn't know the name of the operation, which Jopl has just told us was Operation Separation – quaint. However, while he didn't know what the name of Operation Separation was, he knew that the operation existed. And that its purpose was to provide the CIA with an entirely separate line of funding for its activities.

'The CIA was developing into two separate organisations. One was the one with the public face, which appeared in front of Congressional hearings, which received funding from the American taxpayers that was accounted for by the American government. The other wing was entirely secret – no one in the American government knew about it, other than the president and a few of his closest advisors. There was no mention of it in Congress or Senate – how could there be, as they didn't know it existed. It was funded not by American taxes, but by drug profits out of the Golden Triangle.

'This was the terrible truth that Ben discovered. The CIA was working with the drug chiefs to gain a new line of funding. But the price demanded by the drug barons was high – very high. In order to retain support in their own heartland, they had to keep the local people under control. That required a massive display of power. At that time, there could be no greater display of power than to rid the country of the Americans. That was the price that the drug chiefs demanded. The CIA were facing emasculation, effectively an ending of their power. Some in the CIA believed that they were the only hope for the free world in the face of international communism. Others were simply power-hungry. But whatever their motivation, a cadre of senior elements within the CIA arrived at a single conclusion – they were willing to pay any price necessary in order to guarantee the long-term independence of a part of the CIA. And so they agreed to help organise the American defeat in Vietnam, culminating in the rout from the embassy in

Saigon. In return, they got access to the drug trade, and, through that, a new line of funding.

The professor took another sip of brandy. Laura was about to take another sip of hers, when she realised that her glass was empty – she had drunk it unknown to herself. Rob went to refill her glass, but she asked him for a coffee instead. She knew that she had to stay alert if she was to understand all of this.

'But, Professor, I am still lost. So my father uncovered a CIA plot to use drug money to fund some of their operations. What does that have to do with today? That was decades ago!'

'Yes, Laura, it was, but the beast has grown. What started as a CIA cancer started to spread. The president's office was involved, so this malignancy was embedded in the heart of our glorious country. And from there it spread. Through the 1970s, it became rumoured that if you wanted some dirty work done, and it didn't challenge American policy in any part of the world, then there were people who would mount an operation for you – for a price, of course. But before I go on to that, let me finish the part of the story that directly involves your dad.

'Ben was horrified, but wasn't sure what to do. He knew that he was coming under suspicion himself, as he had been asking a lot of questions, both of the local Vietnamese and of certain Americans. He knew that if the people in the CIA who were orchestrating everything found out that he knew about it, he would be removed. Immediately. And permanently.

'Eventually, he heard from a friend that there was a contract out on him. No one knew where it had come from, but the rumour was that the CIA were no longer prepared to protect him, so there was a suspicion that maybe Ben was a double-agent working for the communists, which was, of course, ridiculous – nothing more than a smokescreen. He went into hiding, with a man he trusted, called Lee Harris, another CIA operative, who had come to Ben with fears and suspicions about what was going on. They were on their own in the forests in Stung Teng province, when there was an air strike almost directly on their position. It was a miracle that Ben survived. Harris wasn't there, because he had gone to a stream about half a kilometre away to get water. When Ben regained his senses after the strike, he racked his brains trying to think how the CIA could have known his position. He thought maybe he was becoming paranoid, because the only explanation he could think of was that Harris was actually working for the bad guys, and had radioed their position while he was away from the camp.

'Ben knew he had to find out one way or another about Harris, so he hid above the ruins of their camp and waited for him to return. When Harris came back, he was talking on a radio – a piece of equipment that Ben thought they didn't have. Ben could hear him reporting on the status of the camp to somebody, and then declaring that he couldn't find the body. Harris listened on the radio for a time, then switched it off and sat down in the clearing.

'Ben came up behind him and held a knife to his neck. He thought he was going to have to try to force a confession out of Harris, but Harris happily told him the truth. He was working for what he called the Provisional CIA. He said that they knew that Ben had stumbled upon their little secret and that they needed him to come in and tell them if anyone else knew what was going on. Ben, of course, laughed at the idea. That was when Harris issued the chilling ultimatum. Ben was to come in and tell them what he knew, and if anyone else knew, or they would kill one person important to him every week until he did come in.'

Laura caught her breath. Now it was her turn to put two and two together.

'Greg knew so much about my dad. He knew so much about what happened. He said he was in the forests in Stung Teng province. Greg is Lee Harris!'

A cry racked her body, caught in her throat. She had slept with the man who had betrayed her father!

'You didn't know, Laura,' said Rob. 'You couldn't have known.'

Jopl looked at her, saying gently, 'Let the dead past bury its own dead. What is done, is done. Look to the future. You have saved the world.'

'Anyway,' continued Symington uncomfortably 'there was a struggle between Ben and Harris, but Harris got away. As he left, he shouted back at Ben, "One week Whiteland, before they start to die." Ben was sick with worry. He needed a way to protect himself against them, he needed some form of smoking gun that he could hold over their head. At first, he hoped to be able to gather enough evidence to force them to dismantle what they had begun, but he quickly realised that everything that he had was slim, circumstantial.

'He documented everything that he knew, everything that he suspected, and deposited sealed copies with people that he could trust. In the course of doing that, he heard that James Carter, the top CIA man overseeing the entire Vietnamese operation, had an illegitimate child with a local Thai girl. Carter was the man that Ben suspected of masterminding the whole strategy. Ben went to see the girl, Li Moon, and found that she was terrified of Carter. He was a violent man in the bedroom as well as in his line of work, but Li Moon was too afraid of him to try to escape.

'Ben promised her that he would help her to escape, with her baby boy. He got them across the border to Thailand and entrusted them to the care of a man he knew in Bangkok. He then went back to Vietnam and turned himself in to his enemy – his employer. He told them that he had hard proof of shipments of equipment from the CIA to Vietnam, and he quoted the shipping number that he had seen as a small example of his proof. They didn't know, of course, that this was about the only proof he had, and even it wasn't much as he had only seen it – he had no paperwork in his possession. He told them that he had deposited copies of the proof with a number of people, and that if anything happened to him, copies would be sent to nine major newspapers around the world. In addition, he said that he had a source who was updating those records over time, and he threatened to expose the entire rotten structure if they didn't dismantle it immediately.'

The professor glanced over at Rob, more uncomfortable than ever, before turning back to Laura. 'I don't know if you are aware of this, Laura, but your mom's death was not the simple car accident that it appeared to be. When Ben threatened them with exposure, they informed him that his wife had been assassinated on their instructions. They offered a truce. They would cancel an order that was already out on your life, and would allow Ben to live in peace, if he agreed to keep quiet about their activities. Ben wrestled with that one through a long hot night. He wanted to tell them to go to hell. He knew that they would kill him, but he hoped that the evidence he had left behind might be enough to destroy them. It was a gamble, and if it was only his own life in the balance, he probably would have rolled that dice. But with your life under threat as well, he couldn't make himself do it. He agreed to their terms, and he came home to the States. The only thing he insisted on was a deposit of tens of millions of dollars into a Swiss account. Not because he wanted the money – indeed, he couldn't use it if he wanted to live an apparently normal life with his daughter. But he knew that men who were as money-conscious as these men were, would assume that he would use the money against them if they ever attacked him again. It also of course gave him for the first time a paper-trail that proved the CIA were into some very dubious activities – after all, they had transferred an incredible amount of money into his account without it ever appearing on a budget-line anywhere. So the money was an insurance policy to help keep them at bay.

'Two years ago, when he found out that he had cancer, he contacted me. He heard about me through some online contacts – Ben never lost the sleuthing skills that he learned in his spying days! He knew that I was investigating some shadowy underworld organisation and he told me that he knew the origins of it. Ben told me everything that he knew, and it made some of what I had been hearing make a lot of sense. He told me that there was evidence, but that it was not written down. He said that the paper records had been destroyed a long time ago but that there was a person in hiding somewhere in Asia, a young man who had all the information that would be needed to attack the organisation that had grown out of what Harris called the PCIA. But he said that he could trust no one with the location of this person. He also said that he would not initiate anything while he was alive, but that he would leave it up to you to decide whether or not you wanted to help us. That is why I sent Rob to see you in the Andes two years ago – I wanted to get an idea of what type of person you were. And I have to tell you, Laura, Ben would have been very proud of you.'

Laura looked from the professor, to Rob, to Jopl, amazement etched into every feature of her face. 'So you are telling me that Jopl somehow has all of the information that you need to bring down this 'Provisional CIA?' she asked incredulously.

'Well, yes and no,' said the Professor. 'Jopl has all of the information, according to your father. We can talk about that in a moment. But just so that you understand the enemy that we are facing, let me tell you that it is no longer just a Provisional CIA. The PCIA has grown into a global organisation, with a command structure very similar to Al Qaeda. They are primarily a loose-knit association of individuals and small organisations, who use the global drug trade to fund their own activities. The only common feature among them is that all activities have to either support, or at the very least not be inimical to, American interests at home and abroad. The CIA still are part of it, as is our presidency. But it has grown much bigger.

'Tell me, have you ever considered why it is that, despite the apparent efforts of governments and police forces around the world, the drug trade is flourishing? The reason is simple. There is a shadow government within the US, and a shadow UN. These sinister bodies have assumed real power in critical areas and succeed precisely because so little is known about them. They are the descendants of the PCIA that used the Golden Triangle as their power base after the Vietnam War. It is them that we have to fight, dislodge, defeat and destroy. Until we do, Western democracy is nothing but a sham, a façade, and the real reins of power and the real decisions are taken by the inheritors of the PCIA.'

Symington spoke fiercely, clearly passionate about the usurpation of democracy and freedom that had been accomplished in the decades since the PCIA was created.

'Now, I will let Jopl take up the story and tell us how he knows so much about the current situation, and the people involved. I have to tell you, Jopl, when Ben told me there was a young man in Bangkok who could help us, I had no idea that he meant someone quite as young as you!'

'Ah, Professor Symington, age is a state of mind, nothing more or less than that. Laura, I hope you will not think that I have deceived you, but you never actually asked me my age. But that is sophistry – I knew that you believed me to be a child and I did not correct you. Therefore, I lied to you by omission as surely as if I had told you a direct lie to your face. I hope you will forgive me this deception, but I believed it necessary, as I felt that something was not right. Of course, I know now that what disturbed me was Greg – he was being untrue.

'My name is Jopl. I am son of Li Moon, son of James Carter. My body is young, for as a baby I was entrusted to the monks of Wat Nák Tong Tieow. I have spent my entire life within the confines of the temple, in an environment of beauty, holiness, peace and contemplation of the mysteries of life. Growing up in such a near-perfect milieu has left my body largely untouched by the years. Thus it is that I appear as though I were a mere child when I am in fact almost forty years old.

'All my life, the monks taught me the mysteries of life, the mysteries of the universe. I have discussed and sought to understand the writings of many of the world's wisest men from across the millennia. I have meditated and contemplated for days and sometimes weeks at a time to understand the world around me.

'One of the skills that I seem to have developed began with being able to recall childhood memories from an earlier age than most. As I meditated upon this phenomenon, it grew within me and so widened the scope of my perception. Soon, I was able to recall memories from when I was in the womb. I can recall my father hitting my mother when she told him that she was pregnant with me. Then, I became able to recall memories of my parents, from before I was born. Still I meditated and contemplated, practised this gift as one must practise any skill to nurture and hone it to the highest point possible. I now have the capacity to know the thoughts of my parents as long as they live. Sadly, I know that my mother died years ago, but my father lives. He lives and he prospers. He prospers on the agony and deprivation of others. He oversees an empire of corruption and greed, an empire that is poisoning the world as surely as their drugs poison those who abuse them.

'This is my calling. This is my purpose. This is my legacy. To fight my father. To undo the wrong that he has done. "For the sins of the fathers shall be visited upon the sons." I will not allow that. I will not permit that. I will not be responsible for the sins of my father. I will hold him accountable. And when this is done, I will go home. Home to Wat Nák Tong Tieow to live out my life in contemplation of the mysteries of the universe.'

If Laura had been amazed at the professor's revelations, she was blown away by Jopl's calm recitation of the facts. She didn't know which was more stunning – his age, his paranormal ability, his legacy, his cold determination to right the wrongs of his father. She was overcome with compassion for him – no wonder he seemed both childlike and ancient. He had spent his entire life in the temple, with no interaction with other children. Of course he took a childlike delight in the outside world. Of course he had a childlike naïveté in not understanding the simplest things about living in the outside world. And yet, no wonder he was so wise. For decades, he had absorbed the wisest teachings of the wisest men.

She was overcome with compassion for this child-man. The load he carried would be crushing to most, but he bore it with grace and humility. He accepted his responsibility, and was resolved to see it through. Laura reached out to her young hero and hugged him close to her, part of her still thinking of him as a child. In truth, he was like a child in body, but in mind, heart and soul he was part child and part superman.

'OK, so where do we go from here?' Rob asked, clearly wanting to get down to business.

'First, we must hide Laura somewhere safe until we have made our move,' said Jopl. 'I want her out of harm's way until this is over, one way or the other.'

'Not a problem,' stated Rob confidently. 'Laura, where would you like to go?'

'I don't know. It's all so sudden, so overwhelming. I don't know what to do.'

'Laura,' said Jopl, taking her hands in his, 'you must be safe. You need to think of somewhere that you know, yet where they would not look for you. Somewhere that you believe you would be safe, somewhere that you could survive. Somewhere that you could stay for weeks certainly, months probably, possibly longer.'

'The Andes,' she whispered, looking at Rob. 'I was happy there, and I think I would be safe.'

'The Andes it is. I will organise tickets for you – you will need to access a small portion of those funds that your dad forced out of the PCIA. We can continue to use the papers that you flew in here with, as they were not picked us either by us or by the enemy. We can fly you out in the morning, routing you through a number of cities to make the trail hard to follow. We will end with an overland trek so that there will be no paper trail at all. Then we can get down to work at this end.'

New Order?

The next day, Laura found herself on a plane bound for Mexico City. From there, she flew through another three cities before landing in Lima, in Peru. From there, she was due to go overland to Puerto Ceticayo in the Madres de Dios Mountains, where she had met Rob two years earlier. Laura decided, however, that she would be safer if no one knew where she was, not even Professor Symington, Rob and her dear Jopl. So she changed her plans and hitched a ride out of Lima, heading west for La Oroya. From there, she worked her way north and slightly west until she got to the town of Pucallpa, near the head of the Ucayali River. Once there, she managed to talk her way onto a riverboat, and floated downriver until she got to Iquitos, the most inland town of a significant size on the mighty Amazon River.

As she spent the week on the riverboat, Laura mourned her love for Greg. He had meant so much to her, and she had put such trust and faith in him that she could scarcely believe that he had been working against her all along. Her heart sank at the thought of how she had confided her deepest fears and her most intimate desires to him. And all the time, he had been merely looking for information that would allow him to destroy what she was trying to save – the fulfilment of the legacy that her dad had left to her. As she thought about this, a fierce raging fire burned within her. Laura cursed herself, condemned herself for her stupidity, resolved to never again let any man so close to her. Never again would she open herself to any man, physically or emotionally. Never again would she leave herself exposed and vulnerable. Never again would she allow any man to see her defenceless and susceptible to being used and abused as Greg had done to her.

As she sat on the deck one late afternoon, letting the heat and the humidity soak into her bones, a shadow fell over her. It was one of the deckhands, a huge black man who seemed to have the strength of ten normal men. 'Excuse me Miss. You seem sad. What is wrong?'

His heavily accented English was difficult to understand, but Laura was just able to decipher it. She smiled to herself at the thought that here she was mourning her stupidity with men, and along comes a man to ask what is wrong with her. The irony was not lost on her, and she smiled to avoid insulting the man as she answered. 'Men! That is what wrong with me. I have been a damned fool. But no man will ever hurt me like that, ever again.'

The big man knelt beside her. Laura was startled, but she relaxed when she saw the look on his face. He leaned close to her and whispered twenty-seven words. 'I hold it true, whate'er befall; I feel it, when I sorrow most; 'tis better to have loved and lost than never to have loved at all.'

Then he arose without a further word, and went back below decks to whatever tasks awaited him there.

Laura looked after the man, amazed. She had assumed he would not be able to read or write, his English was barely decipherable; and yet he had quoted one of the language's greatest writers to her. Laura pondered the words, repeating them softly.

'I hold it true, whatever befall; I feel it, when I sorrow most; 'tis better to have loved and lost than never to have loved at all.'

As she thought about it, a new perspective occurred to her. She had been condemning herself unreservedly for making a mistake, but was that the right way to approach the issue? She thought back to Jopl's words. 'Let the dead past bury its own dead. What is done, is done. Look to the future.'

As she contemplated all that had happened, Laura made a number of resolutions. She resolved that she would leave the past in the past. True, she might draw on past experiences when planning, or to learn from them; but she would not relive them. She would not live in the past, drowning in regret. For in truth, the past is dead and gone. The words of an old Irish song that her dad used to sing quietly came back to her on the breeze.

'What's done is done,

What's won is won,

What's lost is lost and gone forever'

She knew from her conversations with Jopl that the past was not real. We cannot actually relive the past, we cannot change the past. Therefore there is no point in living in the past. Thinking of the things that she learned from Jopl, her second resolution was that she would write a journal, a diary of the things that she had learned from that wise child-man. It would not be a diary of what had happened to her, for she didn't want to have such a potentially inflammatory document lying around. No, it would simply detail the things that she felt she had learned. She would call it 'Lessons Learned', and whenever she felt sad or angry or negative, she would read it and it would remind her of the lessons that she had learned from Jopl, Chanarong, Imno, Tahir and others.

Iquitos suited Laura perfectly – it was big enough for her not to be noticed, yet small enough to have very little through traffic. She found a newsagent that sold foreign newspapers, though they were usually three or four weeks out of date.

She read the papers voraciously, expecting headlines about shadow governments, but saw nothing of the sort. What she did see within weeks was an unusually high number of resignations and deaths from natural causes of well-known figures in the political and commercial arenas. There were also some spectacular victories by the forces of law and order over international drug kingpins. She started to rest assured, knowing that she had done the right thing, knowing that Rob and the professor and Jopl were fighting the good fight, and that they were obviously winning. She had arranged with them that when it was safe for her to come home, they would place a personal ad in the *International Herald Tribune* every Monday until she replied.

Over time, however, the drug victories ceased, and the trade continued as before. No advertisement appeared in the *International Herald Tribune*. Laura worried that the old order may have simply been replaced with a new order. She resolved to write her 'Lessons Learned' journal, in the hope that by doing so, she would arrive at a better understanding of herself, of the world, and of her place within the world.

Armed notebooks and pencils in her backpack, Laura walked into the Brazilian rainforest, comfortable that nature would protect her, as Imno had promised.

ACKNOWLEDGEMENTS

I began this book in the summer of 2005, during a rare quiet period at work. After a month, I expanded my role, got busier, and had to shelve the book. But at least it was started. Looking back now, I want to thank everyone who was involved in giving me that brief quiet moment in the job I held. In doing so, you helped me to realise a lifelong ambition. Thank You!

For the next two years, I was busy, very busy. I changed jobs, and those were extraordinarily busy days. Worn out, and with a very beautiful girlfriend on the other side of the world, I decided to take a few months out to go and visit her. Thanks to all my colleagues in the CSC who helped make that leave of absence possible. A special mention goes to Jacquelyn, because she told me she would kill me if I didn't give her a mention!

In Australia, while my girlfriend worked – I lazed, lounged and eventually started to write again. In June and July 2007, I drafted the book from start to finish. All that was left was the editing. Many thanks to Lee for very many things. Suffice it to mention here the loan of a laptop (even though the 'D' key was missing!), the time, the space, the support, the love.

Thanks to Chook for telling me what the Northern Territory was like – I hope I have represented it accurately here. Thanks to John for taking me fishing – like the old guy in *The Five People You Meet In Heaven*, you don't know how much good that did – how much you did for me. I think that when my time comes, I wouldn't be at all surprised if you were one of my five people. Thanks to Betty across the road for the tea, the delicious fruit cake and the loan of a bed for the kids.

Around the time I started the book, thank you and my deepest and sincerest apologies to Sharon, who taught me the hard lesson of consequences.

Around the time I finished the book, thank you and my deepest and sincerest apologies to Nicola, who taught me the power of the written word.

Thank you to my mum and the rest of my family. They supported me and loved me when I was low and helped through some very dark days. Thanks as well for the Sunday-morning debates when we were kids and teenagers – they helped form the questioning mind that I like to think brought me to this work.

My heartfelt thanks to Mary, who showed me that I was capable of much more than I thought. You showed me that I can make it on my own. Be Happy.

A huge thank you to my kids, who, despite my many failings, have made me feel a success as a parent. You are the light in my life, my beginning and my end. I love you guys, big time.

Having written the book, I then had to see if anyone wanted to publish it. In one way, it didn't really matter. I had written it as a project for myself, to fulfil my own dream; not to get it published. However, publishing would authenticate it – it would be a 'real' book. So many genuine and heartfelt thanks to Tony Clayton-Lea, the first person to read it, and who encouraged me to take the next step in the birth of this book that you hold in your hand right now. Tony is a bloody good author in his own right – Google him or go to amazon.com.

Thanks to Claire, my editor, who polished a rough stone – any remaining faults are mine. They persist despite Claire, not because of her. Her advice, feedback and guidance were invaluable in bringing this work to fruition.

Gratitude to my good friends at Choice Publishing, who supported and assisted the birth of this work into the "real" world.

Be Good.
Anthony.
www.anthonywhelan.ie
Anthony.whelan@anthonywhelan.ie